YEARBOOK

WATCH FOR THE SEQUEL
COMING IN SUMMER 2007

YEARBOOK

A NOVEL BY

Allyson Braithwaite Condie

DESERET
BOOK
SALT LAKE CITY, UTAH

For past, present, and future

high school students everywhere

Especially my boys

Library of Congress Cataloging-in-Publication Data

Condie, Allyson Braithwaite
    Yearbook / Allyson Braithwaite Condie.
        p.   cm.
    Summary: Students and teachers share their struggles in life, the joys they experience, and their testimonies throughout one year at Lakeview High School.
    ISBN-13: 978-1-59038-690-3 (pbk.)
    ISBN-10: 1-59038-690-6 (pbk.)
    [1. High schools—Fiction.   2. Schools—Fiction.   3. Friendship—Fiction.   4. Dating (Social customs)—Fiction.   5. Mormons—Fiction.   6. Christian life—Fiction.]
I. Title.
    PZ7.C7586Ye 2006
    [Fic]—dc22   2006019743

Printed in the United States of America
Malloy Lithographing Inc., Ann Arbor, MI

10   9   8   7   6   5   4   3   2   1

CONTENTS

CONTENTS

ACKNOWLEDGMENTS

I have been very blessed to have the support of my family and friends throughout the writing of *Yearbook*. My husband and children have provided all sorts of help, including (but not limited to) comic relief, positive encouragement, ideas, feedback, and soggy Cheerios. My parents, Bob and Arlene, and my grandmother, Alice, have always given me all of the time and love in the world.

I have benefited enormously from feedback from Elaine, Nic, and Hope, who offered the kind of feedback that is a writer's dream—both honest and enthusiastic.

And finally, many thanks to Lisa Mangum and Chris Schoebinger at Deseret Book. They made this new author feel like she had a story worth telling.

LAKEVIEW
HIGH SCHOOL

It was the first day of school at Lakeview High School, and everyone was afraid of something.

Michaela Choi was afraid that Ethan Beckett was never going to ask her out on a date.

David Sherman was afraid that someone had discovered that *he* was the one who had "streaked" through the seniors' graduation party last summer—wearing running shorts, gigantic sunglasses, a rainbow clown wig, and his father's old moon boots. Worse, he was afraid that someone else might try to take the credit.

Andrea Beckett was afraid that someone would find her weak spot, the chink in her armor, her Achilles heel. She was afraid of knowing what it was herself.

Principal Downing was afraid that she was going to die.

Mr. Thomas, an English teacher, was afraid that he simply might not have the energy to care about his students this final year before he retired. He wrote his name on the board and looked out at his empty classroom. He took a deep breath.

In another part of the school, his son, Owen Thomas, first-year teacher in the music department, was also looking out at his classroom. He felt that he had stopped breathing altogether. He was afraid that the students were going to eat him alive.

Avery Matthews was afraid that she wasn't going to make the volleyball team. She was also afraid of spending too much time by herself. She turned the corner by the gym to look at the final cut list for the team and felt her heart accelerate.

Ethan Beckett, the fastest runner on the boys' cross-country team this year—so far—was afraid of being caught unprepared.

Julie Reid was afraid that no one would notice her. She was more afraid that someone would.

The doors to the school swung open and closed, once, twice, a thousand times, and all the students came in, bumping into each other and walking down the hall together and passing one another. They brought backpacks and watches and notebooks and ideas and heartbreaks and earphones and aspirin and makeup and mirrors and memories and testimonies and doubts and questions. Stories were everywhere.

The bell rang, and the school year began.

CHAPTER 1

SEPTEMBER

Michaela Choi

Friendships can surprise you. You can meet someone and think, "That's impossible, we'll never be friends," and then find out later that you get along perfectly. You can have a best friend and then drift apart over time and lose touch with each other. You can spend half your time daydreaming about how you wish a friendship might turn into something more.

Ethan and I have been friends for a long time. The kind of friends who hang out a lot, who have been in all the same classes since elementary school and who like each other just fine. We're two of a handful of Mormon kids in the area, so we've been thrown together a lot our whole lives. I'd like to think we both know there's a little chemistry there, but I don't know that he even thinks about me as anything more than a friend.

I have been around him too long. The new girls are always more interesting. People always feel bad for the new girls at school, but at least the guys look at them as potential dates when they arrive. That doesn't usually happen to those of us who they've seen throw up during third-grade dodgeball.

I thought about this as I stood at the cooler after practice with the rest of the girls' cross-country team, downing my Gatorade and talking to my teammates. Well, let's be honest. I was also watching Ethan while pretending not to, something I've gotten pretty good at doing these days. He sprinted across the finish line with that fluid, easy run of his, and then turned to yell something back at one of the other guys. From where I was standing, I couldn't hear what either one of them said, but I could hear Ethan laughing, and I could imagine the way his eyes would turn up at the corners when he did, like a reflection of his smile. I've never met anyone who loves running as much as Ethan does.

Like I said, I've known Ethan for years, but this is Ethan's first year running long-distance, and there is something wonderful in the way he discovers something new. I've never seen him throw himself into something like this, without reservation or holding back. I wonder how someone I have known so long can still surprise me. Does he see anything in me that surprises him?

Some of the guys drifted over and joined the girls' team at the cooler. "It's later than usual. Anyone want to get something to eat at Bob's Burgers?" suggested Dave Sherman. "I've got room for four more in my car."

"Sure," said Jana. "I've got room for three." She turned to me. "Mikey, do you want to ride with me?"

"Okay," I said. What I really wanted was to ride with Ethan, but there was no way to arrange that without losing my dignity. "Let me go call my parents." Since I don't have a cell phone, that meant a trip to the school's pay phone. "I'll be right back," I called, turning to jog away, and almost running into Ethan in the meantime. "Hey," I said, surprised by the actual physical fact of him after all my abstract daydreaming.

"Hi, Mikey," he said. "Where's everyone headed? Do I really smell that bad?"

4

A lame joke, but kind of cute nonetheless. "Dave suggested getting something to eat at Bob's."

"That sounds great," he said. "Are you going?"

Of course I was, especially now. "Yeah," I said. "I'll see you there," I called back as I ran off. At first, I felt proud of myself for playing it cool, but then I realized that he probably just thought I had to go to the bathroom really bad or something. I hurried so that Jana wouldn't have to wait for me too long.

. . .

There's nothing that can send a place into chaos faster than twenty hungry teenagers, and I hung back a little as we all piled into Bob's. I ended up standing next to Ethan at the end of the line without too much work on my part. It made me wonder if he was trying to stand by me too. "It's going to take forever to get any food," he said to me.

"Yeah, it is," I agreed.

He leaned in conspiratorially, so close I could see the freckles dusted across his cheekbones and nose. "Good thing I rummaged in Dave's car on the way in and found these." He held up a bag of gummy bears, pale and clumped together in a dusty ball. "I'll even share them with you."

"Thanks," I said, trying to pretend that all kinds of electricity hadn't been running through me when Ethan was close.

"Hold out your hands." I complied, and he shook some of the bears out for me. I popped a red one into my mouth and grimaced.

"Are they as stale as they look?" Ethan asked, eating a green one before I could answer. "Yuck. They're even worse." He looked around. "I guess we should do Dave a favor and get rid of them. Do you want me to take care of yours too?"

I nodded, and our hands brushed as I gave the bears back.

"Save my place for me," Ethan said, and moved toward the trash can.

I surreptitiously tried to remove red gummy from my teeth but was caught by Dave, bearing a tray of burgers like they were precious jewels.

"Beckett!" said Dave as he passed by the two of us. "Don't think I don't know where you found those gummy bears. And don't you throw them away, either. I'm saving them."

"What on earth could he use these things for?" Ethan asked me. "Slingshot ammunition?"

"To poison his enemies before the state race?" I guessed.

"For batting practice?"

Dave passed by us again on his way to get some straws. "For your information, I am going to enter the Sherman Family Gingerbread House Contest this Christmas for the first time ever and take down the competition, namely my aunts and my grandma. And my strategy involves gummy bears. Also gummy frogs, gummy rats, and . . ."

Ethan rolled his eyes and Dave stabbed him in the arm with a straw.

Since we were the last to order, our number was the last one called. Everyone else was almost finished when we finally sat down to eat. The only place left was a booth on the other side of the restaurant from everyone else, so we headed over there together, Ethan carrying the tray and me holding our drinks. The condensation from the drinks dripped down the sides and over my fingers as we wove in and out through the chairs and slid into the booth. I tried and tried, but there was no way I could even imagine that it was a date. Maybe *I* could ask Ethan out. We were sitting alone together. It could happen. I unwrapped my hamburger and took a bite.

My hamburger crunched, which made me mad. What was all that lettuce doing on it? I specifically said *no* lettuce, and no mayonnaise . . . and now there was a splotch of mayonnaise, looking an awful lot like bird poop, that had dripped on my leg.

"They didn't put anything on my hamburger," Ethan said. "Where's my extra mayo?"

I looked at him, and another splotch of mayonnaise dripped onto my foil wrapper. Ethan's eyes caught mine. "I think I have your burger," I said, setting it down. "Do you still want it?"

"That's okay," he said. "You've already started. It's fine."

Did he think I had bad breath, or mono, or just that sharing a hamburger was gross? He bit into my hamburger and made a face at the taste. "You sure don't like much on these, do you?" he said. "This is pretty dry."

Things seemed to have taken a turn for the worse. I was still sweaty from training, wearing the shorts and T-shirt I'd worn for practice. I was eating his hamburger, which was a mess and tasted like some sort of thick salad. I felt like scraping my teeth with the toothpicks on the table. And I could tell that Ethan wasn't enjoying my hamburger very much, either. Should I go ahead and ask him to a movie? I decided against it, seeing as my shirt front was now decorated with his mayonnaise.

Then I got a lucky break. "Mikey," said Jana, stopping by our booth, "I've got to take off. It's later than I thought, and I'm supposed to babysit tonight. Can you get a ride with Ethan?"

Yikes. What would he say? "Sure," Ethan said. "I've got room." He grinned at me. "Now that no one's waiting on us, let's get some new burgers. Yours is disgusting."

While we were eating, we talked about practice that day. His light gray eyes lit up and he kept laughing and gesturing in that animated way that I love. We finished our burgers and then, on our way out the door, I spied the ancient Space Invaders machine. "Hey, Ethan," I said, "I have some quarters. Do you want to be humiliated by a girl?"

Many quarters later, the score was six games to four, my favor. We walked out the door into the night. It was still a little light and it still felt like summer. Maybe better than summer. We rode home with the windows down and the music playing, talking about the upcoming race. I'd run the course last year at state, but Ethan hadn't, so I told him about some of the tough spots. We talked about the English class we have together. We talked about lots of things.

Ethan pulled into the driveway of my house. "You'd better enjoy this feeling, because it won't happen again," he said, as I opened the door.

Stunned, I stared at him. "What?"

"You know, the feeling of beating me. Next time we play Space Invaders, I'm going to win." His mouth twisted into a smile. "Although I might have to go back and practice every night."

Relieved, I laughed. Our eyes locked for a minute before I panicked and climbed out of the car. "You'd *better* practice. See you tomorrow!" He waved.

I carried my shake into the house and lifted off the lid. It was soupy. The taste of mayonnaise and lettuce was still in my mouth, even after the new burger, and my hair felt sticky and sweaty. My autobiography for English class still needed to be written. A trig assignment that I didn't even know how to begin lurked in my backpack. But Ethan Beckett had said, "Next time." It was a perfect night.

• • •

If only perfect nights translated into perfect days. The next day, I was starting to seriously worry about the status of my autobiography for English. I can't stand it when a school assignment consumes my whole life! There were plenty of other things I needed and wanted to think about *instead* of that dumb autobiography: my other classes (trig is NOT going well, by the way), the cross-country meet coming up, and, above all, how to get Ethan Beckett to ask me out on a real date instead of just hanging out together. I was spending more time thinking about how to write about my life than I was actually living it! You can't tell me that there isn't something wrong with that.

Finally, two days before it was due, I threw my hands up in

surrender and went in to talk to my teacher, Mr. Thomas, during lunch. I don't do that very often. Lunch is one of the best parts of the day, and not just because I get to eat. It also means that I get to talk with everyone, and Ethan and I usually sit at the same table with our friends. But, since I have workout after school, lunchtime was my only option.

"How do I know where to start?" I asked Mr. Thomas. I sat on the other side of his huge desk, which was snowed under with papers and student journals. How did he manage to have so much to grade so early in the year, I wondered. "Do I start with all my ancestors, and go from there? Or do I start with what I can first remember? Or when my parents met?"

Mr. Thomas smiled. "Yes."

Well, *that* was helpful. He could tell that I was confused, so he continued.

"Any of those would be a good place to start," he said. "Think of writing as unraveling a sweater—grab a thread and start pulling. All the connected strands will start unraveling too. Everyone is full of stories. What you need to find out is how and where your stories connect with the stories of others. Then you'll see what people and events are important for you to write about. One of the most important parts of life, Michaela, is realizing that the things you do affect other people. You can't do anything without it impacting someone else, and they impact you too. You're more than just a face in the yearbook or a name on a roll . . . and so is everyone else."

Mom has been reminding me of the Golden Rule—you know, "Do unto others as you'd have them do unto you"—my entire life. It was strange to hear a version of the same thing coming from Mr. Thomas. I don't know if he's a member of the Church or not. Instead of asking him, though, I nodded my head and went to my next class, thinking about what he'd said.

• • •

That night, I sat down at the computer, determined to get something on paper. I grabbed a thread—my first memory, which was of rescuing earthworms left stranded on the sidewalk after the rain, wearing my favorite yellow plastic boots with ducks on them—and started pulling. As I wrote, a lot of different people showed up in the pages. My parents, of course, and my little brothers. My best friend, Krista, who just moved to Colorado. My third-grade teacher, who told me I was the worst student at math she'd ever had. Talk about scarring someone for life! My Beehive leader, who was the funniest and kindest person I've known. My grandparents, who live in Korea, where my grandfather is a mission president. Lots of people were running around in my autobiography. I bet some of them would be surprised. Little did they know what I remembered of them from when our lives met up! Little did they know what I was documenting, both good and bad!

I wrote for hours. I wrote about *most* of the things that were important to me. When I say "most," I mean just about everything that didn't involve my crush on Ethan, which has existed in some form ever since he was the new boy in my kindergarten class, looking little and serious and wearing a Teenage Mutant Ninja Turtles T-shirt. I saw the way he smiled and the way he colored very carefully, always staying in the lines. I saw the way he played every game well at recess, and I knew he was the boy I loved. I think it's the combination of familiar and surprising that intrigues me most about Ethan. I know him, but there is also a lot more to him than what I know.

I wish that Ethan showed up in the pages of my autobiography as more than just a friend. But, just because I *wish* that we were dating doesn't mean anything. You can't pick who you want to be your friend or your boyfriend. They have to choose you too. There's such a complicated interplay of how you affect other people and how they affect you and what you all decide to do about it. It made me wonder: Exactly how much of our lives are really just our lives, and how much are connected with others' lives? That's probably part of what Mr. Thomas was trying to point out when he was talking about our stories affecting one another.

Another thing that I didn't write much about at first was my testimony or my church. It felt a little bit fake to mention it, like I was showing off or something. So I left it out.

But then, when I was partway through, I got a feeling—it felt like sitting in church and knowing that you need to bear your testimony or you're going to regret it. My little brother once described it as, "My insides started to feel like Sprite," which I think is the best description I've heard. You feel all sparkly and clear and like you want to overflow with what you're feeling—with what you *know*. I felt that way as I sat at the computer, so I decided to mention it after all. Mr. Thomas said to write about the things that were important to me, and my testimony definitely is one of those things.

I wrote about my baptism, and the way I felt when I came out of the water and saw my father smiling at me. Everything seemed so clear and beautiful—the light on the water, the light in my father's eyes, the brilliance of the warm feeling running through my veins. I wonder what it would feel like to stand at the side of the font and see someone get baptized and know that you had helped them learn about the gospel. I wrote about how my grandparents were part of many baptisms in Korea, and how they wrote about each new member with so much love in their letters. I wondered if Mr. Thomas had ever been baptized, or been to a baptism.

Sometimes, in the back of my mind, I've wondered about sharing the gospel. How do you know how much is enough and how much is too much? I decided to start praying every night that I would be guided to the person the Lord wanted me to share the gospel with and that I wouldn't be too chicken to bring it up when I did find someone to talk to about it.

At the end of my autobiography, I wrote, "It is true that many people impact our lives, for better and for worse, as Mr. Thomas told me when I was writing this. We'd be in a lot of trouble if everyone judged us by our picture in the yearbook. I need to remember that there are stories behind the faces and the appearances. I need to remember that my decisions, good and bad, affect other people all the time. I need to live the way my religion teaches me to live, and the way I know the Savior wants me to live, so that my testimony shows in all the ways it can, little and big. Writing this autobiography has reminded me of all these things."

I shut down the computer and felt much better. I wondered what Mr. Thomas would think, and that made me nervous, but I felt like I had done the right thing by writing what I had. I read it again the next day and felt the same way. My autobiography was done. I could start thinking about other things again. And I did.

I finished well in a race, I failed a trig test, and I found my shake from that night at the restaurant with Ethan. It was still in the freezer, frozen to my spoon like a giant popsicle in a Styrofoam cup. I thought about saving it, but that seemed too weird, so I ate it instead. Partway through, I found a rock-solid yellow gummy bear that *someone* had snuck in there when I wasn't paying attention.

That night, I prayed about being a missionary. I also prayed for Ethan—not that he would ask me on a date, although that thought did cross my mind, but that he would have a good day the next day. Small things like that.

When it was time to hand in my autobiography, I printed it out, put it in a blue folder, and handed it in before class, before Mr. Thomas even called for them. I've always liked handing in assignments, even though I don't like doing them very much. It feels good to say, "Here you go—it's *your* problem now!"

When I handed the folder to Mr. Thomas, he looked at me with those gentle blue eyes of his and thanked me. There's both comfort and stress in knowing that he will read every word. Teachers who don't are both easier and more frustrating. I wondered what he would think about the last paragraph.

As I was walking back to my desk, Ethan, who sits behind me, said, "Mikey, you already handed it in?" I nodded.

"Here's mine." He held up a bunch of notebook paper stapled together. "My printer ran out of ink at midnight, so I had to write it all out by *hand*. I couldn't get on the computer until then to print it out because Andrea has been working on her stupid college applications night and day." He shook his head in disbelief. "At least I started with kindergarten, because that was the first thing I could really remember enough to write about, so I only had eleven years to cover instead of the whole sixteen."

"Can I see it?" I wanted to see if Ethan had written about our kindergarten teacher, Mrs. Crenshaw, and the day she bent over and her orange sherbet pantsuit split along the seams. That was what I remembered about kindergarten. That, and eating paste in the corner with the boys when Mrs. Crenshaw wasn't looking.

"Sure," he said, handing me the sheaf of paper. Ethan has pretty decent handwriting, for a boy. I read the first two lines in his paper: "When I started kindergarten, I was in Mrs. Crenshaw's class. I don't remember very much about it except the day her pantsuit split."

I looked up and laughed. "I wrote about Mrs. Crenshaw's pants splitting too!" I started reading again. The next two lines were, "I thought kindergarten was going to be terrible, until I found out where I was sitting. It was by Michaela Choi, the cutest girl in the class."

I was getting *very* interested when Ethan yanked the paper away from me. I looked up into his face, startled, and I could see that he was embarrassed. "Uh, there might be some personal stuff in there that I didn't want anyone to see," he said, and I could tell that he had just remembered what he had included in that first paragraph.

"Oh, I understand," I said, smiling inside. I didn't want him to be embarrassed, so I pretended I hadn't read any further. The bell rang and I turned around and sat in my seat, still beaming.

Mr. Thomas called for everyone to hand their papers forward, and I turned around to take Ethan's from him. I passed it on to Avery Matthews, who sits in front of me, and then felt a tap on my shoulder.

I turned around to face Ethan. His face was a little red, but his gray eyes were as bright as ever. He leaned forward and said very, very quietly, "I still think you are the cutest girl I know." Then he sat back, turned a little redder, and pretended to pay attention to what Mr. Thomas was saying. I turned around and stared at Mr. Thomas too.

And right then I had a strange feeling. It's not that I thought Ethan and I were going to get married or something. But, I suddenly thought, *Ethan Beckett, I think I'm going to take a chance. I think I want to let you know how I feel about you, and see what you and I decide to do about it.*

I glanced back at Ethan. I looked right into his eyes and gave him the biggest smile I could.

LATE SEPTEMBER

Mr. Thomas

I have been grading eleventh grade autobiographies for over thirty years. You would think that I would be tired of reading the trials and tribulations of today's troubled youth, but they are still interesting, endearing, shocking, and revelatory. Usually there are several things that surprise me.

Usually. But after reading fifteen of them this evening and preparing to read approximately fifty more, I contemplated taking my retirement immediately instead of when school ends in June. It was hard to care enough to correct, once again, the same grammar mistakes I've been correcting for what feels like eons. I hadn't come across a particularly dazzling autobiography yet. I started wondering why I had even bothered to make the assignment. That often happens when I'm grading. I was having a bad moment. When I have one of those bad moments, I take a break.

I left the dining room table where I had been working and went into the kitchen to get a drink. The fridge that was once full of gallons of milk and bushels of fruit and tubs of cold cuts now has just enough for two. It used to be that this room was full of boys. Boys eating, boys yelling, boys laughing, boys doing dishes at a very high decibel level, boys stealing extra dessert. Now, the youngest one is gone to college, the oldest has a baby of his own, and the middle one, Owen, is living with me and teaching choir at Lakeview. They are all good boys. They all make me proud. In fact, I remember grading Owen's autobiography. Owen was—and still is—our most difficult, prickly child, and I had been pleasantly surprised in my reading when he mentioned that he thought that he was lucky because he had "especially cool parents." It felt good to read that. I showed it to my wife.

I stood by the kitchen window and closed my eyes. One of the last papers I'd read belonged to Michaela Choi. A good girl, one of the skinny, bright-eyed, hard-working types. She is a good writer— not a brilliant one, but decent, and, thank goodness, not the kind that tries too hard to be dark and serious and profound. Although, in their own way, those student writers are touching too. Michaela looks a little like my boys—dark eyes, dark hair, tall and thin. I always thought it was a little bit of a shame that the boys looked so much like me. Their mother was beautiful—thick blonde hair, elegant facial features—but I guess a boy would rather be told that he looks like his father than his mother, no matter how much he loves her. They do all have her eyes, though.

At first glance, Michaela's paper had been a perfectly average paper about a perfectly average teenage girl. But there was something about the end of it that had caught my attention. There was an earnest, if clichéd, paragraph about making decisions and realizing that you may impact others, not just yourself—and that your decisions and the decisions of others are all intertwined, as are your stories. She mentioned her religion, which I thought was rather courageous of her, and her belief that she needed to live like Christ to help others as she interacted with them. I suppose she took my little speech at our lunchtime meeting to heart.

I believe what I told her. How could I not? The decision that some teenager made almost a year ago affects me every day, a thousand times a day, because it killed my wife. His bad decision one night became our reality every night for the rest of our lives.

What I felt like writing in the margin of Michaela's paper with my pen was, "What is the point of going on when everything you do can be wiped out by one bad choice? Why even try? How do you know that Jesus wants you to do those things? How do you even know he's there?" But you can't ask those kinds of questions of a junior in high school, not when you yourself are an adult and can't figure out the answers. Can you?

I put my head in my hands.

The door opened, and I straightened up. Owen walked in, whistling. "Hey," he said. "How are the autobiographies coming?"

I made a thumbs-down sign. "Remind me again why I assign these things every year," I said.

"Because you like to torture kids. And because you like to make them think about their lives—where they've been and where they're going." This second sentence was delivered in his best James Earl Jones voice.

I had to laugh. It was exactly the line I'd delivered this year and the one I'm sure I delivered when Owen was in my class seven years ago. "Owen," I asked, "whatever happened to your autobiography?"

"I don't know," he said. "Mom probably put it somewhere in a box. She liked to save all our stuff."

"I know," I said. "I haven't really cleaned things out yet, especially not in the attic."

There are pictures of my wife all over the house, even some of her clothes left in the closet, many of her files left in the filing cabinet. Sometimes people ask if it isn't too painful for me to see her everywhere. I don't bother explaining to them that no matter what I do, I would still see her everywhere. The obvious reminders are a small fraction of those things. I see her in the tulips in the front yard, in the colors of my boys' eyes, in the paint she chose for the living room. Those same people who want me to get rid of the pictures would say, "Then why don't you move?" But then I would still see her in the mountains, in a brand of ice cream she liked at the grocery store. I would still hear her in a song on the radio or in the sound of a lawn mower cutting grass, which is what she did every Saturday. To be honest, I don't want to escape her memory. I would rather feel the pain of seeing remnants of our life together than have emptiness instead.

"I could help you do that," Owen said. "If you want to go through the attic, I could help you with it."

"I don't think I'm ready yet," I said. "But I would love to have you help me when I am."

"What I won't help you with," Owen said, "are those autobiographies. Look at me and learn. Give assignments sparingly. I taught today, and now all I have to do is write a lesson plan. No papers to grade, because we sing. Assignments and tests only occasionally. It's the life, Dad. You should give up English and follow my lead."

"It sounds like it."

"I'll make you a deal, Dad. Grade five more autobiographies and then we'll go get something to eat."

"Agreed." Neither of us bother to make dinner very often. Last night, we ran into each other in the kitchen at midnight in our pajamas with bowls of cereal. We hadn't remembered to have dinner until then. I can only imagine what my wife would have said about that.

"I'm going to go upstairs and change into some jeans. Yell when you're ready." Whistling, he went upstairs. It must have been a good day.

After he left, I broke my end of the bargain a little. I didn't grade right away. I thought about Owen, and my two other sons. I am connected to the boy who killed my wife, but I am also connected to these boys, her boys, whom she loved, and that connection is everything to me. Our best hope of being all right is to keep moving, keep trying, keep caring about each other. *Keep moving,* I told myself.

Maybe you can ask Michaela for the name of her minister or someone, and ask him where they find the answers to their difficult questions. I heard the floorboards creak upstairs as Owen walked down the hall.

"All right," I muttered and reached for the stack of papers. I took the cap off my grading pen. I picked up the next paper: Avery Matthews. I kept moving and began to read.

CHAPTER 3

LATE SEPTEMBER

Avery Matthews

SIXTEEN

"Take your backpack," my mother tells me.
I ignore her.
"How can you go to school without a pen, a piece of paper?" she shrills.
I pick up the backpack and walk out the door.
She smiles, satisfied.
What she doesn't know is that the backpack is empty.
I am empty.

It's easier to let yourself drown.
Why struggle and slip and swim and choke?
Better to let go now.
The water is black and cold and deep and dark
I slip beneath.
It's so easy.

Teachers ask for assignments.

Gossip and whispers surround us.
Teams lament losses, exult in wins.
I swim below everything.
I see only their ripples on the surface.
Nothing moves me here below.

There are monsters here in the deep.
Dark, some of them.
Beautiful and terrible, some of them.
I can swim around in my own sorrow, in my own anger.
No one notices, or if they do, they understand and swim by.
Better to feel anger than to feel sorrow.
Better to feel nothing than to feel sorrow.
Better not to feel.

But something in me still wants to rise up out of the dark water.
Wants to feel the sun on my wet, cold skin.
Something inside of me wants to put my feet on hot, grainy sand
And run along the beach.
Even though there is glass that might cut me buried beneath.

CHAPTER 4

OCTOBER

Ethan Beckett

The very best day of my life was today, and I really can't believe that so much happened so quickly. I want to rewind, replay, and relive it a million times. I bet I'd never get sick of it. Who knew that one day could be such a big deal?

Today was the State cross-country race. I was ranked fourth in the state, which was huge for me. I don't mean to sound cocky, but running has been going really well for me. It has been a surprise, in a way. Last year, I ran track, and it was great. I didn't make the soccer team the fall of my sophomore year, so this fall, the fall of my junior year, I figured I would try cross-country instead. You don't get cut in cross-country. That's pretty appealing, if you ask me.

Anyway, by some miracle I turned out to be pretty good at running long distances (a race in cross-country is three miles). I guess playing basketball in the winter and soccer in the summer has kept me in good shape. I knew I was fast. I didn't get winded like the other guys did, but I've always been sort of average at everything else. I'd avoided cross-country because it's always been my sister Andrea's thing, but this year, I figured that she didn't have a monopoly on the sport.

It's been awesome to find out I was good, seriously good, at running. I guess I shouldn't have been so surprised because Andrea is State Championship material and the fastest on the girls' team, but I was.

It's also cool because the girls' team goes on the trips too, and there are a lot of cute girls on the team. I think that one girl in particular, Michaela Choi, is a lot of fun and very pretty. She's in my stake and we went to elementary school together. I've liked her for a while; I've known her forever.

Anyway, I figured it couldn't hurt to join the team. Imagine how shocked I was early in the season when I started beating the older guys, and guys on other teams! It was incredible. I started to *feel* that I was good—I could taste the victory in my mouth and I could tell what I needed to do to catch someone.

I couldn't wait for today—the State Championship race—and at the same time I wished that it would never come. The girls' championship race was first. Michaela was running in it. She isn't the fastest, but she's solid and she works really hard. Andrea was standing apart from the rest of the team, as usual. They all respect her, but she doesn't really make friends. Last year, her junior year, she took second at the State meet and I know not getting first almost killed her. Andrea doesn't like to take second in anything. I saw Mikey wish her good luck and Andrea respond briefly.

One of the things that I like about Mikey is that she knows what to do a lot of the time. I did the stupidest thing in English last month. Well, it turned out fine, but it could have been really, really bad. I basically told her, flat out in the middle of class, that I liked her. I don't know *what* I was thinking! And what did she do? She smiled at me and somehow that let me know that it was okay. After class, she waited for me, and when we walked down the hall to our lockers, I got up the guts to ask her if she wanted to go to the football game on Friday and get something to eat afterwards. Ever since then, I think we've been sort of going out. I like to see her smile the minute she looks at me. I like how she cheers for me when I run and I like cheering for her too. Some of the guys, namely Dave Sherman, give me a hard time about it, but everyone likes Mikey just fine and so I don't think they really mean much by it. My mom is okay with it because Mikey's such a good girl. Not in a dorky way, just in a really nice way.

I saw her standing by herself saying a little prayer and so I didn't bug her, but I did give her a little wave later. She waved back. She looked really nervous. I know it meant a lot to her to run a good race and not let the team down.

When I went down toward the bull pen to warm up for the race, I stopped to get some last-minute words of encouragement from Coach Roberts. He is a great guy—the kind of guy you would like to have as your dad, or maybe your uncle.

"Ethan, are you feeling ready?" Coach asked. "Do you want to talk through the race, or do you feel like you're clear on what you need to do?"

"Do you still think I should start fast?" The field was a big one. I didn't want to get boxed in.

"I think you should take off fast, but I don't think you should lead," Coach said. "One of the things you do best, Ethan, is pick people off as you go along. I've told you that before and I think it's a good strategy for today. There are going to be some guys setting a very, very fast pace. I think your best bet is to maintain contact with that lead pack, but don't try to lead it. You'll need to charge them eventually, probably near that big hill partway into the course, and when you do, you can start to pick them off at the end. I know you can do it. If you need to change your race, you'll have a feel for it as it goes. Trust your race intuition—yours is as good as any I've seen, including Andrea's." He looked at his watch. "I have to go—the girls are starting. I'll be cheering for you at the end of the first turn. I think we have a chance of placing in the top three as a team if you all have the races of your lives." He shook his head. "That would be amazing."

Coach jogged away with the coordinated stride of a guy who has been running for a long time. He had given me a lot to think about. I knew that he would never get upset at me no matter how I ran. But, I have to admit, I was still pretty worried.

So was Mikey. I could almost feel her nervousness as I watched her jogging around to keep warm by the starting line. Her being nervous made me even more stressed. When the starter called out for them to line up, I thought *I* was going to throw up. When the gun went off, though, all my concern was just for her. Was she going to get blocked in? Was she going to do okay? "Go, Mikey!" I yelled, but I'm sure no one could hear. I wasn't worried about Andrea. I knew she was going to do great and I would pretty much bet my life savings on that, if I had any savings. And if I believed in betting. You know what I mean.

I ran over to where the runners would be coming past as they looped through their first mile. According to the plan, Mikey should be somewhere in the top thirty runners, and she should be about fourth on our team. There were hundreds of runners in the race, so I looked for the green and white of her uniform as hard as I could. While I waited, I jumped up and down to keep warm. I'm sure I looked like a loser, but I didn't care.

Andrea was in first and she had that expression on her face that meant everyone else had better watch out. There were two girls closing in on her but it almost seemed like Andrea was toying with them. I could tell she was working hard, but she didn't look half as drained as they did. I didn't cheer for her because she feels like cheering is a distraction. She flew by.

Where was Mikey? There she was. I furiously counted the runners ahead of her—she was in sixth place! *Oh, man, Michaela,* I thought, *I hope you didn't start out too fast.* "You're doing great!"

I yelled as she ran past. I wasn't sure if she heard me. She's pretty focused when she races, which is how I am too.

Jake Clark, our team captain, ran over to me. "Hey, Ethan, we're meeting in the bull pen now. It's time to warm up."

I had to leave the course and get ready because our race would begin the minute the girls finished. The starting line was in a different place from the finish line, so we wouldn't get to see who won. So, that was it. I wondered how it would turn out. I was worried about Mikey, but I have to admit that now I was even more worried about myself and about the guys' team. This was my first State race and a lot of people were counting on me. I didn't want to let the other guys down. They'd been great all year, totally welcoming me even though most of them had been running together since middle school.

I waved to my parents standing on the sidelines as I headed over to the bull pen. They got divorced three years ago, but they have been doing pretty good at talking and getting along recently. My dad was a high-school basketball star and I'm actually pretty surprised and happy that he gets into my running so much. He lives in Portland, but he still makes it to the big meets.

Andrea won't talk to either of them before or after a race, though, so they end up standing around my starting line a lot. That's another one of her rules, like the "no cheering during the race" rule. She has a lot of rules.

I thought about what Mikey had done before her race, so I bowed my head and said a little prayer too, asking that I could do my best and not be disappointed in the results. I looked up and noticed a couple of the guys staring at me but I didn't care. Andrea, who hasn't been into any church-type stuff since the divorce, would have rolled her eyes at me. Jake waved me over and he gave us all a little speech about running our best for the team and for ourselves. I don't really remember much about it, but Jake is a good guy and a good runner and we all respect him. Then we all yelled, "Go Lakeview!" and headed out to the starting line to warm up.

Across the field and behind a fence was the track where the runners finish. A voice from the loudspeaker announced the girls as they crossed the line. Our team yelled out for Andrea, who won the whole thing—and I do mean the whole thing. She took State. It was expected, though—Andrea has been winning everything all year and getting about as much enjoyment out of it as she does out of anything in her life, which is not much lately. Still, I was relieved to see that long reddish braid of hers bobbing in the lead, and I was glad to hear her name called first. I've been feeling lately that all it's going to take is one misstep and Andrea is going to snap.

I listened to the announcer as he listed everybody else's names. Another of our girls finished in third.

"Crossing the line in seventh is Michaela Choi, from Lakeview High!"

Michaela had taken seventh! *She must be so excited,* I thought. *That's the highest she's ever finished.* I craned my neck around, but the track was shielded from our view by its fence, bleachers, and trees. She'd be on the All-State team now. That was awesome!

But I couldn't think about Mikey anymore. Or even Andrea's big win. I had to think about my own race and what I had to do. I was happy for both of them, but I knew I couldn't think about how well they'd done, or I wouldn't be able to do anything myself. It might sound selfish, but it's true.

I wish I could describe exactly how it feels to stand on the starting line of a big race. I've heard people describe the taste in your mouth as being metallic, and I think that part is true, but I don't agree with the description of butterflies in your stomach. I feel like the metallic taste in my mouth comes from the huge, solid, metal weight sitting there in my gut, making me feel heavy and worried right when I need to feel light and unconcerned.

The other guys seemed nervous too. Even Dave, who is a senior and who has run at State all four years, wasn't making any jokes. I couldn't stop looking at the other guys and worrying that I would let them down. It's been great to be the fastest runner on the team, but all of a sudden there on that starting line, I realized what that meant. They were all pulling for me as Ethan the individual, sure, but they also needed me to race well if we were going to stand a chance of placing as a team. If I messed up, I would be disappointed in myself, but I would have also let the whole team down too. Dave, Jake, all the rest of the guys—they were my friends, and I wanted us all to do the best we could as a team. I took a deep breath and reminded myself that we could do this. That *I* could do this.

When the gun went off, I started out fast. It was almost as though I had to do it. I didn't even think about the advice Coach gave me; I didn't think about how Michaela had started out fast too. I could just feel what I needed to do. That doesn't happen to me very often. I usually have to strategize and calculate, but once in a while I just run.

Like now. The lead pack was starting to break away from me— not far, but away. I had to make a move. I moved in right behind them and kept my eyes on their heads, on their feet, on them. I could feel that we were going fast. I could feel that I was running hard, that I was hurting, but I wasn't hurting too much. Not yet.

We came around the bend of the curve that marked the first mile. I knew Coach was probably standing there somewhere, yelling advice, but I didn't spare the time to glance to the side for him. The pace was too fast to blink. I knew that if I lost focus, I would lose them.

The interesting thing about cross-country, even the State race where there is a bigger than normal crowd, is that there is a lot of the race that you run alone. The start and the finish have big crowds and so do some parts of the race. But most of it is in the middle, when it's just you and the other runners crossing the terrain with a few observers and some officials to make sure you're not cutting corners.

Most of the race is the feeling of solitude and of listening to your own breathing and feeling your own pain and your own speed. It is

becoming more acquainted with yourself with every step. It is thinking furiously and it is also not thinking at all. You are so alone with
yourself that you don't have to frame words in your mind while
you're thinking—you just know what you need to do by instinct.

When three guys broke from the first pack near the hill, I didn't
think, *I have to go with them.* I just went, but I had thought it somewhere deep inside without words. When I started running the hill
and I passed two of them, I didn't think, *Two down, one to go.* I just
ran as hard as I could for as long as I could to the finish line. I
crossed in second place, just a few steps behind the first runner, who
outran me at the end with a killer sprint.

It comes as a shock to interact with people again after a race like
that, to say "thanks" for the cups of Gatorade the volunteers are
handing out, to turn and accept congratulations from runners
behind you, to hear your coach yelling your name excitedly. But
there is a great moment where it all slides back into focus and you
feel all the excitement and adrenaline electrify you and you scream
and yell and grab your teammates and hoist your medal and smile,
smile, smile.

They took pictures of us, because the boys' team won the whole
thing. I've never seen a group of happier guys. Dave Sherman
grabbed me in the world's biggest bear hug and swung me around
and I was laughing so hard I wasn't even embarrassed. We kept slap-
ping each other on the back and giving each other high fives and pos-
ing for pictures with our parents.

The girls' team was doing the same thing because they had
placed in the top three. Their celebration was different: they were
squealing and crying the way girls do. Coach had tears in his eyes,
even when we dumped the cooler of Gatorade on him. We all felt
like a million bucks. I kept saying, "Thank you, thank you," in my
mind. I *felt* that prayer of gratitude running through me, like
electricity.

My parents were freaking out, and they took about a million

pictures of Andrea and me once she'd turned up. She hadn't been celebrating with the rest of the girls. I didn't know where she'd been. There were some newspaper photographers snapping pictures too. I heard one of them say, "Now if the brother had won first place *too* that would have been an even better story," but even that didn't make me come back to earth.

I kept catching Mikey's eye and smiling at her, but I didn't get a chance to actually talk to her until we were on the bus, going home.

On the bus, sitting there with the guys, I looked up and saw Andrea sitting alone and I realized that she never has that moment where it all slides back into focus. She stays in the mind-set of being alone and driven and running flat-out the whole time. She is one of the most beautiful girls in our school, according to all the other guys, but she doesn't seem to notice. I decided to break one of her rules. I was going to talk to her, even if it was just for a minute. It was her senior year, her last race, and the last time we would ride the bus back together from a cross-country meet.

She had earphones in and it took her a minute to notice me standing there. "Ethan," she said flatly. Her trophy was on the seat next to her and all of a sudden I felt sad to see it. She had surrounded it in sweatshirts to keep it protected and it was her only company.

She pulled out her earphones, but she didn't move over for me to sit down. "Andrea," I said, "congratulations."

"You too," she said. "That was a great race." She almost said something else, but then stopped. Then, "Don't forget—Mom only left the one car at the school, so we need to drive home together." She put her earphones back in.

"Okay," I said, hurt by her dismissal. I wished we could have sat and talked about everything that had happened, compared notes on our races, but there's a coldness in Andrea that I can't seem to get past. In spite of myself, though, I patted her on the shoulder on my way back to my seat.

I plopped back down next to Dave Sherman, who was regaling

the back of the bus with his version of "Eye of the Tiger," which I have to admit, is pretty funny. Legend has it that when they were both sophomores, Dave got Andrea to laugh once on a bus trip. That alone is a reason to like the guy. He's in our ward and it's so weird to think that he'll be going on a mission soon. That means my turn is coming up too.

It was getting dark, and we still had a while to drive. The traffic was rough. The coaches were being pretty lenient since this was the last meet of the season, and they let us pick the music to play on the bus's ancient tape deck and they didn't get mad if the guys sat with the girls or vice versa. I think they figured a little freedom wouldn't kill us or, more importantly, them.

I noticed Mikey sitting with her friend Jana a few rows ahead of me. At first, I thought about different ways to play it cool, but I suddenly decided I didn't care. I guess I was still feeling confident after my race which had gone better than expected. I stood and walked up the aisle. "Hey, Jana, could I trade you seats for a little while?"

"It depends," said Jana. "Who are you sitting with?" She craned her neck around and saw David, who was currently gorging himself on Cheese Puffs. "Oh, great. David!"

She had a point. But Mikey smiled up at me and I knew I couldn't let this opportunity pass. "Come on, Jana. Just for a few minutes."

"Since you *are* the second-fastest runner in the state, I *guess* I can cut you some slack," Jana said. She headed toward the back and David hoisted the Cheese Puffs in her direction, grinning with his orange teeth.

After she had gone, I slid into the seat next to Mikey and ignored the interested stares of some freshmen junior-varsity runners who had come along to cheer at the race. "Hey, I've been wanting to talk to you, but it's been kind of—well, it's been happening really fast."

"I know," she said. "You did a great job today. What a race. It was unbelievable to see you come around that bend. You were flying!" She cupped her hands around her mouth like a loudspeaker. "Ethan Beckett!" she called. "How did it feel to hear your name announced like that?"

"You should know," I said. She looked puzzled. "They announced you too! I heard them say you finished seventh when I was lining up to start. I knew you made the All-State team and I was really happy for you."

"Thanks," she said. "I'm happy for me too and for Andrea. *And* I'm happy for you. Second in the state!"

And she honestly did look happy for me. She was smiling and she smelled like the fresh-cut grass on the course and the bus was very dark, since it was late now. There was a little, tiny bit of coolness in the air because it was fall, but it still felt summery and golden. I wanted to take this day and keep living it over again. How was I going to go back to school and real life and days where I didn't have close-to-perfect races and the chance to sit next to the girl I liked on a bus in the dark?

"Next year," I whispered into her ear, "I'm going to be first."

"I know," she whispered back.

So I kissed her.

OCTOBER

Andrea Beckett

Stupid, stupid, stupid. That's what I was. I don't know why I couldn't have waited one more day to break up with Connor. He'd been driving me crazy for weeks—what was one more night?

But no, we had to break up the night before the Homecoming game.

It's during the Homecoming game that they parade the royalty out at halftime and announce the Homecoming Queen and King in front of the whole crowd. I had been elected to the court, and I was supposed to be escorted by my date for the dance, which happens after the game. Homecoming is a huge deal at our school—the parents come and watch and take pictures, and the whole student body shows up for the game and to see who's crowned.

Our school is big on pomp and pageantry and so we all have to be up there on the makeshift stage in the middle of the field when they announce the results of the student vote. It's almost like the Miss America Pageant, but more ridiculous and serious at the same time. It would cause a lot of consternation if I didn't show up. People would call my house; they would make a fuss; they would act like idiots. But once Connor wasn't my date, I didn't have an escort. I didn't mind missing the dance; it's so shallow and juvenile anyway. I knew it would be humiliating to walk across the stage without an escort, but I decided the alternatives were even more degrading.

I didn't want to ask Ethan or my father to escort me—that would be unbelievably pathetic. I'd rather walk alone. I also didn't want to explain to my family that Connor and I had broken up. They could figure that out for themselves later. And finally, the last alternative was to ask someone from school to be my escort. I absolutely did not want to do that. There was no reason to make a bad situation worse by groveling.

As for actually being the Homecoming Queen, I wasn't sure if I would win. I win at a lot of things. Lots of people think I'm lucky, and maybe I am, but I also work hard too. I won the State cross-country meet this year, which was a big event. I was on the front page of the newspaper and colleges started calling about scholarships. I had been working toward winning State for years and I was surprised at how I felt when I won. Sure, I felt happy, but it was more a relieved kind of happy as opposed to a wild and exhilarated happy. It was the way I felt when I got away with something when I was younger and had tricked my parents somehow.

I hate losing. I'm so competitive, in fact, I don't have time for a lot of friends. I never realized until now that you can be popular without having a lot of friends. I have people I sit by in every class, people to eat lunch with, people to call about homework assignments, but I don't really hang out with anyone on the weekends. I think that was one of the problems with dating Connor.

Connor is very good-looking and I liked having a boyfriend, but all I could think about when we were kissing was, *I have so many other things I need to be doing right now.* And everything he did seemed so mundane and predictable. That's what our fight was about. He wanted to take me somewhere to celebrate my State Championship, and his idea of something special was dinner and a movie. I realize that isn't such a ridiculous idea and that people do things like that all of the time. But that, in my mind, is precisely the problem.

"Can't we ever do something a little less asinine and high-school? Maybe go to a play, or to the ballet, or something?" I asked. Connor pointed out that I was never satisfied with what we did and that I never seemed happy with him and that I really was the Ice Queen everyone thought I was. That was enough. I got out of the car and stalked back into the house. He called out, "What about the dance?" and I called back without turning around, "You'll have to find someone who's easily satisfied."

Sometimes I hate my nickname. Sometimes I do my best to live up to it.

On the surface, it looks like I've had a perfect year—winning everything. What people don't know though is that I've been losing a lot this year too. It's similar to running up a trail when it's wet—you might look like you're gaining ground, but sometimes you can feel that you're going to fall and it's simply a matter of time. I felt that way when my parents were fighting before the divorce. I knew I was going to say or do something that would make it all worse somehow, so when I did, it wasn't a surprise.

The night of the Homecoming game, my mom dropped me off before she took Chloe into the bleachers to watch the game. Ethan had begged and pleaded with my mom to let him use the other car for the night, so I was out of luck and had to catch a ride with the family, just to make my night even more magical. I went into the dressing room in the gym before halftime, slipped into my dress and did my best to make everything look perfect. I had to be perfect. Everyone was expecting me to be. And I don't disappoint.

I saw the other two girls elected to the court and we made small talk. The girls who were the escorts for the boys on the court were there too. I wondered who Connor had found to replace me on such short notice. He probably hadn't had too much trouble.

"All right, everyone, it's time to go," Principal Downing said. She herded us all to the edge of the field where the guys were waiting for us. "Everyone pair up with your escort." Everyone did. Except for me, of course. I stood there and did my best to appear cool and unconcerned. But Principal Downing still noticed. "Andrea," she began.

I saved her the trouble. "I don't have an escort," I said, daring her to say another word.

"All right," she said, after a pause. "Let's put you at the very beginning, then."

At first, I thought that was a good idea because that way I didn't look like a little tag along, like someone who decided to attach themselves to the rest of the court as an afterthought. Then, as I stood there and heard everyone whispering behind me, and as I turned around and met Connor's eyes for a brief second before looking away, I knew that leading everyone out would be even worse. I'm always conscious of appearances and I knew that it would be much more noticeable if I paraded out there alone before everyone else as if I were already the queen or something. When Principal Downing wasn't looking, I moved out of the way and told the couple behind me to go first. They looked startled, but everyone was waiting, so they had no choice. I slipped back into line after them.

That was a long walk. The red carpet seemed to be a red version of Astroturf, prickly and cheap and synthetic. But it was much better than trying to walk across the wet playing field in high heels. I could just picture myself sinking deeper with each step into the grass. This way, we were able to hang onto a shred of dignity as we marched out in front of everyone. The crowd was cheering and I couldn't tell if anyone had noticed I didn't have an escort yet.

It was better when we stood up on the stage and they separated us out, the royalty grouped together with the escorts standing at the back, waiting to walk up with us when they announced our status. I was safe in a group for a moment, but I knew that when they called out my name, whether it was second attendant or first attendant or Queen, I would be the only one who walked up to the front of the stage alone. That was what finally made me lose my poise.

Standing and waiting for them to announce who would be the Homecoming Queen, I think I almost had an anxiety attack. The stadium lights up there were so bright and I was standing next to two girls who were wearing gallons of perfume and I was wearing a silver dress that was catching and reflecting a lot of the light. I knew my mom was sitting in the audience, rabid, with her camera at the ready.

I felt my muscles tense like they do at the start of a race and I had to hold myself back so that I didn't run. I felt sweaty and cold. I felt some of the sweat gathering on my face and I didn't even care that it might make me look bad. I didn't think I was going to make it. The crowd was quiet, waiting for the announcement. I felt myself get ready to spring.

It was right at that moment that Ms. Downing leaned in to the microphone. "Let's give our Homecoming Court this year a round of applause before we make the final announcement." The people in the stands obliged. I couldn't see any individual faces in the crowd, only smeary streaks of color, a lot of green and white because most people were wearing the school colors to the big game.

After the applause and catcalls died down, Mrs. Downing announced, "We've tallied the votes, and the race was very close. Our second attendants are Kate Larkin and Connor Manwaring." Kate and Connor stepped forward and everyone cheered. A small tide of relief washed over me. At least Connor and I didn't have to stand together. Connor and Kate accepted their little crowns and their roses and waved to the crowd. I stared straight ahead and willed myself to stay put.

"Our first attendants are Jade Winters and Michael Walker." It took a moment for that to register. That meant . . .

"Our Homecoming Queen and King this year are Andrea Beckett and Corbin Gray!" The crowd went wild. But Corbin was the quarterback and he was still in the locker room prepping for the second half of the game, so everyone's attention was on me. I walked up to the front of the stage alone. I felt the urgency to run leave me and I collapsed a little inside. It was ending. It would be over soon. I felt detached from everything again, which was a welcome relief.

I don't remember much about being crowned or accepting the roses and tiara and sash, or even really walking over to the other side of the stage for the required yearbook pictures. *Look,* I thought, *there I am being crowned Homecoming Queen. Isn't that interesting?* It was eerily similar to the way I felt when I was accepting my trophy for running. *Look, there I am winning the State Championship. Isn't that something?*

I almost made it. But then, at the very end, when we were about to leave the stage, that disengaged feeling stopped again. The anxiety was back, even worse this time. As I stood there on the stage, waiting for my turn to step off and go back into the gym, away from the lights, I wondered why people had voted for me, since I don't have many close friends. Did people vote for me because it's all about the eye candy and I happen to be five foot ten inches with long hair and the long legs of a track runner? Did they vote for me because I'm smart, or at least have that reputation? Did they vote for me because the crowd I've been hanging out with is Connor's crowd, the crowd that always wins these things? They probably voted for me because of those reasons.

I don't think anyone voted for me because they actually *like* me. No friends were waiting for me in the stands to watch the rest of the game together. No girlfriends would be ready to tell me how exciting it was that I won. I found myself wondering what my old friends from church would have said. Probably something comforting about how it's what's inside that matters and that not having a date to the dance didn't matter at all. But I would know that there wasn't much inside me anymore and even those words, meant to be comforting, would hurt. They'd probably hurt the most of all. I felt sick. The cameras flashed in our faces.

During the walk off the field, I was alone again while everyone else had their escort beside them. I still didn't run, although it took everything I had not to bolt across the wet grass and into the night, past the lights and the staring faces and the gossip and the questions that would come later. Wasn't it ironic that I could run faster than anyone in the state except for the one time I really needed to be able to flee? And even if I did run, I couldn't outrun myself.

I didn't go into the dressing room with everyone else to get my stuff. I veered toward the parking lot as soon as I was out of sight from the bleachers in the stadium. I heard someone call out my name but I ignored them. My one thought was to get out of there before anyone could find me. I didn't want to explain things to my mom, to Ethan, to Connor, to anyone.

I took off my heels, crammed the roses into a trash can, and started running across the parking lot. My feet are tough from years of running, and I ran right on the cold asphalt, feeling the rocks making indentations in my feet. The pain was almost welcome. I ran fast and quiet and smooth—until I ran right into someone. He had stepped out from his car and I slammed into him, knocking my shoes and tiara out of my hands and onto the ground. What was left of my composure crashed too.

The moonlight glittered off my tiara and my hands starting shaking like leaves. I felt tears running down my face, wreaking havoc with my mascara. But I didn't care at all. I knew I had to start running again or I might disintegrate. I didn't even look at who I'd collided with, I just mumbled, "Sorry," and stared hard at the sharp edges of my tiara. I was a grotesque caricature of Cinderella—both shoes missing, no coach, no fairy-tale ending on the way because *this* Cinderella was angry and bitter and didn't deserve one.

"Andrea? Do you need a ride home?" said the voice. I saw hands reach down to pick up my shoes and my crown.

I looked up. It was David Sherman, a guy I know fairly well from when I used to go to church, and from running. He was looking worried and serious, which wasn't his usual state. He was tall and gangly with the world's biggest smile, which he used often as the class clown. But he wasn't smiling then.

It was an out. "Yes," I said, climbing in the door he held open and pulling it shut before he could say anything. David got into his dilapidated car and looked over at me. He must have decided that it was better to just get going because he grabbed the keys out of the cup holder and started the engine. "You still live on 137th, right?" he asked. I nodded.

He drove through the dark night and I sat there and cried as though I would never stop. I didn't know it would feel so terrible and so good. I couldn't think of the last time I'd cried. David didn't say anything, but he handed me a roll of toilet paper from under the seat. I don't even want to know why that was there. I went through almost the whole roll in the few miles to my house. When we pulled into the driveway, I started crying again, and I couldn't seem to pull it together. I said, "Pull around the corner. I don't want anyone to see me." He did it without comment.

It started to rain when he stopped the engine. It's always raining here. The streetlight near the car reflected light off each droplet as it sparkled and fell to the ground. The air was thick and humid and sometimes the drops that landed on the windshield stayed there for a while before they slid lazily down to join other drops of light, making bigger and bigger jewels that eventually vanished from the windshield altogether. I followed the tracks of several drops, watching them merge and absorb and disappear, watching them as I cried. Something about it became mesmerizing and soothing, and I stopped crying after a while. I'm not sure how long.

I looked over at David. All I could see was his profile in the streetlight, his face very sad and serious, looking straight ahead and his hands still on the wheel. He turned to look at me. "You all right?"

he asked. There was no laughter in his eyes, but there was something very kind in his face. I felt a rush of gratitude toward him. It was thoughtful of him not to watch me while I cried.

I nodded shakily and tried to give him a smile, a confident smile, an "isn't this funny?" smile. I don't know what it looked like, but it didn't have quite the effect I'd intended. I'd wanted to put him at ease, to make him think that I was simply having one of those days and would be fine, to make him crack one of his signature jokes, to make him let me go. Instead, it made him reach out and take my hand, the one full of mascara- and tear-stained tissues, and hold it tight for a second before he let it go. I opened the door. I realized I had to get out or I was going to start crying again.

"Thanks," I said a little too cheerfully. I climbed out and started toward my house, hoping he didn't see that the tears were starting again. I couldn't keep being vulnerable this way. It had already gone straight past embarrassing to humiliating and was rapidly approaching ludicrous. I was a few steps away when I heard the car door open again.

"Wait!" David said. "You forgot your tiara!" He was standing there by the car, holding it out in front of him like an offering, his skinny arms sticking straight out in front of him. The crown looked garish and fake and not nearly as beautiful as the rain falling everywhere. But he was serious.

"Keep it," I said. I tried to smile again and gave him a little wave. Then I started running up the sidewalk. He knew enough not to come after me.

OCTOBER, PHOENIX, AZ

Tyler Cruz

It was ridiculously easy to forget that nothing was the way it should be. I forgot for a few hours tonight that my world as I know it is about to end. Funny what a conversation with a good-looking girl can do to you.

After work today, my dad came home and announced that he was going to ruin my life. Then he told me I should be excited about it, that I should think positively. What he said was, "I got the job with Microsoft in Redmond! They want me to start as soon as I can."

My mother, who is a pediatrician, beamed at him. "That's wonderful news!" She was thrilled because her parents live in the Seattle area and she's always wanted to go back. She'd already been in touch with a practice that she wanted to join and all we needed was for my dad to get the right job. Everything was really coming together for us, my parents kept saying, forgetting that there was a third person to this family. Me.

We'd lived in Phoenix for ten years, long enough that it was the only place I really remembered, and therefore, the only place I really belonged. I had friends in Phoenix and a history in Phoenix.

Not all of it was perfect, but all of it was mine. I'd never been on board with this plan and they both knew it.

After hugging each other and giving each other congratulations, they both looked at me with a little bit of fear in their eyes. We were standing in the kitchen where I had risked my mom's wrath by starting to eat my dinner before it was done. I'm an only child, which is lonely on the one hand and also kind of nice on the other. What I say carries a lot more weight, I think, than if I had a bunch of brothers and sisters. But, in this case, I could have used some backup.

"You both know I don't want to move," I said. "I'm not excited. I'm not happy about this. I don't want to go." I put my spoon on the counter and grabbed the keys to the car. "I'll be back. I'm going to the gym to shoot around."

Neither of them tried to stop me. They just shot those significant looks at each other that annoy me. As I backed out of the driveway, I could see through the kitchen window. They were sitting at the table, talking. As much as I hoped they were saying, "Well, Tyler's upset, so we'd better just stay," I knew they weren't. At least I was missing some of the excited planning that was going on in there. I had known this was coming, but now that the axe had fallen, I felt more anger—and more sorrow—than I'd expected, and it was ticking me off.

I wondered if I could talk them into letting me stay behind to finish out the basketball season. We'd started some informal practices in the past two weeks and it was obvious that the team was going to be phenomenal this year. I wanted to be a part of it, not a part of some other team in Seattle.

As I drove to the high school, I hoped that Coach would be staying late and that the gym would be open. I needed to run fast down the court, to see the ball sail through the air into the hoop, to drive hard to the basket, to feel the way the basket springs back under my hands after a slam dunk, to feel my feet slide along the hardwood floor. Basically what I had in mind was a completely sensory experience—feeling and seeing and not thinking at all.

The side door to the gym was unlocked. Perfect. I opened it and went in, then stopped. There were people and newspapers and paint and wire all over the gym. "What's going on?" I asked the girl closest to the door. I must not have done a very good job at keeping the frustration out of my voice. She turned and looked at me with a smile on her lips.

Talk about a sensory experience.

Our school is huge, but I would have known if I'd seen this girl before. It wasn't so much that she was pretty, although she was. It was more that she was interesting-looking. Her eyes were really big, bright green, and alive. And she smelled like cinnamon, or something else spicy and different. She definitely didn't smell like the gym. Her blonde hair was pulled back in a long braid, and she was wearing jeans and flip-flops and a T-shirt. Nothing showy, but still she caught your eye. "They're working on a float for the Homecoming Parade," she said. "Are you here to help?"

"No," I said. "I was hoping to play some ball. Who are you? You don't go to school here."

She laughed. "No, I don't. I'm here for the weekend, visiting my cousins. I'm from Tucson."

"Who are your cousins?" I asked.

She pointed to our student body president, Libby Snow, who was obviously in charge tonight. She stood in the center of the activity, coordinating the efforts. "Libby's my cousin. She brought me along tonight to help. I'm in charge of this." She pointed to a huge pile of tissue paper squares. "I'm folding them into flowers for the float."

I raised one eyebrow at her, which girls usually find attractive and sardonic. "That's kind of a mind-numbing project for a Friday night, don't you think?"

She raised one eyebrow back at me, which I found attractive and sardonic. "It would be more interesting if I had someone to talk to. Lib's pretty busy with supervising those guys over there, so she abandoned me. She smiled. "I owe it to her, though. Last year, when I was in charge of the junior prom at my school, she helped *me* decorate."

I weighed my options. I could leave and go home to face the music, leave and head over to Max's house to hang out with my friends, or stay and fold tissue paper flowers with a girl who didn't even live here. I chose the path of least resistance, which also seemed the path of most interest for some reason. "All right," I said. "Show me how to fold the flowers. Might as well donate an hour or two in the name of school spirit."

"Really?" she said. Smiling, she handed me a square of blue paper. "I'm Maya, by the way."

"Tyler," I said, sticking out my free hand. We shook hands and I sat down next to her on the floor. She showed me how to fold the paper and staple it. It was a pretty mindless job. But that was good. I could still talk to her, think about how angry I was at my parents, and staple away.

"When you're done, throw them in here," she said, tossing one into a clean plastic garbage can. "Then, when it's full, we'll take them over and attach them to the float."

"Maybe I'll get a chance to practice my game after all," I said, aiming my tissue paper flower straight into the garbage can.

"Are you on the basketball team?" she asked.

"Is he on the basketball team? He practically *is* the basketball team," said Libby, who had come up behind us. "Hey, Tyler."

"Hi, Libby," I said. "I came here to play, but it looks like you've taken over the gym."

"Yeah, I guess we did," she said, looking around at the mess. "Sorry about that. It looks like you've met Maya. Maya, you should know that Tyler is the only guy who could ever give Noah a run for his money on the court."

Noah was Libby's older brother. He had been a huge star on the basketball team, but he graduated right before I got to high school. Everyone still talks about him and it's his records I'm out to beat.

"How is Noah, anyway?" I asked. "He ended up taking a basketball scholarship to that school in Utah, right? But then Coach said he was taking a break for a couple of years, going to New Zealand or something?"

"Yeah, he went to Australia," Libby said. "He took a two-year leave to serve a mission for our church. That's why Maya is here. He just got home this week and everyone came to see him and hear him give his talk at our church meetings this weekend." She stopped, distracted. "Oh *no*. Those guys are starting to attach the balloons to the frame and it's nowhere near time for that yet . . ." And she was gone.

Maya tossed a flower toward the can. She missed by a mile.

"Not your sport?" I teased her.

She laughed. "Not at all. I'm a swimmer. It doesn't require any hand-eye coordination."

"No wonder you're so tan. You must have been a lifeguard this summer."

She nodded. "It's the perfect summer job. What did you do?"

"Nothing, really," I said. "I went to a lot of basketball camps so there wasn't much time to get a regular job. But when I was home, I worked some for my neighbors doing yard work, helping one of them frame his garage, stuff like that."

"No wonder *you're* so tan," she said.

"Yeah, but that's about to change." I threw some more flowers into the can a little harder than was necessary. "My parents just told me tonight that we're moving to Seattle. All it ever does there is rain."

She looked at me with what appeared to be true sympathy in her face. "You're moving? Now?"

I nodded. "Well, as soon as my parents find a house, which won't take long. They've been scoping out neighborhoods and homes for months and they know the area really well. That's where my mom is from. And even if we don't find a house, we'll rent something. They want to be up there for me to start school there in January. It sucks."

"I hear you," she said. "We moved from Utah to Tucson my freshman year in high school. Talk about an awkward time to change schools. I was insecure enough about starting high school anyway. I was so mad at my parents that I didn't speak to them for a week." She laughed. "They actually probably appreciated that since all I'd been doing before then was whining. I have three brothers too and all *they* were doing was whining."

"I'm trying to decide which one I should do, myself," I said. "I'm an only child, so if I quit speaking to them, they'll notice for sure. So maybe griping about it nonstop would be better. I should decide soon so I can get started."

Maya walked an armful of flowers over to the garbage can and started letting them drift down into it, one by one. I noticed that she had stuck one of the flowers into her hair, which was the golden-yellow color of the hardwood floor in the gym.

"Nice touch," I said, standing up and bringing my flowers over to the garbage can.

"What?" she said.

"The flower in your hair," I said, leaning in close enough to pull it out.

She laughed. "I was getting bored until you got here."

"Are you bored now?" I said, sticking the flower back into her braid. Then I stepped back to admire the effect and to see what she was going to say.

Maya grinned. She had one of those smiles that took over her whole face, crinkling her eyes and wrinkling her nose. It was cute. "Nope," she said, walking back to the tissue paper pile. I followed her.

"It's good to talk to someone who doesn't know you once in a while," she said. "It's fun to talk to people who don't have any pre-conceptions about you and what you do and who you are and who will give you a chance the first time they meet you. That's one of the things I liked about moving, once I noticed it. Of course, not everyone was like that. There were jerks in Tucson just like there were jerks at my old school. But it felt good, in a way, to have a clean slate. And it was also good to feel the same way about other people—every new person was a potential friend. I didn't have all the preconceptions about people that everyone else did because they'd all grown up together, you know what I mean?"

"I bet that came in handy when you ran for junior class president," I said.

"It did, but that's not why I ran. I ran because I wanted to get really involved and give back to a school that I felt like had given a lot to me." She stopped. "Hey—how did you know I was class president?"

"A guess," I said. "Why else would you be in charge of the junior prom? And I would vote for you in a second."

"Speaking of preconceptions, I'm trying not to have any about you," she said. "But it's hard when you keep coming up with these little pickup lines. You're one of those guys who's always sweet-talking the ladies, aren't you?" There was some sarcasm in her voice, but enough warmth in her eyes and smile that I didn't take offense.

"Maybe," I said. "But, preconceptions aside, what do you think?"

She surprised me by getting very serious. "I think you're a good guy. A good person."

It was quiet for a second. I don't know why it felt so good to have a perfect stranger tell me I was a good person, but it did. Then the teasing look came back into her face. "But I've been wrong before."

We talked for the rest of the evening and into the night, until every tissue paper flower was stapled and thrown into the garbage can and then until every flower in the can was glued onto the frame of the float. Somewhere along the way Maya acquired a lot more tissue paper flowers in her hair—I may have had something to do with that—and I picked up a lot of advice about starting over in a new school.

When the float was finished, Libby went to the student government room to put some things away, and Maya and I sat on the bleachers to wait for her. I didn't want to leave until they did. The gym was empty except for the two of us, the float, and the basketball standards at either end. Maya said, "Are you going to be okay with your move?"

"I don't know," I said. I didn't want to think about the future, just the present. I told her that, and she laughed.

"I understand," she said. "What are you going to miss the most about living here?"

"Basketball, and the guys on the team," I said without hesitation. "And the way night feels in the desert." She gave me another raised-eyebrow look. I held up my hands. "Not a pickup line. Haven't you noticed the way it feels here? So dry and dark but alive. I love that."

"Yeah," she said. "That's true. It does." We sat there for a second, thinking. I was remembering a camping trip with my dad a few years ago, one I hadn't thought about in a long time. We had been camping up on a mesa in his little two-man tent that he'd had since college and we'd had one of our deeper conversations. At night, we'd warmed up cans of Dinty Moore stew on his camp stove. We'd each had our own pan and we'd sat there together eating the stew right out of the pan with our spoons and sticking big pieces of French bread in there to mop up the rest. We're big eaters, my dad and me. The sun went down, and the night sounds in the desert were picking up. I could smell the sagebrush and the smoke from our campfire. When I'd finished sopping up the last of my stew, my dad had put some more brush on the fire and we'd started making s'mores. (Like I said, we're big eaters.)

I remembered laughing really hard when my dad brought out a bunch of those yellow marshmallow chickens that they sell at Easter to use in our s'mores. I don't know how old they were, but they were definitely on the stale side. My old man cannot resist a bargain. The stick was kind of short, which meant my fingers got too hot after a while. My dad and I took turns spearing the poor Peeps with the little dry sticks and roasting them over the fire. "This is kind of sadistic," he said, and I had to agree. We spent a long time cracking jokes and stuffing our faces. Then we'd sort of had a talk after the sun went down and we were both resting in our sleeping bags. His tent had kind of a skylight. He unzipped the window in the roof of the tent and we looked out through the netting.

"Check out all the stars, Ty," he said from his sleeping bag.

"There's a lot more here than in the city," I said. There were about a million of them.

"No kidding," he said. "It always makes me feel kind of small."

"What do you think is out there?" I asked him. I'd never really known how my parents felt about religion or what happens after you die. I tried not to think about that too much.

"I don't know, kiddo," he said. I remember feeling proud that he felt like I was grown-up enough for him to be honest like that with me. "I'd like to think that there's a God and that more stuff happens after we die, but I've never been really sure."

He was quiet for a few minutes. Then he steamrolled over me in his sleeping bag and we started laughing so hard that we forgot all about the other stuff.

I didn't know what Maya had been thinking about while I'd been remembering, but I soon found out.

"You could negotiate a deal with your parents," she said after a moment. "Tell them that if they'll let you stay behind or if they postpone the move until after the basketball season, you promise to be happy about the move and give it all a fair chance. It's worth a try."

"You think that would work?"

"It might, if you really mean it and live up to it when you do move," she said. "I don't know your parents or anything, but it could be worth a shot. There has to be someone they would trust leaving you with, or something they could work out for a couple of months if they felt like it would be a good thing for your family."

"Yeah," I said, feeling hopeful for the first time. "They might go for that. The season's only until March. Maybe it would be worth a couple of months to them to have me be a happy little camper." The minute I said that, I thought again about that camping trip, and I decided that my dad and I would have to find some good places to go camping in Washington if it quit raining for a minute. That was one thing to look forward to, at least. I'm sure it wouldn't smell or feel the way camping in the desert does, but I bet we could find some cans of stew and I *think* we could still both fit into that little tent. On second thought, maybe we should invest in another one.

The float was done. It was time to go home. Libby, her boyfriend James, Maya, and I were the last ones left. We walked toward the parking lot in a group, but Maya and I lagged a little behind.

"I wonder if I'll see you again," I said. "This has all been kind of surreal."

"You could come to Noah's homecoming," she said. When I looked blank, she said, "You know, that meeting he's speaking at, about Australia. The one at our church. It's Sunday at 9:00 A.M."

"Nine in the morning on the *weekend?*" I said. "You've got to be kidding me!"

"Coach is coming," Libby added, turning around. "And some of the guys from the team will probably be there. We'd love to have you."

"Okay," I said. "I'll think about it. That's pretty early, but it might be cool. You don't think Noah would think it was weird that I came? I mean, I don't really know him."

"Oh no," Libby said mischievously, winking at Maya. "I think he'd understand." We arrived at Libby's car. "Let me write down the address for you," Libby said, opening the glove compartment and pulling out a pen. Maya donated a tissue paper flower from her hair to write the address down on and handed it to me.

"Thanks," I said, waving as they all climbed into their car. "Thanks for everything, Maya," I added. "The moving advice, all of that."

"No problem," Maya said. "See you Sunday." She gave me one last smile.

I grinned back, feeling the softness of the tissue paper flower in my hand.

I love the way night feels in the desert. I drove home, thinking about how to ask my parents to stay so that I would be able to leave.

CHAPTER 7

NOVEMBER

Julie Reid

I used to wish I had never been born. I first wished it when I was little and my parents were fighting. I wished it again every time my brothers broke the law and caused trouble. One time I didn't was two years ago when my stepdad asked if I wanted to be adopted and have his name instead. I wouldn't have to go to school at the beginning of each year and have the teachers all say, "Julie Cox . . . Are you Kevin and Mark's sister?" I always had to say "Yes," because if I lied, they'd find out eventually anyway. The teachers would get this look on their faces, like now they were going to have to keep an eye on me or something. They'd always try to hide their surprise when I turned out not to be a troublemaker. I didn't want to surprise anyone anymore.

Even though it helps to have a different last name, there are still plenty of people who know who I am. The other kids know about my brothers and the teachers usually do too. I knew that, of all people, my music teacher, Mr. Thomas, would know who I was and what my brother had done.

I couldn't believe it when he arrived as our teacher. I had never been assigned his dad's English class, and if I had, I would have changed it immediately. I had no idea that Mr. Thomas, the son, would be teaching choir. My schedule said "Mrs. Durham" because Mrs. Durham had been the music teacher forever. I had decided to take beginning choir to fill my cultural arts requirement since my brothers had always taken art. I figured I'd have a better chance of the choir teacher not knowing that I was related to them. Plus, I really like to sing, though I only really dare to do it when I'm alone. Anyway, I thought I would be safe. I never am.

On the first day of school I was sitting in the third row from the back. I think that's the best place to sit. The teachers always notice you if you're right in front, but if you sit clear in the back they think you're a troublemaker, which is sometimes true. That's where Everett always sits.

I was watching everyone come in and talk to each other. Girls hugged like they hadn't seen each other in years. Guys called out to each other. Everyone was kind of checking each other out to see how people had changed over the summer. Some people had changed a lot. There were a few people who had gotten new clothes, new hairstyles, new everything. I've wondered what it would be like to do that—have a complete makeover and throw away everything I had before—but we've never had a ton of money the way some kids' families do. I was wearing *some* new clothes, but they were ones I'd picked out that would blend right in: jeans and a gray cable-knit sweater. I wondered what it would be like to wear an outfit that demanded attention.

Everyone else was all talking a mile a minute when a young man came in. He was tall and thin and looked sort of familiar somehow. He smiled, a little nervously, I thought, and walked to the front of the room. He tapped his baton on the top of his black metal music stand. No one noticed, except for me. He tried again. Nothing. Then he walked over to the piano and started playing the chords from what I later found out was Beethoven's *Fifth Symphony* as loud as he could. Everyone stopped and looked at him.

"Thanks," he said and walked back to the music stand. "I'm your new choir teacher, Mr. Thomas." People looked at each other in surprise. I was surprised too, but I hadn't made the connection yet. "Mrs. Durham decided to retire over the summer, so I'm taking her place."

And then someone asked the question that changed everything for me. "Are you related to Mr. Thomas the English teacher?"

"Yes, I'm his son," said Mr. Thomas. He made kind of a lame joke about not holding that against him, but I wasn't listening at all. I felt like someone had slapped me hard and quick across the face when I was in the middle of laughing. I had felt so safe and kind of excited about being in choir, and then this. I hadn't known he was related to Mr. Thomas.

I hadn't known he was the son of the woman Kevin killed that awful, awful night.

Ever since the first day of school, I've wondered if Mr. Thomas hates me. He is perfectly polite. He says hello to me and he didn't even miss a beat when he called roll the first time. He's been nothing but kind so far. But there might be something underneath.

I feel like I'm waiting for the storm to hit. Every day I go to class and think, *Today's going to be the day he gets mad at me.* Or, *Today, he's going to take me aside and ask me to quit choir.* I don't know how much longer I can keep going to school because I have a sick, waiting-for-something-bad-to-happen feeling all of the time. There are two people I'm terrified of right now—Mr. Thomas and Everett Wilson. I felt like I could deal with either one of them alone, but the combination of the two of them is too much. I wanted to start all over and it was beginning to feel impossible.

Something had to give and one day it did. I passed Everett in the hall right before choir. He leaned over to me as I stood by my locker and whispered something gross, something humiliating. I didn't even turn to look at him, but he laughed when I dropped my notebook. "I can still get to you, can't I?" he said, and then he went down the hall. I took a deep breath and picked up my notebook. I shut my locker and turned around. A few people were looking at me. I didn't want anyone to see me with Everett, ever. I hurried to choir as fast as I could without even thinking about where I was going, which was right from one scary situation to the next.

When Mr. Thomas walked up to the front of the room to begin, I felt all the worry and exhaustion weighing right behind my eyes. I felt like I couldn't see clearly. He started us off on the first few lines of our song and I tried to sing along with everyone else, but I couldn't seem to get enough air. All of a sudden, my legs gave in and buckled like a baby's. I sat down on the floor, dizzy. Everyone turned to see what trouble I was causing. I felt like crying but tried not to, because I knew that would only make everything worse. First Everett drawing attention to me in the hall, now falling apart in choir. I knew everyone was murmuring and whispering about me. I heard the sharp *click* as Mr. Thomas set down his baton and the sound of his shoes as he walked over to me.

"Are you okay?" he said.

I nodded. I didn't make eye contact. "I'm fine. I think it's just a little hot in here."

"You look like you could use a drink," he said kindly. "Michaela"—he turned to the girl next to me—"will you walk with Julie down the hall and make sure she gets to the nurse's office all right?"

"Sure," she said, looking at me with concern.

Mr. Thomas helped me up and, when he could tell I really was okay, handed me over to Michaela. He smiled and turned back to conducting the class. Michaela kept a grip on my arm, firm but kind.

"I feel a lot better," I said shyly to her as we walked down the hall. "I'm sorry for bothering you and making you leave class. That was really embarrassing."

"Don't worry about it, seriously," she said. "I've had that happen to me before. I was in church and I had to give a talk. I didn't sit down like you did, but I came really close. It was awful."

"I don't think I need to go to the nurse's office," I said. "I feel better already. Maybe I'll just splash some cold water on my face in the bathroom."

Michaela studied me. "You do look better. It's always so hot in there," she said, as she pushed open the bathroom door.

As we walked in, we both heard someone throwing up in the bathroom stall. It didn't sound good, not that throwing up ever sounds good, but this sounded awfully bad. It sounded like Kevin after a long wild night of partying, but I didn't tell Michaela that. We looked at each other for a minute, then Michaela walked over to the stall door and gently knocked.

"Are you okay in there?" she said.

"Yes, I am."

Whoever it was, it sounded like an adult, maybe a teacher or a staff member. Michaela looked as startled as I felt. "I'm just not feeling so well today," the voice said.

I could relate to that. "Do you want us to get the nurse or anything?"

"I think I'll be fine in just a moment," the voice said. "Thank you."

Michaela and I looked at each other again. "We should do something," I whispered.

She nodded.

"I have some gum," I said. Right after I said it, I thought, *That's a stupid idea.*

Michaela didn't think so. "That will help. She'd have to go the rest of the day smelling like barf. And it sounds like she might be a teacher or something." We spoke quietly, but I'm sure that whoever was in there could hear us whispering about her. That's a terrible feeling. I feel it all the time when I walk by Everett and any of his friends.

I stuck my hand under the door, nervously, as though I were feeding some sort of caged animal that I couldn't see. An animal that might bite my hand right off. "Here," I said. I felt her hand take the gum from mine. "Are you sure you're okay?"

"Thank you. I do feel better." There was a little more energy in her voice. Michaela said, "All right." I motioned to her that we should leave. I didn't want whoever it was to be embarrassed when she came out and saw us.

We stopped at the drinking fountain outside of the bathroom, and I splashed my face with the cold water.

"I wonder who was in there," Michaela mused. "I guess you're not the only one who felt sick today."

I agreed. "At least I didn't throw up in front of everyone. That would have been even worse than what I did."

"You know what?" Michaela said. "My worst fear is that I'm going to stand up in front of the class to give a presentation sometime and I'm going to wet my pants."

I laughed. "Really?" I didn't know Michaela very well, even though we'd been in school together for a while, but that fear didn't seem to fit my image of her. "You don't seem like a class presentation would make you very nervous."

"Oh, it does," she said, laughing along with me. "That was a really good idea about the gum, by the way. I wanted to do something, but I didn't know what."

"I felt the same way," I said. "I feel like that a lot. Like there's something I should be doing and I always mess things up somehow and do the wrong thing. And once you've made a mistake, you can't go back. At least she seemed to want the gum. You never know how people are going to react sometimes."

We were walking away from the drinking fountain when we saw her come out of the bathroom. I know that neither of us hid our surprise very well when we saw that familiar spiky blonde hair and those sharp eyes. It was Principal Downing. She smiled at us and said, "Thank you for the gum." She moved off down the hall at a brisk pace.

Michaela and I stared at each other. "Poor Ms. Downing!" I said.

"Who would have ever thought we'd hear our principal throw up?" she said. "That's so weird! What's she doing at school if she's so sick?"

"Maybe there was a meeting or something she really had to go to," I said as we walked down the hall toward our music class.

Our high school has gray linoleum floors that always seem scuffed and dirty. I've gotten here early in the morning, though, and they are spotless, shining away under the fluorescent lights. I wonder if it makes the janitors mad that we mess up their halls every day and they have to keep cleaning them. I feel like that's what I'm doing sometimes. I feel like I'm getting up and starting over, not only cleaning up all my mistakes but the ones Kevin and Mark made too.

Right before we got to the choir door, Michaela stopped me. "This is going to sound really weird," she said, "but I have to tell you that you're wrong."

"What?" I said, surprised. "I'm wrong about what?"

"What you said earlier, about not being able to go back after you've made a mistake. You can't go back and change what happened, but you can be forgiven for it and be clean again if you really want to." She looked a little uncomfortable as I stared at her. "That's what my church teaches. I wanted to tell you that for some reason. I didn't want you to feel like you couldn't fix whatever it was that was bothering you, or at least feel better about it."

Tears stung my eyes. Did she know about me? Did she know about my brothers?

We opened the door to our classroom. The students were all singing and Mr. Thomas was conducting. A few people turned to look at us. One of them was Mr. Thomas. He raised his eyebrows at us while his hands flew through the air. I mouthed the words, *I'm okay,* as Michaela and I slid back into our places. He smiled and gave me a thumbs-up sign.

As Michaela picked up our music and looked for the place, she whispered, "Some of us are going to a church activity tonight. Me and Ethan Beckett—do you know him? And David Sherman. Do you want to come with us? We're just playing floor hockey in the gym at our church and then having some food, but it will be fun, I think. It's not like an actual church meeting or anything, just something fun."

"Sure," I said. No one has asked me to hang out in months, not since Everett. I didn't know how to play floor hockey, but I felt reckless, in a good way. I smiled at Michaela. She grinned back.

I opened my mouth to start singing again and the words came flying out with the music. They floated around the room, and I felt weightless too. I felt fine, or like things could be fine, for the first time in months.

NOVEMBER

David Sherman

Ah, journal writing. Something I do about every decade. I haven't written in here in so long. The last entry was about receiving the Aaronic Priesthood—that was almost six years ago! Back then my worst fear was that I would mess up what seemed to be the really complicated formations that everyone else knew by heart when it was time to deliver the bread and water for the sacrament to exactly the right spots. Or that I would spill the water all over someone. And I think I was also probably pretty worried that my voice wouldn't ever change and that I would never get to dance with a girl at a stake dance. Some things change, including my voice (thank the powers that be for that).

Back then, Andrea's parents were married and she still came to church. I don't think I thought much about her then. I knew she was there, of course, but she has always been so far

61

out of my league. A few years later she quit coming altogether and her father moved away and now it's just Ethan and his mom and his other sister. I know my mom, who was Andrea's Mia Maid leader, tried to get her to come back, but finally she gave up and said that Andrea needed some time. Andrea doesn't even come to early-morning seminary at the church, which her mom teaches. Andrea and I have both been on the cross-country team for four years and I know her brother Ethan pretty well, but I haven't thought that much about her, to be honest. She kind of moves in a different circle. Plus, high school for me has been one big good time. I haven't ever done anything really sinful or anything, but there was a lesson in early-morning seminary a few weeks ago that kind of hit me between the eyes.

Our teacher, who, as I mentioned, happens to be Andrea's mom, was talking about sins of commission and sins of omission. I'm sure I've had a lesson on the same subject before because all the church lessons seem to go in rounds, like the pride cycle. There's the one on the sacrament, the one on morality (my personal favorite because, whatever else it may be—embarrassing or awkward—it's never boring), the one on Joseph Smith, the one on the priesthood, etc., etc. I'm not saying that's a bad thing. I need all the repetition I can get, I bet. Anyway, on this particular go-around, it was the part in the lesson on sins of omission that really got to me.

I've been congratulating myself lately on making it through high school without any especially grievous sins. No immorality problems, no drugs, no alcohol, I've been decent to most people, I think, no huge dramatic arguments with my parents (well, none that resulted in me getting shown the door, anyway). Sometimes with the world the way it is today you get to thinking that's a pretty big accomplishment. I'm not saying that I was thinking I was the greatest guy ever or that I'd never been tempted to do anything wrong. But I was feeling pretty good about making it to senior year with my life still in order (although my parents do think that I could be more serious a lot of the time).

Then, in our lesson, Sister Beckett talked about how sometimes the worst sins can be the ones that we don't actively commit, like going out and getting drunk, but the ones we fail to do, like treating someone the way the Savior would. She told us about how it was especially sad when we committed those sins because we knew better and were giving up a chance to become even more like the Savior than we could be if all we did was follow the rules. She pointed out that the Savior didn't just obey the laws and do the right thing; He also actively sought out others to serve and looked for things He could do for people. I'd never thought of things that way before. It surprised me and it made me think, a lot. I stayed awake in all my classes for the rest of the day, which doesn't always happen after early-morning seminary. I kept thinking about Sister Beckett's lesson and decided to try to do better over the next few weeks. Try to help people like the Savior would.

Two weeks ago, I was at the Homecoming Game with a bunch of my friends. We were going to go to the dance afterwards. Most of the other guys' dates were there, but my date, Holly Clark, was on a volleyball trip and wouldn't be getting back until just in time for the dance. Halftime came and it was time to see who the Queen would be (and the King too, I guess, although that little piece of political correctness always cracks me right up, since no guy in his right mind really wants to be paraded up there as the King, does he?). They called the names and there came Andrea Beckett, walking across the red carpet totally alone with no escort. Her boyfriend Connor had an escort, though.

I've never heard gossip start in a million places simultaneously before. It was really weird. It was like there was this pause in the crowd as everyone breathed in and then everyone started talking. "She doesn't have a date!" "Ooohh . . . I wonder if Connor dumped her last night so he could take Katherine!" "She's hot . . . I'd be her escort in a second." "She's always so stuck up . . . it serves her right." "Wouldn't it be great if she won Queen and had to go up there all alone?" And on and on like that. Not one person I could hear was interested in Andrea the person, just Andrea the potential scandal.

I was sitting pretty close to the front and I could almost see the expression on Andrea's face as she was waiting for them to announce the Queen. I might have been imagining it, but it seemed like she was scared and going to panic. I couldn't take it anymore. I decided to go home in case my date got home early, or something. I told my buddies, but they were too interested in watching what was happening to really care. I headed out through the crowd to my car, trying hard not to pay any attention to what was going on over the loudspeakers.

Well, not that hard. I paused partway across the parking lot to listen and I heard them announce her name. I wondered what people were saying now. No matter what, it was going to be tough for her to walk that walk all by herself. I couldn't help but admire her. I was just glad I hadn't had to see her face or listen to anyone around me when she won.

By the time I located my old beast of a car, I saw her. She was running toward me across the parking lot, like Cinderella with her ball gone horribly awry. (Did I spell that right? Posterity, you'll have to check it for me. I'm too lazy to find a dictionary right now. Besides, you're lucky to be reading a journal entry from me anyway!) I could tell she wasn't really paying attention, but I didn't think she'd run right into me, which she did, and everything went flying and she started to cry.

It was really weird seeing Andrea Beckett cry. I'd never thought of her crying. She's so beautiful and she's always winning everything. She's like Midas, with a golden touch. But she was really crying, tears everywhere, makeup everywhere, no holds barred. I couldn't stand it.

I mumbled something about a ride home, and to my surprise, she agreed. She got in the car so fast and slammed the door so quickly that I could tell she wanted out of there right away. I didn't know what to do so I handed her the roll of toilet paper that's been rolling around my car since the last camping trip (I think my mess kit is in there somewhere too). She used up almost the whole thing crying.

She had me pull around the corner of her house, so no one would see her if they came by, I guess, and I asked her if she was all right (like an idiot) and of course she lied and said yes. I sat there the whole time and wished that there were something I could do. I got the feeling that she was crying about more than the whole Homecoming thing and being alone on the stage. But how do you ask someone to explain what's wrong when it's fairly obvious their heart is breaking? I couldn't even think of any jokes to make that wouldn't make everything a hundred times worse. She tried to smile at me like everything was okay, but I knew it wasn't, and so without thinking I reached out and held her hand. She let me for just a second before she reached for the door to leave.

She was partway up the walk when I noticed she had left her crown behind. I grabbed it and jumped out. "Wait!" I yelled. "You forgot this!" I held it in front of me. She smiled at me and told me to keep it and ran inside. I wanted to go after her and talk to her, but it didn't seem like the right thing to do. So, I took the crown and went home and went on my date later that night.

It's been two weeks now and nothing has really happened. We say hello in the halls but don't talk any more than we did before. I took the crown to school once to try to give it back to her, but there's no really subtle way to pass someone their Homecoming crown on the sly, so I brought it back home and buried it in my closet somewhere. I need to give it back to her.

Even if she doesn't think so, that crown represents something. It's just a fake crown that the student body officers ordered for the occasion, but it represents something more than that stupid Homecoming mess to me now and I wish that I could explain it to her.

Andrea really is regal. I knew that when she marched up to take her state trophy and I knew that when she was crying in the car. It's like I saw for a minute how she really is— maybe how the Savior would see her—kind of alone and just like the rest of us, hurt by things that happen. I think she feels like people won't respect her or something if they think she isn't perfect. But, even though she's not perfect, she's still a person who matters. Everyone matters. I wonder if she doesn't come to church because she can't see that anymore. Could I talk to her about something like that?

So what do I do? If I bring things up and everything goes wrong, I'll feel like I made her feel worse and hurt her even more. But, if I sit around and do nothing, I might miss my chance to help her. And I admit it. I've fallen for her.

It was a lot easier being a deacon. Even though I did spill the water that one Sunday.

CHAPTER 9

DECEMBER

Avery Matthews

Yesterday I was suspended for smoking on the school grounds again. It's the second time (they caught me in November too), so now everyone is getting very serious. Please. Like kids don't do worse things every day. Ms. Downing, our stupid principal, gave me a little speech about how I should have pride in myself and treat my body with respect. Whatever. She's not looking so hot herself. I wouldn't be surprised if *she* were doing a little something on the side. Her eyes have been absolutely bloodshot all week.

So today I couldn't go to school because of the suspension. My parents, who were obviously not happy with the whole situation, didn't really know what to do with me. They yelled, I yelled, I got grounded for some indeterminate, completely ridiculous amount of time, and then they were stuck deciding who was going to "monitor" me for the next few days while I couldn't go to school. They ended up deciding to call every hour to see what I was doing and that they would take their lunches at different, undisclosed times so that they could come home and make sure I was there. What do they think this is? A major espionage endeavor? If I want to leave, I'll leave. If, like right now, I can't seem to find the energy, I won't.

So here I am, listening to my music as loudly as possible and drinking—a double latte, nothing more. As a day goes, it could be worse. It could also be better. Yesterday was only the third or fourth time I'd smoked. I don't think that smoking a few times is nearly as bad as, say, Everett Wilson. That guy is pure poison, but he never gets in trouble for anything. Not even for the way he treats girls.

The term hasn't been going so well for me. It started going downhill the very first day of school. I found out then that I had been cut from the volleyball team, which really surprised me (and the assistant coach, by the way). I started not liking the way I looked. And the weather—I hate the winter. It's so dark and long and depressing. Why get up in the morning if you automatically know it's going to be cold or raining? Better to cut your losses and stay in bed.

I got bored with listening to music, so I decided to watch some talk shows. Those always make me feel better about myself in a hurry. The people on there are so messed up that they make me look like Avery Matthews, Adolescent Genius.

I was halfway through a particularly pathetic show when my dad walked in the door. I turned the TV off and assumed a look I like to call "Bored Nonchalance Version Five" when he came in.

"What are you doing?" he asked.

"Nothing," I responded.

"Well, then, if you're not doing anything, I think you should clean out your binder." He dumped it unceremoniously on my lap. "I found it in my car and it is a complete disaster. There's no way you'll start doing better in school until you get organized."

Ahh. Organization. The Palm Pilot King speaks.

"I am going to make some copies, and then I'm going to get your sister from kindergarten and we're all going to lunch—you, Caitlin, and me. I want you to have this backpack organized by the time I get back. And I want you to think about the kind of example you are setting for Caitlin. She's your little sister. Do you think this is good for her to see? Do you want her doing things like this?"

I sat very still. Make it go away. My dad isn't a bad guy, but he's also completely out of touch with anything that goes on in my little universe.

"Avery. Camille. Matthews." Eye contact. "Do you understand?"

"Yes." I picked up my backpack, grabbed a handful of papers out of it, and feigned being industrious. Satisfied, he gave me a little wave and left.

I flopped back on the couch. I glanced at the paper on top of the pile in my fist. "My Life, by Avery Matthews." What is this? When did I write this?

Oh yes. I remember now. Our autobiographies. We turned them in way back in September and Mr. Thomas took almost a whole month to read them and give them back to us. He said it took so long because he was really giving each one his time and attention and doing what it took to be a fair grader. Please. I'm sure he's just lazy and has things going on that he thinks are more important than we are. Actually, that's not entirely fair. He gives me too many speeches about *trying* and *doing* and blah blah blah, but he is a decent teacher and I'm sure he did try to do a good job. For what *that's* worth.

I looked at the grade at the top of the paper. I got an A on this paper? I couldn't believe it. I thought I had quit caring by that point. Then I remembered that he had told me I could do a special assignment. "Since you like writing poems so much," he had said after noticing that I was doing that instead of writing in my journal or doing assignments, "maybe you could write a poem for each year of your life as an autobiography instead of writing a more traditional one. I'd let you pick the topics—anything, as long as it's something that relates to your life for each year. What do you think?"

I hate it when teachers feel sorry for me and make exceptions for me, but I'm also not stupid, and I also don't like to work any harder than I absolutely have to work. If I could do something I liked and get a good grade to help my average when I didn't do other assignments later (because, let's face it, that's what was going to happen), then why not? I'm sure that Mr. Thomas felt that he had won some sort of small victory. He got the withdrawn, angry student to do an assignment. Teacher of the Year.

Thinking back on this, I snorted. How disappointed he must have felt when I failed last term in spite of this A, this "special assignment." I had stayed up all night finishing this one, and then I didn't turn in anything the rest of the term.

I started reading the first poem. It was about being one year old and being adorable for the last time in my life. Not great, but not bad. The poem about being two was about the terrible twos and was sticky sweet and totally fake. I kept reading.

"Sixteen" jumped out at me from the last page. I remembered writing about how it felt to be sixteen. I remember choosing to include the color black because everyone always asked why I wore so much black, or, as my mom phrased it, "Why do you look so . . . I don't know, so almost *Gothic* all of a sudden?"

I knew that I thought this was the best one, but I couldn't remember why. I read a few lines of one of the last stanzas:

> *Better to feel anger than to feel sorrow.*
> *Better to feel nothing than to feel sorrow.*
> *Better not to feel.*

I could remember exactly how I felt when I wrote that. It was in the middle of the night, on one of those nights that I stayed up to avoid sleeping and dreaming the dark, thick, scary dreams that I have. I have them when I'm awake too, but they are more vague and there are other things going on. At night, the dreams are all that I see. They scare me. I had started to write simply to keep myself awake, but I remember feeling my mind engaging in the poem more than it had engaged in anything else I'd written this year.

As I reread the poem, I was surprised to see a tear hit the paper, like a sharp staccato note. I was crying. The poem made me feel sorry for myself in a different way than I had been. It made me feel sad for that girl in September who wrote this, sad for anyone who felt this way. *How long has it been,* I wondered, *since I felt happy?* How long has it been since I got up in the morning without a dark feeling pulling me down? How long has it been since I didn't cry in the shower, or *feel* like crying in the shower? Lately, I haven't been able to figure out what the purpose is behind anything. No matter what we do, we're still going to die. Why bother with anything?

This morning when I got up, I felt so *heavy.* It had nothing to do with the smoking or anything else I'd been doing. It had everything to do with feeling like it was just way too much work. Just way too much work to eat breakfast, way too much work to interact with my parents, way too much work to run a comb through my hair. I must have felt the same way when I wrote the poem. I do remember feeling better for a little while after I wrote it, but obviously the feeling hadn't stuck around for long. People always act like writing is so cathartic, and it is, but it's not like it fixes everything. Although I guess anything that helps a little might be worth doing.

Mr. Thomas had written on the page, "Please see me. This is one of the best pieces of writing I've seen in a long time. I'd like to publish it in the school paper. I am also worried about how you might be feeling."

I hadn't seen him after class, but a few weeks later I'd been called into the school counselor's office. Mr. Thomas must have tipped him off. I guess I can see why he did it, although it's still not really any of his business. If the poem made me feel sad, it probably made him feel sad for me too. He is the advisor for the paper so he keeps asking me to look into writing for the school newspaper instead of having a free period for study hall (I never go) on Tuesdays and Thursdays.

I reread the part about writing again. "This is one of the best pieces of writing I've seen in a long time." He should know. He certainly assigns enough pieces of writing.

A little part of me remembered what it felt like to be good at something. I used to be good at volleyball. I used to like hearing people cheer for me and I liked feeling as though I was better than other people at something instead of inferior. The same little part of me also remembered what it felt like to get up and go to school and live my life without having to pull myself through every act. It was the part of me that made me want to try to swim back to the surface, the way I'd talked about swimming up again in the poem.

For the first time in a while, I felt like maybe it was possible to be that person again. I don't want to be this sad anymore. There has to be an answer to my question about what the purpose of all of this is. Do I have the energy to try to find out what it is? It might take a long, long time. I'm not sure I have what it takes to care again.

• • •

My dad drove me to school the next day, making a big deal about where and when he would pick me up. I went straight to English before the bell rang and before I lost my courage. He was sitting at his desk, as usual.

"Mr. Thomas?"

"Yes?"

"I was wondering if maybe you would like to print this in that little spot in the paper where you guys do poems?" I handed him my "Sixteen" poem.

He glanced at it and I saw that he recognized it. He looked at me with kind eyes. "I think it would be an excellent contribution. In fact, I think we could run it this Friday."

That soon? I panicked. "Actually, I was also wondering if you could print it without a name?"

He studied me for a moment. "We don't usually like to publish anonymous pieces. We want students to have accountability—and recognition, of course—for their writing."

"Oh, okay." I took the poem back and walked back to my seat. I felt like I might burst into tears, which made me sit down in the wrong seat. The worst part of all is that I sat in Michaela Choi's seat. She is one of those churchy girls who has never had a bad thing happen to her in her whole life. She's cute and athletic and smart and has a nice boyfriend and thinks only happy thoughts, I'm sure.

"Avery?" she said. "I think you're sitting in my seat."

I didn't even look at her. I just grabbed my stuff and started out the door. The bell hadn't even rung yet.

I was halfway to my locker when I heard someone say "Avery!" I turned around. It was Mr. Thomas. He had my poem in his hand.

"Avery," he said. "I think it would be a good idea to publish your poem, and I think it's an important enough poem that I think we'll make an exception and let you be anonymous."

"I don't want you to publish it just because I left class. That's not why I left."

"I know," he said. "But I had time to reread it while the others were coming in, and when I looked up, you were leaving. I had forgotten how good it was. I think this needs to be printed."

"Why?" I said.

"Because you describe how it feels to suffer."

"Why does that matter?"

"There are more of us out there who are suffering than you, and it feels good to know that we are not alone."

"We?" I stared at him.

He looked out the hall windows, not directly at me. "I lost my wife last year."

I had forgotten. I didn't know what to say. "I'm sorry."

He faced me and his eyes looked sadder than any I'd seen, including mine in the mirror most mornings. "Will you let me publish it?"

I nodded.

"Will you come back to class? The bell's going to ring soon."

I nodded again. "I need to go to the bathroom first."

"Okay. I'll see you in a minute. And thank you, Avery, for writing the poem. And for letting others read it."

I gave him kind of a smile and ducked into the bathroom. I waited there for a few minutes before heading back to class. I felt better. Don't get me wrong. I know that only the nerds and teachers read the Poetry Corner in the school paper. I know that the people who read it might not like it and that probably only a handful of people will even get it, and those people who do might be people that I wouldn't even want to hang out with or that I don't even know. But it still felt good, and just plain good was a feeling I hadn't had in a long, long time. I mean sometimes it feels *very* good to me to be angry and dark. But this was the simpler kind of good. Not an answer to my question, but maybe a step in the right direction.

On Friday when Mr. Thomas passed out the school paper in English, he said, "I'd like everyone to take a minute to read the Poetry Corner. It's particularly good this month." Then, as he always does on paper day, he let us have a few minutes to read before class started.

I pretended to be reading as I looked around. Not everyone was reading it, but some people were. I felt a more complex feeling than just feeling good—I felt proud and scared and I also felt interested and alive.

I think I'm going to show the paper to my parents this evening. I think I might ask Mr. Thomas about writing for the newspaper. I wonder if he knew anything would come from what he wrote on my paper. I wonder how he found the time and energy to write on it when he is suffering so much.

There are lots of questions to answer. One by one.

DECEMBER

Anna Beckett

If my twenty-year-old self could have looked sixty years into the future and seen me now at eighty, I wonder what she would have thought. My husband died young, or what I think of as young—sixty-five. That was fifteen years ago. Five years ago, I moved to Seattle to be near my son, my only child, whose marriage would soon end in divorce. When he moved to Portland, I stayed behind in a retirement home named Azure Bay to be near the grandchildren.

What would I have thought of myself—an old woman, marooned from her friends and her life and the home that she built with her hands and her heart, watching the rain out the window and hoping for a visit from her family? Wondering how her son ended up alone and why marriages sometimes don't work? Wondering what happened but not daring to ask?

When I was younger, though, I didn't have the gospel. Perhaps that should make more of a difference than I allow it to sometimes. Still, God bless those missionaries who knocked on our door. I think of them often, now that time has slowed down a little for me and I can look back over my life. The important things stand out and draw your eye to them.

It is much like the Christmas tree in my room, which draws the eye of everyone who visits. My son, sheepish and smiling, brought it on his last visit. Azure Bay doesn't allow real trees because of the fire hazard, but this one was a blue spruce and looked more real than most.

"Is it all right?" he asked as he set it up. "I thought a blue spruce would be a good choice for you because it's unusual. Plus it reminds me of the one we had in our yard when I was a kid."

I told him that it was fine, which it was, but I thought to myself that he had certainly could have picked a smaller tree. He had had to leave soon after and we hadn't decorated it, but it was growing on me in spite of myself. It was nice to have a seven-foot-high tree in my room, even without ornaments.

It was fun to watch the nurses walk in and see it for the first time. "Oh my," they'd say as they walked in the door, surprised at being confronted by a barrage of plastic needles. "How nice," they inevitably decided, and though at first I was amused by their reaction, I gradually came to agree with them. It was a nice Christmas tree.

A week later, I was sitting by my window, thinking, when my grandchildren Ethan and Andrea arrived, lugging a large box full of ornaments that their mother had sent for the tree. I was a little surprised to see Andrea. It had been some time since she visited. Usually, Ethan and Chloe, my youngest granddaughter, visit with their mother. Or their mother comes alone. I greeted them with enthusiasm and watched Andrea take in the tree with a glance.

"Looks like we'd better get to work," she said, and started unpacking ornaments with her characteristic brisk efficiency that borders on the abrupt.

"Where should we start?" Ethan asked me, holding up a filigreed glass ball covered with gold. "I'm not very good at decorating." His hand hovered near the tree. "It's kind of hard to put the first orna-ment on because there's so many places it can go. Grandma? Where do you want this one?"

"I don't know," I said. I felt a brief and temporary wash of home-sickness for my old home where I knew exactly where and how to arrange everything. I knew where to place each ornament and every wreath. I knew to wind the pine garland around the banister and to place the fresh, homemade nutmeg eggnog and platters of cookies right on the entry table for anyone who came by to visit. "Andrea, where do you think this one should go?"

Andrea took the ornament from Ethan and hung it on the tree, decisive as always.

Ethan handed me an ornate blue glass ball. "This one is beauti-ful," I said. "Did your mother send me all her best ornaments?" I still love my daughter-in-law and I know she still loves me. That is some-thing to be grateful for, I told myself, something more important than having garlands on the banisters. I know that Christmas isn't about the trappings, but sometimes I have to remind myself. Sometimes I want to remind other people too. For example, there was a ridiculous moment the other day when they brought a man dressed up as Santa around to see the residents. "I'm an elderly woman, not a child," I told them, and shut the door politely but firmly. Growing old with dignity isn't quite as easy as I'd hoped.

"Actually, she did," Ethan grinned. "She didn't want Chloe to break them, and she thought they'd be safer with you."

Ornament by ornament, the tree began to take shape. I put on a CD of the Mormon Tabernacle Choir singing Christmas music, and I caught myself humming along to it as I watched my grandchildren decorate the tree. I even added some ornaments myself. Andrea found a pomander-type ornament that smelled like nutmeg, which I have always believed to be the perfect Christmas smell. Some of the ornaments from my old tree, the ones I'd given to my daughter-in-law when she first married my son, appeared from the box.

We had a bad moment where we broke one of the newer orna-ments, a beautiful one made of faceted glass. It acted like a prism and threw rainbows across the room. I was sure that it would be impos-sible to replace, but Ethan said he was fairly sure that had come from a glass store in the Bellevue Square mall. His mother had been excited to find it there on sale last year.

"Why don't we go and find one before she comes to visit and notices that one is missing?" I asked hopefully. "We could go over to the mall and pick it up."

To my surprise and excitement, Ethan agreed. "We can do that. I have to get Michaela a Christmas present, anyway."

"Why don't you call your mother and let her know about our plans while I get ready?" I said. "It won't take me but a minute. You're coming too, aren't you, Andrea?"

She thought for a moment. "There's some shopping I haven't done yet." I supposed that was an answer in the affirmative.

I hurried—well, as much as I could hurry—to my closet. I found an outfit that I hoped wouldn't be embarrassing: black pants, a white blouse, and a red cardigan sweater with matching red garnet earrings. They were my favorite earrings, brought by my husband from Italy, but they've been harder for me to put on lately.

I went to the bathroom sink to freshen up and make sure the outfit looked nice. I was combing my hair but froze when I saw my reflection in the mirror.

My smile was so hopeful and happy and my face was so old. I felt pathetic. I was acting as though I were going on a date. And the kids probably didn't even want me to go with them. They were probably just being kind. I felt very small and was tempted to climb back into my rocking chair and tell them that I had changed my mind after all.

"Grandma!" Ethan knocked on the door. "We're ready! Where are your keys? I'll go get your car." I opened the door and handed him the keys from my purse. He took off. I don't drive much anymore so the grandkids are often the ones who chauffeur me around. It is another way things have changed.

"Let's go wait in front for him," said Andrea. We walked slowly together down the hall and out the front door. "You look pretty," she said. "I remember that sweater. I wanted to get one that color, but I never could match it. It's such a perfect shade of red." It was the kindest, most personal thing I'd heard her say in a long time.

Do grandchildren know how much power they have? They can make us feel wonderful or terrible, depending on what they say and do, without even thinking. I suppose it is only fair. I'm sure I had the same power over them when they were small. We are all vulnerable at different times in our lives.

We climbed in the car together, Ethan and me in the front and Andrea in the back. I saw Andrea send Ethan a glance in the rearview mirror as we pulled away from the curb. Consequently, I think Ethan drove much more carefully than he usually does. He also parked very carefully, without swinging suddenly into a parking spot the way I've seen him do before. It was thoughtful of him but unnecessary. I still enjoy a good burst of speed and a bit of excitement on occasion.

The moment we stepped into the mall, though, I knew I'd made a mistake. It was chaos, and chaos of the very worst kind: too many people moving too quickly and talking too loudly. People everywhere were doing their last-minute Christmas shopping. There were screaming children and frustrated mothers. There were men looking for the perfect gift for their wives. There were men looking for *any* gift for their wives. And most of all there were teenagers.

I stopped in my tracks in the doorway of the big department store. Traffic flowed around me—a little old lady in the middle of the real world.

I felt Andrea link her arm through mine. "Don't want to lose you," she said.

Ethan emerged on my other side. "I think the shop where Mom found that ornament is right over here."

I took a deep breath and it seemed as though everything would be fine after all. I reminded myself that I had delivered speeches to crowds bigger than this one. We swam through the crowd to the glass shop.

Once we'd purchased a replacement ornament, we went to a toy store so Andrea could find something for Chloe. "The more pink it is and the more plastic involved, the more she'll like it," Andrea said, finding something that did indeed meet those requirements.

Next was the search for something for Ethan's girlfriend. It was quite an endeavor. I'd forgotten how tiring shopping can be. I was giving all the grandchildren money this year, which seemed a bit impersonal but their mother said it was what they'd want.

At one of the stores selling athletic equipment, Ethan saw a young man working at the counter that he seemed to know. He and Ethan nodded at each other. "Are you two friends?" I asked Ethan as he hunted for a present for his girlfriend. I didn't think he would find anything here. Why was he buying her clothes? All these clothes looked to my eyes to be athletic and unfeminine. He held up a gray hooded sweatshirt. Could he really be serious?

"Yeah," Ethan said. "He's in our ward and on the track team. He's a really funny guy. I think he has a crush on Andrea."

"That's what *you* think," Andrea said. "Let's get out of here. I'm sure we can find Michaela something else."

Ethan hung the sweatshirt back up and we wandered out of the store. Andrea pointedly did not look at the boy behind the counter as we left, even though he tried to catch her eye and smile at her. Boys are always trying to catch Andrea's eye. She *is* stunning.

"Would you two like some lunch?" I asked. "My treat, of course."

"Sure," Ethan said. I knew I could count on his desire for free food to overcome any fears he had about being seen with his grandmother. "Where do you want to go?"

"Do they still have that little place at the end of the mall? The one where you can sit down and there are plants and music and those comfortable booths?" I asked.

"Yeah, but it's kind of expensive, Grandma. We could get a hot dog or something if you'd rather."

"No, no," I said hastily. "What else would I want to spend my money on besides my grandchildren?"

I was relieved when we slid into the booths and I could rest my feet. I was having a remarkable time being out with my grand-children in their brightly colored world but, like any tourist, I was overwhelmed by all the sights and sounds and needed a rest.

The restaurant had round glass vases like bubbles on the table with evergreen branches and cranberries in them. They made the table smell festive and wonderful. I breathed in deeply. I caught Andrea looking at me with a worried glance. I didn't know whether to be insulted or touched that she was looking out for me. Andrea, who had burst into tears at the sight of Pluto at Disneyland and who had sobbed into my shirt and clung to me, was worried about me! Things have changed.

Lunch was delicious. It felt a bit decadent to eat something that didn't come from Azure Bay. We had a good time talking about our past trips to Disneyland. Ethan ate so much so quickly. I forget how teenage boys are. I could tell he was frustrated that he still hadn't found something for Michaela.

After the plates had been cleared, Ethan said, "I'm going to go look for a CD for her. Is that okay? I'll be back in twenty minutes."

Andrea stayed with me. We decided to share a piece of straw-berry cheesecake for dessert. I was grateful for the added reprieve of a few extra minutes. We'd only been out for about two hours, but my bones felt fragile and I had had to walk more slowly than I wanted.

"So," I said, "what was wrong with the young man in the store? He seemed to want to talk to you."

"Oh, Grandma, it's not really a big deal," she said.

"Oh," I said. "I didn't mean to intrude." Andrea acts like she's tough as nails, but I know that part of her is still the trusting, happy, little girl who found the world to be a wonderful place. The divorce, and everything connected to it, have made her afraid to be that person.

"He helped me out once and it's been awkward ever since. I feel like I should thank him but I don't really know how. That's all." She scooped her long auburn hair out of the way of her straw and took a drink.

The waitress slid the cheesecake and two plates, two forks, and a knife in front of us. Andrea reached for them. "I'll split this up," she said. I watched as she scored the cheesecake with her knife exactly down the middle before she cut it. She even bisected the strawberry on the top precisely in the center.

"You could write him a thank-you note," I offered. The look Andrea gave me as she passed me my plate made me feel instantly both ancient and chagrined. "I guess that's an archaic idea. I'm so old that I still think of things that way. But there are few things as pleas-ant as knowing that you've done something good for someone else, note or not. If he knows he helped you out, then he shouldn't need a note."

Andrea turned and looked at me with the full intensity of her gaze. She reminds me so very much of her father when she does that. "Actually, I don't know that he does. I never really thanked him or acted grateful."

Her directness startled me. "Oh," I said. "You know, there was a very kind nurse in the hospital who taught me how to care for a baby after your father was born. My mother had died and I didn't know anything about babies. That nurse helped me with nursing and with baby care every step of the way. But I never truly thanked her. She wasn't there when we checked out of the hospital and I never went back or sent a note. I should have. I think I didn't want to do it because I felt so vulnerable and she had seen me in that position."

"That's probably why I haven't, either." Andrea looked fierce. "I *hate* feeling vulnerable."

"We all do, but I think you and I hate it more than most," I said, laughing. "That's one of the reasons I never went on a mission with your grandfather. He always wanted to go and I always put him off with excuses about wanting to be near our family. It was true. I wanted very much to be near my grandchildren. But one of the real reasons, and one I didn't even acknowledge to myself until years later, was that I was scared. I was scared to put myself and my beliefs on the line and go through the pain of rejection. I didn't want to admit to your grandfather that I was scared, because he'd always called me his 'tough cookie.' I should have told him. He would have helped me through and we would have been stronger because of it. It's one of the things I regret most." I pulled out a handkerchief and blotted at my eyes, a bit sheepishly. "I'm sorry, Andrea. I don't know why I'm telling you all of this. I haven't told anyone before. I hope you don't think less of me."

Andrea gripped my hand. "I don't think less of you. You know I have doubts about the Church. Sometimes it's good to know that other people have weaknesses too." She looked at me quizzically. "You know it's true, though, don't you?"

I nodded. "I do, Andrea. I put the Lord's promise in Moroni to the test when the missionaries knocked on my door years ago. I do know. But I have been selfish in not sharing my testimony as often as I should."

"Maybe I should read the Book of Mormon again. It's been a long time. That promise in Moroni has always seemed a little like a sales pitch to me, though. You know, 'If you believe, then you'll get your answer that it's true.' Do you really think that promise works?"

"If you have a pure heart, and pray with real intent, then yes. It's much more than a sales pitch, Andrea." I looked closely at her. "We are a lot alike, Andrea. We both have to study and research and analyze everything. I think that's very important in life. I know that it will help you gain a knowledge of the Church because I know you won't believe something you haven't bothered to study and ponder. But I also know that there comes a time when you have to allow faith to take your study and prayer and turn it into a testimony. That was a hard step for me because it meant letting something happen that was out of my control."

Andrea nodded. "That sounds exactly like me," she said. "I can't decide if I want to start reading again because then I'll have to act upon it if it's true. And I like being in control."

"I've found, now more than ever, that being in control is a myth," I told her. "It's taken me eighty years to learn that. You can control aspects of your life, but you'll never be completely at peace that way. Peace comes with the acceptance and faith that come with a strong testimony. And happiness comes with serving others the way the Savior would have us do."

"I didn't know this shopping trip would get so serious," Andrea said. She didn't seem angry, though, for which I was grateful. I had wanted to talk to her about the Church for a long time.

Ethan walked through the door of the restaurant, looking dejected. "Did you find anything?" Andrea asked.

"No. We can go home. Girls are way too hard to shop for. I'll figure something out later." He looked at us and at our partially eaten dessert. "Do you two need some help with that?"

After the three of us had finished up the cheesecake, I paid the check and we walked back through the mall the way we'd come. Andrea had her arm linked through mine again, and I was grateful to have her to lean on. When we walked by the store where we'd found the glass ornament, I had an idea.

"Ethan! Why don't you buy Michaela one of those beautiful prism ornaments, like the one we bought your mother? You could have it wrapped in one of those gold boxes tied with the red velvet ribbon that they have in there. And on the card you could tell Michaela that the ornament reminds you of her. That she makes your life more beautiful and colorful. That she brings rainbows into your life." It was what I would have done if my husband had still been alive.

Ethan stopped walking and stared at me. I felt my face flush a little. I had obviously gotten too carried away for the gray-sweatshirt generation. Something that seemed romantic to me would probably seem overblown and laughable to him. I laughed nervously and started to say something, anything, to change the subject.

"Grandma," Ethan said, "that's *perfect!*"

Andrea agreed. "That's very romantic, Grandma."

Driving home in the car with the holiday music on the radio and my grandchildren humming along, I felt completely happy and utterly exhausted. Ethan was driving so I held the velvet-ribboned boxes with the prism ornaments inside. I felt as though they were for me and held them very carefully to make sure they were safe. I leaned back against the headrest and closed my eyes, but I could feel the boxes in my hands and I didn't fall asleep.

After the kids had dropped me off and kissed me good-bye, I went in and hung the replacement ornament on my tree. I stood there for some time as the light from the lamp near the tree reflected off the ornament and bounced rainbows into the different areas of the room. It made me think of a testimony. In its red velvet-lined box, the ornament was pretty, but once it was taken out and light was allowed in from different angles, it was truly beautiful. It was time to take my testimony, precious as it was, out of its box.

The phone rang several hours later. It was only eight o'clock, but I was already in bed. "Hello!" I said, trying to sound bright-eyed.

"Grandma, it's Ethan. I gave Michaela her present tonight since she's going out of town for the holidays and she *loved* it. Seriously, Grandma, she even *cried.* I just wanted to call and thank you."

"Oh, you're welcome. I'm so glad she liked it."

"Yeah, she really did. Oh, and my mom says we'll pick you up at five tomorrow for Christmas Eve dinner at our house. Or earlier if you want. Just call."

"Thank you, Ethan."

"Bye, Grandma."

I hung up the phone. I felt more awake after talking to him. I sat up straighter and reached for the rolling desk next to my bed. I pulled my writing tablet and my scriptures over to me. I decided to do something I'd been thinking about for a while. I'd write a letter to each of my three grandchildren, to their mother, and to my son, and let them know how I felt about them and about the gospel. I had been putting it off but now it seemed there was no time like the present. I could give the letters to them as birthday presents in the coming year.

I pulled the lid off my black fountain pen and wrote names on top of five envelopes: Rachel, Andrea, Ethan, Chloe, Ben. Who should I write to first?

I was once a "fun" grandmother. I went to Disneyland every year with them; I played ball with them; I helped them with their homework. When I first moved to the Seattle area, I lived in an apartment and they liked to come over and watch movies and have popcorn. Now that I am having so much trouble getting around and they are in high school, those parties are a thing of the past. I am eighty, after all. It's amazing I've held up as long as I have.

It has all caught up to me, though. It catches up to all of us. I think that I had somehow anticipated being the first elderly woman to sail smoothly into old age without any noticeable aches or pains. I imagined myself as wise and serene. I certainly did not imagine myself in an "assisted living" home called Azure Bay, heating up my cocoa on a hot plate and having to call a nurse to help me unfasten the clasps on my red garnet earrings.

One of the things you lose when you grow old is the ability to provide comfort for someone else. Something else you lose is the ability to be genuinely useful to others. People are always comforting you, coddling you, helping you to do things—or leaving you completely alone.

I am one of the lucky ones because I am treated very well. The nurses give me a pat on the arm after they bring my morning pills. They grip my shoulder kindly when they help me walk somewhere. Rachel, my daughter-in-law, hugs me, as do my grandchildren and my son. The other day in fact Chloe jumped on my lap and hugged me with such enthusiasm that her mother looked worried for me.

My family will bring me things I ask for, since I don't drive as much anymore. Just yesterday morning Rachel drove over with a particular brand of licorice I like and some soft, cushiony tissues, not the cheap hospital-type they have here. My son, Ben, calls every day or two and comes by often on the weekends. He'll even drive me to my hair appointment and wait there with me.

I knew, however, that it had been some time since *I* offered physical or emotional comfort to someone. To have comforted Andrea even a little at lunch, to have helped Ethan find something special—it felt wonderful. I needed to remember those feelings and to bear my testimony more often to my family and to others. Perhaps I had missed the chance to serve a mission with my husband, but there were others to share my testimony with, including my very own granddaughter.

So I started writing the first letter very, very carefully. I wanted it to look and sound perfect. I knew it might take a few drafts. I had time, though, as long as I started now. A little rainbow from the prism ornament danced on the page.

The next morning, I put a Book of Mormon on the table in the residents' living room. It was gone by that evening. I decided that the next day, I would talk to someone in Azure Bay about the Church. What better time than Christmas?

CHAPTER 11

JANUARY

David Sherman

Today they handed out the ballots for the senior class awards—Funniest, Most Likely to Succeed, Most Beautiful Eyes, etc., during seventh period, which is journalism for me. I write just the comics and a sports article once in a while, so I can spend most of my time bugging the other kids or finishing up my homework for other classes. Anyway, I was filling in the blanks on my ballot when I heard my friend Jake behind me say to someone else, "Funniest? That's easy. I'm voting for Dave Sherman." The someone else said, "Me too." Then they went on to discuss the next category.

I looked down at my ballot. Although I had felt flattered at first when they said that, now I wasn't so sure. Was that all anyone ever saw me as? A funny guy? I've done other things in my life. Just because I have a good time doesn't mean that I'm always feeling like life is funny. Although I have to admit there are a lot of things in this world that are hilarious. But still, why wouldn't they vote for me for something else? How about Most Likely to Be President Someday? Now there's something I could really enjoy. And who's to say that it couldn't happen?

"What are you freaking out about?" asked Avery, the cranky new girl assigned to the computer next to me.

"Nothing," I said.

"Then could you try to quit snorting and grunting like a water buffalo in heat? Some of us are trying to get stuff done instead of spending hours on those stupid ballots."

Ouch. "Pardon me," I said sarcastically. "What are you writing about over there, anyway? Something profound and soul-searching like"—I paused dramatically—"'The History of our School Mascot' no doubt."

That was a cheap shot—I knew it and so did she. That had been the last article she'd written. She'd been assigned to do it because she was the newest staff member, the low man on the totem pole. Plus no one else had wanted to do it. Articles like that are the worst. They're no fun to write and none of the other students read them; I don't even think any of the *teachers* bother to read them. Which gives me an idea for the next time it's my turn to write an article like that. . . .

Anyway, it really was a lame article to write because our mascot is the joke of the state of Washington.

We're the Lakeview High Skippers. The Skipper is some poor soul dressed up in a little sailor outfit, wearing a gigantic papier-mâché head with an idiotic grin and a papier-mâché sailor hat attached. The Skipper does not strike fear into the hearts of our opponents. The Skipper, in fact, may be one of the most counter-productive mascots ever. He makes our opponents want to beat us up even more. And it's hard to get pumped up over a hyperactive, frantic sailor running around, exhorting us to win.

The worst part of all, though, is the part in our school's song where the Skipper does his little hornpipe dance, skipping about gaily and generally doing irreparable damage to our fearsome image. And the song itself—"We are the Skippers, the mighty Skippers"—makes me think of an army of plastic, pink Skipper dolls marching out to battle with Barbie and Ken. It's so bad it's almost funny. Almost.

Avery looked like she was getting ready to say something, but then she stopped. I could feel Mr. Thomas glaring at me even before I turned around. "David, why do you have to give her such a hard time?" he asked.

"She gives me a hard time too, in case you hadn't noticed," I said. "Not five minutes ago she told me that I sounded like a water buffalo in heat."

Mr. Thomas is good at holding in his smile even when he thinks something is funny. "That wasn't very nice of her. But your constant battling is interfering with everyone else's work. So since you've both managed to disrupt the whole classroom, I'm sending the two of you out with the survey on the school's dress code."

"No!" I moaned dramatically. Whenever we do a "serious" article about "serious" student opinions, we take surveys to all the classes during seventh period and have the students fill them out. I could not care less about what students think about the dress code. I know what I think about it and isn't that enough? Plus the worst part of it is that there are so many surveys, it's impossible to carry them all and make the rounds of the whole school in forty-five minutes. So Mr. Thomas has one person pull—get this—a little red wagon while the other person runs into the classroom and drops off the surveys. It's like an insane, childish mail delivery service. He does the same thing when it's time to deliver the school papers.

Avery was barely able to control her anger. Several choice comments floated through my mind, but I didn't say them. She started whining again. "But I have to finish my article! You shouldn't punish me because *he's* an idiot!"

Mr. Thomas gave me the handle of the red wagon and Avery a list of the classrooms. "Check off each classroom number as you drop them off. You'd better hurry."

It didn't go well. The surveys were *huge* and bulky and our school is so big there were hundreds, maybe even thousands, of them. It wasn't exactly easy to drag a wagon full of them down the hall at lightning speed. Avery was mad at me because I wasn't fast enough but she wasn't making it any easier either.

She just grabbed the top bunch off the wagon, stalked into a classroom, laid them on the nearest desk, then stalked out again. No explanation to the teacher, no small talk with any kids in the class, nothing. I, on the other hand, kept running into people or teachers I knew and wanted to talk a little. What was the problem with that?

Avery thought there were about seven hundred problems with that. "You're slowing us down! You're talking too much! I can't believe I have to do this!" For someone who cared so little about how she looked or about anyone else in the world, she was sure worried about getting this done.

Finally, I'd had enough. "Listen," I said, "you pull the wagon if you think you can do a better job. I'm sick of listening to you." We were standing right next to the doors of the upper level of the gym, which meant that we still had about half the school to go, and I refused to listen to her screechy little voice for the rest of the trip.

Avery grabbed the wagon handle right out of my hand. She was *strong*. In fact, she was *too* strong. She yanked the wagon out of my hand, but she'd pulled with such force, she couldn't keep her own grip on it. The wagon went careening through the gym doors and between the guardrails on the upper deck, sailing toward the gym floor below . . . and the Skipper.

"Watch out!" I called, but the Skipper didn't move. I watched in horror as the wagon crushed the Skipper's skull, bits and pieces flying everywhere. Then I realized that there wasn't any blood. Only papier-mâché. No one had been wearing the costume; it had been sitting on a chair on the gym floor, waiting for some unlucky freshman to put it on and give it life for the pep rally later that day. The Skipper, or at least the soul of the Skipper, still lived.

Down on the gym floor, the wagon lay on top of what was left of the Skipper's head, which looked like a busted piñata. I saw a flash of movement and a blonde head. The beady little eyes of Principal Downing peered up at us. Avery and I stood there like deer caught in the headlights. Avery's mouth was wide open. The gym was absolutely quiet for about two seconds.

Then I heard a tapping sound. Was someone clapping, happy to witness the Skipper's grand finale? Perhaps the poor underclassman who had been conned into serving as school mascot and would now never have to be humiliated again by wearing the Skipper's head? Nope. It was Principal Downing's high heels stabbing the floor as she made short, furious strides up the bleachers to us. A wagon wheel skittered across the floor and clanked to a stop against the other end of the gym. The last few surveys floated to the floor, in memoriam.

What could I do? I sat down on the floor and laughed so hard, I couldn't get air. I couldn't breathe. Something about the whole situation just killed me. The wagon flying through the air, Avery's anger and how she'd hurled the wagon straight through the bars onto the floor, the Principal's outrage, the Skipper's head obliterated, the fact that we were careening around the school with a little red wagon in the first place—I was dying.

"Shut *up*," said Avery and something in her voice made me pay attention. "Do you think this is funny? I am going to be *expelled* for this. The last time I was in her office, she told me that I was going to get expelled if I pulled any more stunts."

"Why do I care?" I said. "I've seen you smoking on the school grounds. If you care so much about school, why didn't you think of it before you messed up the other times?"

She looked completely pale and shaken. "I didn't care then. I'm still not sure how much I care now. But I do *not* want to be expelled because I threw a wagon onto the Skipper's head."

That started me laughing again. I couldn't help it. Avery shot me a look of pure hatred, and Principal Downing, out of breath, climbed the last bleacher and stood in front of us, her hands on her hips.

"What are you two doing?" she said.

Avery folded her arms and stood there. She didn't say a word. I kept laughing, even though I felt bad for her.

Principal Downing asked again, louder, "*What* are you two doing?"

"I'm sorry, Principal Downing," I said. "I seem to have lost control of my little red wagon." I snorted with laughter. I felt Avery turn to stare at me.

"Why did you have a wagon in the school in the first place? And why are the two of you are wandering around unsupervised during class time? The mascot is ruined! What were you thinking? We needed him for basketball season! I don't believe this."

"It's not our wagon," I explained. "It's Mr. Thomas's. He uses it for the school paper—to distribute it and stuff. We were handing out surveys for an article. We were pulling it along in the hall and it sailed right through the door and . . . squished the Skipper." I tried not to laugh again, but it was useless.

Principal Downing marched us right back to Mr. Thomas's room, where he confirmed our story. She asked him how he expected her to pay for the damage to the Skipper and he looked tired and said he was sorry. He would have the newspaper staff do a fundraiser to help purchase a new head. (Loud groans and evil stares at me from the newspaper staff.) He sounded so subdued that I saw Ms. Downing look at him with something like understanding and say, "Thank you very much. That will be perfect." And later she brought back the remains of the red wagon and apologized for being so upset which I thought was weird.

But the weirdest thing of all happened after I'd been running track that day. I went out to my car and found Avery Matthews sitting on the hood, wearing a huge parka with the hood pulled up against the cold. She was hunched over her notebook, writing, and stopped when I came up.

"What are you doing?" I said, sitting next to her. "This is my car."

"I know," she said. "I wanted to thank you for explaining everything to Principal Downing." She still seemed pretty mad about the whole thing, but somehow she also seemed to mean it when she thanked me.

"That's okay," I said. "We were both acting like jerks and it wasn't worth someone getting expelled over it. Besides, I told her the truth. We *were* pulling it down the hall and it *did* fly onto the Skipper. It was both our faults. And I have a clean record, so it was better for me to do the talking."

"How can that be?" she said. "You're always doing stuff like running through the graduation party in moon boots." She seemed amused in spite of herself.

"You know that I did that?" I asked, diverted.

"Everyone knows," Avery said. "I'm sure the administrators do too. But if they haven't said something by now about it, they're not going to."

"I wonder why they didn't suspend me. Probably because they don't think it would do any good. I think they warned the principal about me. I was a wild little kid in elementary school and so everyone always expects me to act like I'm insane."

"So that's your secret?" Avery asked. "Low expectations?"

"Yup," I said. "Look how surprised you were when I took the fall for the Red Wagon Incident."

She looked at me thoughtfully. "I guess that's true. But don't you like getting so much mileage out of it? Making people laugh? People love that. They eat it up."

"I know," I said. "I like it when people laugh at me, most of the time. I think the world is pretty funny. I really do. I mean, come on. Didn't you even feel like laughing at all today?"

Avery smiled. It had taken some doing, but we were on the same page, even if it was for only a minute.

Just then, Andrea Beckett walked by on the way to her car. When she saw me with Avery, she hesitated for a second, then she marched right over to me. "This is for you," she said, handing me a note with my name on it. She smiled at me and then headed for her car. I watched her go. I may have gone into slight cardiac arrest, but Avery brought me back into reality.

"You like her, don't you?" said Avery bitterly. "Everyone does."

"So what?" I said, tucking Andrea's note into my pocket. "Are you going to freak out at me again, or do you want a ride home?"

"Sure," she said, "but I don't live very far away."

"I know. I live right by you. I see you walking to school all the time."

We got into the car and I reached into the cup holder. It was empty. "Oh no," I said. "Someone must have borrowed my car and forgot to put the keys back."

"You leave your keys in your cup holder and tell people about it? How naïve *are* you?"

"Someone will give them back to me tomorrow. And if they don't, I'll have another set made. Everyone knows this is my car. No one would steal it. It's ugly as sin."

"I guess that's true," she said, climbing out of the car.

I got out too. "Hey, I will walk you home, though."

She shrugged her backpack over her shoulders. "All right then. Let's go."

As we were walking, I realized that I owed her an apology for some of the things I'd said earlier. "Hey, Avery," I said. "I'm sorry about saying stuff earlier. You know, the stuff about you smoking and not caring what people think and all of that. I shouldn't have said that. I was being a total jerk. I take joking around and trading insults too far sometimes. I've been trying to work on it and I didn't do so well today. Anyway, I'm sorry."

She kept marching. "That's okay. I wasn't being a sweetheart to you, either."

We walked a few more steps when she turned to me. "Did you take the fall for me because you're religious?"

"Where did that come from?" I asked. "First of all, I told Principal Downing the truth. I did lose control of my little red wagon. Second of all, I *am* a Mormon, but how did you know that? We've never talked about it."

"I've been working on this article for the paper next month about different religions at Lakeview High. One of the girls I interviewed was Mormon and a lot of you guys hang out in that same crowd, like you and Ethan Beckett and his girlfriend. I started out the interview thinking that Mormonism was kind of weird."

"Thanks a lot," I said, pretending to be outraged. Inside I was stunned. Wow. I guess you never *do* know who's watching. It made me a little uncomfortable to think of the example I'd been setting for her. Even though I've been trying to not judge people by the front they present to others, especially since the night of the Homecoming game, I forget too often. Which is hard since I, personally, don't always like being labeled as just a funny guy.

"But Elizabeth—the girl I interviewed—was pretty cool. She seemed normal. Anyway, *is* your religion why you took the fall today?"

"I guess you could say I did it because of my religion in a way, because my religion is a big part of who I am, but it's not like I sat and thought, 'I should do this because of church.' It just kind of happened. I just wanted to do it. And I should have been nicer earlier and not been such a jerk. I'm sorry again about all of that."

"Okay," she said. I wondered what was going on in her head. Maybe she was interested in Mormonism. Unlikely, but I decided to go for it.

"Hey, do you want to come to church with me sometime?" I asked and held my breath.

She stopped dead in her tracks and turned to stare at me. "Are you *serious?*"

"Um," I said. Maybe that hadn't been such a good idea.

She thought for a minute. "No," she said, and started walking again. We were almost to her house. I didn't quite know what to say. I opened my mouth to make some dumb comment about the wagon or the Skipper, but she spoke first. "I might come someday, though," she said. "Ask me again sometime. I'll see you tomorrow." And she went inside.

The next Friday the newspaper staff all chipped in and Avery and I went to Costco after school. We bought Mr. Thomas a pink Power Wheels Barbie car to deliver the newspaper stuff instead. He laughed really hard and then made Avery and me take it back to exchange it for a new red wagon.

I haven't seen the Skipper since (except for a papier-mâché eye I found later when I was hiding from Principal Downing under the bleachers—but that's another story). May he rest in peace.

I also haven't asked Avery about coming to church again yet, but I am going to. I think I will know when it's the right time.

And I don't know what to think about the note from Andrea. It was a thank-you note:

David,
　　I wanted to write and thank you for being a good friend on the night of the Homecoming Game. I apologize for taking so long to let you know that I appreciate what you did.
　　　　　　　　　Thank you,
　　　　　　　　　Andrea Beckett

P.S. I bet you look stunning in that tiara.

It's not much, but I have a feeling it might be a good sign. Meanwhile, I've got to figure out a way to get that tiara back to her without seriously endangering my pride.

May the force of the Skipper be with me.

CHAPTER 12

JANUARY

Julie Reid

"This has to be too good to be true," I told Mikey. She looked up in surprise. She was unpacking her backpack so we could study for an English test and I was finishing reading a chapter in the Book of Mormon that she had given me for Christmas.

"What are you talking about?" she asked. "Something in the scriptures?"

I thought about saying, "Everything." The truth was it all seemed too good to be true. It seemed too good to be true that I had a best friend, someone who knew a lot about me and about my family and still liked me anyway. It seemed too good to be true that my signing up for choir had turned into a class that I liked and something that I might be really good at besides. It seemed too good to be true that I was so far removed from where I had been last year— hanging out with Everett. And now, the things that I was learning from Mikey and the missionaries—they all seemed too good to be true too.

But specifically it was Book of Mormon that I thought might be too good to be true. "This whole chapter," I said. "Alma 22."

Mikey got a big grin on her face. "Do you want to talk about it for a little while before we start studying?" She loves talking about the Mormon Church with me, with or without the missionaries. She's really good about letting me bring it up and not pushing it on me, but she's always ready to talk when I am. I can't get over how much she knows about the Book of Mormon and the Bible and what she believes. Sometimes I worry that I'm too far behind and that I'll never know as much as she does about being Mormon, but she keeps promising me that that doesn't matter at all.

"Sure," I said. "That would be great."

"Let me find it in my scriptures," she said. That was another thing. She often—not always, but often—had her scriptures with her. She had a matching set, with her name engraved on the covers of both the Book of Mormon and the Bible. I'd never known anyone who carried around religious books so they could look at them all the time. It seemed a little weird to me at first, but now it makes sense that you might need them for looking up stuff. She even takes a religious class called seminary before school starts. She says that her teacher is really good—it's her boyfriend's mom, of all people—and that she keeps things interesting even though it's so early in the morning. I keep telling her I'll come sometime, but it's hard to get up before dawn!

"Okay, Jules," she said. "I'm ready. Where's the part that's too good to be true?"

"Well, the first part is pretty great. I love how the king asks Aaron all the different questions and the way Aaron answers them. The king asks so many of the same questions I had: Is there a God? Is there anywhere we go after we die? What do I have to do to get to heaven? And then Aaron gives the answer in verse sixteen: 'If thou desirest this thing, if thou wilt bow down before God, yea, if thou wilt repent of all thy sins, and will bow down before God, and call on his name in faith, believing that ye shall receive, then shalt thou receive the hope which thou desirest.'"

I looked up at Michaela. I'm sure I had mispronounced things and I'm not the fastest or smoothest reader, but she never seemed to notice or say anything. "This is the part that seems too good to be true. How can I really be forgiven after everything I've done, just by repenting and praying?"

"It is amazing," Mikey said quietly. "It does seem too good to be true in a way that we could do so many things wrong and still return to heaven and still have eternal life and still receive so many blessings."

"How can that be?" I said. "How can it all work out so well?"

"Because of Jesus Christ," Mikey said. "He suffered for us and paid the price for our sins."

"That's something that confuses me," I admitted. "He died for us, but haven't lots of people died for other people? I know that parents have died for their children and friends have died for each other. What is it that makes his death so much more important than all the other ones?"

Mikey nodded as I spoke and said, "I remember having the same question. He did die for us and it was something special because he *chose* to die for us, even though he was the Son of God and very powerful. But that wasn't all he did. He also suffered in Gethsemane, so much that he bled at every pore. He suffered for every single person's individual sins and so, if we repent, he has already paid the price for us." Her voice was quiet and awed. "In fact, it was such a hard thing to do that he prayed to Heavenly Father to release him from having to do it. But when he realized it had to happen that way, he chose to do it for us." She turned to her Bible.

"Here," she said, handing it to me. "Read this part. Luke 22, starting in verse 40. This is where Jesus goes to the Garden of Gethsemane."

I read the verses slowly, wanting to make sure that I understood everything. Jesus really did ask Heavenly Father to let the cup pass from him, but he still suffered for us, even though it was agony beyond anything I could imagine. I read verses 43 and 44 once to myself, and then again out loud, wanting to hear them and make them even more real: "And there appeared an angel unto him from heaven, strengthening him. And being in an agony he prayed more earnestly: and his sweat was as it were great drops of blood falling down to the ground."

For a moment, my heart ached. I couldn't imagine either of my older brothers doing anything like that for me, but Jesus Christ, who Mikey and the missionaries both referred to as "our elder brother," had done that for me. He knew even more about me than they did and chose to suffer for me anyway.

There are two main times that I've suffered in my life. One of them I didn't cause; the other one I did. The first time was the night when the police station called to tell my parents that Kevin was there and that he'd been arrested for killing a woman while he was driving drunk and stoned.

That was a horrible feeling. It was beyond feeling sick, beyond feeling scared, beyond feeling sad.

After that phone call, my mom seemed like she had gone very far away for a few days. She went down to the station, she talked to Kevin, and she made sure he had an attorney lined up. Then she started writing. It was a letter to the family of the woman in the car Kevin hit. For six or seven days, she sat at her desk in her bathrobe and wrote. She kept throwing the letters away and starting over.

I stood in the doorway of her room and watched her once. She didn't notice me, or if she did, she didn't care. She would write a few lines, chewing on her bottom lip, and then she would stop and reread them. She would get angry about what she'd written because it wasn't good enough and she'd throw the paper onto the floor and grab a new sheet. She was quietly crying almost the whole time she did this. The whole area around her desk was littered with letters.

I stood watching her for a long time, but I didn't know what to do. My stepfather came home and found me there. He gently but firmly made me go back to my room. I don't know what happened to the letter. I don't think she ever finished it. After a few days, she stopped trying to write, but it was still a long time before she seemed like she was going to be okay again. I knew that she kept thinking about the woman's family, just like I did. I wondered if Kevin was going to destroy two families—mine and the one of his victim. I hated him.

The time I caused my own suffering was when I was with Everett.

My eyes filled with tears and I looked up at Mikey. She put her arm around me. "I still don't understand," I said. "Why would Jesus be willing to go through this for me? For my stupid, stupid sins?" I was crying harder. "Mikey, some of the things that I did when I was with Everett—they're not just little things. How could Jesus be willing to take care of all of that for me?"

"Because he loves you," Mikey said simply. "He loves me too and did the same for me. I know. And I know that he truly loves you, mistakes and all." She turned the pages in her Book of Mormon. "And once you are baptized and confirmed, you receive another special gift. The gift of the Holy Ghost."

"I know you and the missionaries keep talking about that, but what exactly does that mean?"

"The Holy Ghost is often called the Comforter, because the Holy Ghost comforts you and gives you promptings or feelings about what you need to do and helps you. Here." She pointed to a verse: Moroni 8:26. "I'm saying it badly, but this says it better." She read, "'And the remission of sins bringeth meekness, and lowliness of heart; and because of meekness and lowliness of heart cometh the visitation of the Holy Ghost, which Comforter filleth with hope and perfect love, which love endureth by diligence unto prayer, until the end shall come, when all the saints shall dwell with God.'"

I didn't say anything for a minute and Mikey was quiet too. If there was one thing in the world I wanted, it was a Comforter. To never be alone, to always have guidance and love and help and assistance and peace.

"What do you think?" Mikey asked softly.

"It still seems too good to be true," I said, and Mikey smiled at me. "But I can tell that it *is* true. I can feel it. He loves me even though he knows what I've done and the bad feelings I've had toward my brothers. I can feel that he loves me that much even though it's kind of hard for my mind to understand it."

"He loves you that much and he knows you that well," she said. "He knows how wonderful and important you are. He will help you through all your suffering because he understands it and you. He feels that way about every single one of us. Isn't that amazing?"

"I want to get baptized," I said. I could see Mikey's face light up with surprise and happiness, reflecting what I was sure was on my face too. "I'm going to ask my parents tomorrow."

• • •

I don't think I've woken up so many times in one night since I was a little girl and it was Christmas Eve and I was waiting for Santa to deliver presents under the tree. I wore my watch to bed so that I could check the time. 1:15 A.M. 3:43 A.M. 4:02 A.M. Finally it was 6:00 A.M. and I couldn't stand it any longer. I went downstairs to get some cereal and wait for my parents to come down. They are usually early risers, even on a Saturday, and I kept looking at the kitchen door, hoping that they would come through and I could tell them my decision.

I sat on the bar stool at the counter, swinging my feet impatiently. I looked out the big kitchen window to the trees beyond. It was dark and I could only see a little outside, just what the kitchen light and the very faint light of dawn revealed. It was like my belief in the Church, I thought. I couldn't see everything yet and some of what I could see was because Mikey was illuminating it for me. But I could see enough to take that first step outside of myself and into something new. I turned away from the window to see my mother walking into the kitchen.

She smiled at me. "You're up early," she said.

I smiled back. I wasn't sure how to start the conversation so I blurted it out. "I want to get baptized into the Mormon Church."

"Oh, Julie," my mother sighed, sitting down on the stool next to me. She didn't sound excited at all. I guess I should have expected that. I expected her to be a little angry, but I figured that she had been through worse with my brothers. Certainly my finding a church I believed in couldn't be anything like what they had put her through, so I didn't expect her to feel sad, which is how she looked.

Tears filled her eyes. "Julie, what have I done wrong? I don't want to lose all of my children. First Mark moved away from home, then Kevin . . ." She didn't finish with Kevin. "And now you want to join a strange church?" She shook her head. "I've been so happy with the way you've been finding yourself this year, and I don't have anything against Mormons—Michaela is a sweet girl—but I don't want to lose you too."

"Mom, a big part of me finding myself and being so happy about everything has been this church." I felt like there had to be words to help her understand if I could just find them. Maybe they were in the Book of Mormon! If I read her the chapters Mikey and I had discussed, she would have to feel the way I did and understand how important this was. "Wait here," I said and ran upstairs to find my scriptures. It took me a few minutes, but soon I ran down with the Book of Mormon and Mikey's Bible in my hands.

My mother still sat there, and my stepfather was there with her now. He is a kind man, a quiet man, and I love him for the gentle way he treats my mother, but there is rock underneath. "Julie," he said, "your mother has been telling me that you want to get baptized into the Mormon Church."

I nodded. "I do. I really believe that it is true."

He sighed. "I know it's been important to you lately and your friends seem like good kids. It's been wonderful to see you develop such good friendships. I don't think either your mother or I have any problem with you associating with them. Right?" He looked to my mother for confirmation, and she nodded. "But we don't want you to get baptized."

"Why not?" I asked.

"I already told you," my mother said, reaching out to hug me. "I don't want to lose you."

"How would you lose me?" I asked, completely taken aback. "I'll still be here. I'll still be your daughter. I'm not going to move away or anything."

"Yes, but you'll become a part of something I don't understand. I don't understand all about the things the Mormons teach. I know polygamy was a part of their history somewhere. And I've heard they believe that women should stay home with their children and you have such a fine mind and so many talents. I don't want it to all be wasted. There is too much to this church that I don't understand."

"I could help you understand it!" I said, excitedly. "If you would read the Book of Mormon and meet with the missionaries, just like I've been doing, then—"

She broke in. "I'm sorry, Julie, but my answer has to be no. If you are still interested in the Mormon Church when you are eighteen, there's nothing I'll be able to do to stop you, and you can go ahead and be baptized. If you're still interested in it two years down the road, then that's a different matter. But for now, it's not something I can give my permission for you to do. I'm sorry, sweetheart."

I stood there holding the Book of Mormon in my hands for a little while longer while my parents turned away to fix breakfast.

If she had just let me read this to her! I kept telling myself. When Mikey came over later to see how it went, I had to tell her. It was awful to watch the excitement drain from her face. "I know," I said. "I feel terrible." I started to cry. "I feel like I finally found the one thing that would work for me and now it's being taken away. But I can't disobey my mom and I know that the missionaries said the Church believes in having your parents' permission before you're eighteen, so what am I going to do? I'm already so far behind with these things. Now I'll never catch up."

To my surprise, Mikey laughed. "Julie, you're learning so much so fast. Catching up is the last thing you have to worry about. I was excited to get baptized when I was eight, but I definitely didn't understand how beautiful and powerful it was. Not like you will. I wish that you could get baptized right now, today, but your baptism will be beautiful no matter when it happens because of the faith you'll bring into those waters."

"But what if I really do have to wait two years?"

"Remember that scripture in Alma we read? If you ask Heavenly Father, believing that you will receive, he will give you hope." She smiled at me. "You will be blessed because of your belief, and he will help you through however long it is until your baptism. You'll have hope and you won't give up."

I knelt to pray after she had left. I didn't know how to start, so I just started by asking, over and over, "Heavenly Father, please give me hope. Please give me hope and help me know what to do." Then I thought of something else. "Please help me to truly repent so that when the time comes to be baptized, I will be absolutely ready."

I looked at the clock. It was almost time for Mom to leave to visit Kevin at the prison. I've never been. I've never wanted to go, and she's stopped asking me if I want to come. I've been afraid to visit because I don't want to see Kevin in there, because I'm scared of both the prison and of him. I'm scared of all the feelings I'll have when I see him, especially now that I know Mr. Thomas personally and know that he lost his mother because of Kevin's choices.

I knew in my heart what I should do and I acted as quickly as I could before the fear took away the hope again. I put on my coat and went out to stand on the front porch. It's cold in Seattle in January; the rain has an icy edge to it that it doesn't have later in the year. I usually put my hood up to shield my face. Instead, I lifted my face to the sky and let the rain freckle my face, spangle my hair, jewel my eyelashes. And hide my tears.

When my mother came out to the car, she found me waiting in the front seat. She didn't say anything. She climbed into the driver's seat and started the car and the heater, rubbing her hands together to get them warm before touching the chilled plastic steering wheel. Before she started to back out of the driveway, she reached over and gave my hand a squeeze. I could see the rain mingled with the tears on her face. I reached over and hugged her. I had enough hope for both of us. Maybe even enough for Kevin too.

FEBRUARY

Andrea Beckett

There was a glaring blank spot on my college applications this fall. The part where I'm supposed to list "community service." I hadn't worried about it before because I knew that my essays were perfect, that my running accolades were impressive, and that my grades in my college-level course classes spoke for themselves. I thought I was the epitome of the well-rounded student that schools would be looking for and wanting to accept. And in a way, I was right. Cornell, my number one school, had already accepted me. I was set.

Until I wanted to apply for a summer internship at the cancer center in Seattle and found out that the community service part of *that* application was the biggest part of all. I wanted that internship desperately since being a doctor someday is my target career path. The internship would look great when I applied to med schools later.

I don't have time for service after school, with track practice and homework and all, so I wasn't sure how I was going to fit it in, but I knew it had to be done. At first, I thought I might count my time visiting Grandma as community service. She does live in a retirement home after all. Then I felt a little ashamed about doing that. It seemed like I was using Grandma and something inside of me didn't want to do that.

Finally I remembered that David Sherman did peer tutoring one period a day during school. That seemed like a perfect solution—I could schedule the community service right in where it would fit. It would mean giving up orchestra, but I could probably spare it since I had met the fine arts requirement for graduation and was already on track for college. Plus I was getting a little tired of sawing away on the violin day after day and year after year. It would be good to try something new.

I went to the counseling office to make the change. Even though the new term had started, I was sure they would make an exception and I was right. Mrs. Barlow, the counselor, practically fell over with joy. "I think this is a *wonderful* idea," she said. "It will mean so much to those students to have your help. We lost a few peer tutors last semester and I know that Mr. Newman will be thrilled to have more. You can start today. I'll make the change in your schedule effective immediately. This is so sweet of you!"

I felt slightly uncomfortable with all her praise, considering that the main reason I was even making the change was self-serving, but I didn't say anything. Why disillusion her?

"Now," Mrs. Barlow said, handing me the paper, "you'll need to get Principal Downing to sign this, and then you'll be all set."

"Principal Downing?" I asked.

"Yes. She has to approve all course changes this late in the year, especially for seniors. I'm sure it won't take long."

My lunch period was already halfway gone. I went to the principal's office and luckily she was free. I sat down across from Principal Downing and wondered again what had made her decide to chop off all her long blonde hair and replace it with this less-than-flattering haircut. I have a lot of respect for Principal Downing, though. It takes a tough woman to be a principal and I know the district office has come calling for her to be superintendent a time or two. But she's dedicated to Lakeview High so she stays here. I don't know if that shows she's smart or not. She could make a lot more money as superintendent.

"You want to be a peer tutor?" she asked. It was a little unflattering how surprised she sounded.

"Yes," I said. "I don't really need orchestra anymore. I have already fulfilled the fine arts requirement."

"But what about the upcoming concerts?" she asked. "Are you leaving Ms. Hall in the lurch?"

"No," I said. "I'm not first violin and I don't have any solos. There's plenty of violinists. I'd like to do something different."

"Are you sure?" she asked, her pen hovering over the slip.

"I'm sure," I said, a little irritated. She didn't even really know me and now she was questioning my sincerity?

"Why this sudden interest in peer tutoring?"

Honesty is the best policy, right? Besides Principal Downing is like a human polygraph test. No one can slip a lie past her—she sees right through them. "I'm applying for an internship at the cancer research center in Seattle this summer." She looked up at me suddenly and I paused, but she didn't say anything, so I continued. "I need more community service on my application if I'm going to get in. I know I'm weak in that area, but I think I'd be good at the research if I can just get in. And I could probably use a little work on my bedside manner if I'm really going to be a doctor. Peer tutoring might help with that too."

She gave me a look that was hard to read. "Well, if you think you can handle it, then it's all right by me." She signed the slip and handed it back to me. "You can go ahead and report to Mr. Newman after lunch."

I took the paper back with her crisp black signature on the yellow paper and thanked her.

Lately, it's been way too awkward to eat in the cafeteria with everyone whispering about me, so I've been going home for lunch instead. We live close to the school so I can make it there and back if I hurry. My mom is at work and Chloe and Ethan are at school so I have the house to myself. It is a lot healthier than eating at the school, a lot easier than packing a lunch, and a lot lonelier than eating with everyone else.

Today there wasn't time to go home and I hadn't thought to pack a lunch, so I had to brave the cafeteria. Going without food when I run so much simply isn't an option. The least offensive entrée in the place was a chicken salad—rubbery chicken reclining on a wilting lettuce bed. I doused it with ranch dressing so that I could choke it down. I heard Principal Downing behind me in line, ordering the same thing.

I took my salad into the cafeteria. It had been a long time since I'd been there—a few months, in fact. The atmosphere was as raucous as ever and almost all of the tables were full. I didn't see my old group. They must have gone out somewhere to eat, which was probably a good thing.

Before our breakup in the fall, I used to eat with Connor and his friends. I'd eaten with them since my sophomore year. It was a big group, full of football players and cheerleaders and student body officers. Lots of people refer to it as the popular group, but I am realizing more and more that there is no such thing. It was strange to realize that fact after all the years of trying to get into Conner's group and then the years of being part of it. Now, I would call my old lunch group the High-Visibility Group—the people that do things in front of the school, like play sports and organize assemblies. There were some good people in that group that I missed, but there had been some jerks too. It's probably like that with most groups, but since I don't really belong to any group these days, I can't be sure.

I scanned the tables, looking for somewhere to set my tray. High school is full of decisions like these—little ones with lots of variables and huge repercussions. I couldn't sit down uninvited with people I didn't know, and no one seemed to be inviting me. I had to pretend that I was looking for someone, so no one would notice that I was alone and didn't have a place. I had to keep out of the way of the people coming through the door behind me. I had to balance my backpack and my salad and the signed slip I was holding and stick the change from lunch into my pocket without spilling anything. And I had to do it all fast. Hesitate for a minute, and they'll eat you alive in this place.

One thing I've learned is that it's important to always look like you have a purpose. My eye caught some people leaving at the back, so I made a beeline for their table. I wish I'd thought to bring one of my textbooks. Then if anyone noticed that I was sitting alone, they would think it was because I had studying to do.

I set my salad down in the middle of the refuse the other group had left behind and pulled the scarred orange plastic chair up to the table. I intended to set another school record. It would be the record for the fastest lunch consumption ever to take place in the Lakeview High School cafeteria. I speared the lettuce and chicken and stuck it into my mouth.

One of the rules of life is that someone will always ask you something as soon as you've filled your mouth with food. Another is that your dentist will always ask you lots of questions while he's working on your teeth, which is absurd because there's no way to answer them.

"Can I sit here?"

I looked up and saw Principal Downing. I nodded, since I couldn't speak, and she sat down next to me.

"How's the salad?" she asked with a wry grin. "I always pack my lunch and it's always extra healthy, but I forgot it on the counter at home today."

I swallowed. "Passable." There were only ten minutes left until the bell, thank goodness. I didn't mind sitting with the principal; I'm sure no one thought I was in trouble and at least I wasn't alone.

However, I wasn't sure what we were going to talk about for those ten minutes. The people at the next table looked over at us and then looked away. There wouldn't be any food fights or talk about crazy weekend antics anywhere near us for the rest of the lunch hour.

She took a bite and chewed it. "Good adjective," she said, taking a big drink of water. "Passable about covers it." She pulled out a little plastic container full of pills and swallowed them down. I was watching, even though I pretended not to be.

She knew it too. "I'm on a lot of meds," she said, without looking up, as she put her pill case back into her purse. Then she startled me with a direct gaze. "Nothing exciting or recreational, I'm afraid."

"I didn't think that," I said, caught off guard.

"Now *this* is my vice," she said, pulling a plastic bag out of her purse. "Homemade chocolate chip cookies." She popped one into her mouth. "Takes away that chalky pill aftertaste and it's delicious. Do you want one?" She held one out to me. "Mr. Thomas brought them into the office for the faculty meeting later today and I snuck some into my purse. I keep trying to get the recipe from him and he keeps forgetting to give it to me, so I thought I was justified."

I didn't know what else to do, so I took it. "Thanks," I said. I guess taking food from teachers and principals is safe, right? I took a bite. It *was* delicious. "This is good," I said. "He should market them."

"That's what I keep telling him," she said, a little absently. Then she turned and looked at me with another one of her direct gazes. "Andrea, I'm sorry about giving you the third degree earlier. If you want to be a peer tutor, that's wonderful. I was just surprised."

"Why?" I asked. "Don't I seem like the type?"

She laughed. "No, it's more that you are so busy. You remind me a lot of myself when I was younger. You have your mind set on the goal at all times. I'm glad you're taking the time out to help someone else. I've been getting better at that, but it's taken a while to learn." She had another bite of salad and made a face. "This is getting less and less passable by the minute. I'm going to go buy a carton of milk and eat cookies instead." She scooted her chair back and headed back into the cafeteria line. Students moved to let her pass and she waved to some of them. They waved back.

My face burned after she left. She thought I was taking time out to help someone else, but really it was all for my application. *But working at the cancer research center is helping others,* I told myself, and this was what I had to do to get there. It didn't make me feel better about my motives, though.

Principal Downing came back with two cartons of milk and handed one to me. "Here you go," she said.

"Thanks," I said, surprised. She plopped a couple of cookies on my plate and dug into hers with relish. I watched her while I started to eat mine. I'd never seen an adult enjoy cookies so much.

She caught me looking at her again and smiled. "I've been on a diet for the past few months," she explained. "I haven't had cookies in a while, especially not ones that tasted this good."

"A diet?" I asked, surprised. "But you're already thin."

"It was a different kind of diet," she said evasively. "Anyway, my apologies again about the interrogation. I think you'll be a good peer tutor."

"Thanks," I said, as the five-minute warning bell rang. "I haven't done anything like this before, so who knows how I'll do." Admitting weakness to the school principal? What was coming over me?

We both stood up to clear away the rest of our lunches. The unfinished salads went into the trash can next to our table. "It will be a learning experience," she said, smiling at me. "Good for you for giving it a shot." She waved good-bye as she walked off in the direction of a cluster of students known for needing a little extra supervision. "Okay, people, let's get to class," I heard her say.

I picked up my backpack from the table and started walking to Mr. Newman's room. The halls after lunch are impossible and impassable. I'm not above using a little elbowing here and there to get through. You have to look out for yourself, after all. It's like the starting line of a big race, except the crowd never thins out until after the bell rings and by then it's too late.

I made it just in time. Mr. Newman peered at me over his glasses without much excitement, looking at me with scrutiny. "What qualifications do you have?" he asked.

"I have a 4.0 GPA, I've taken calculus, advanced English—" I started. Here we go again. I didn't think I'd have to prepare a resume to be a peer tutor!

"That's nice that you have good grades, but that's not what I mean," he interrupted. "Have you worked with youth or with peers before? Have you taken any workshops on peer tutoring, like the one we offered last summer?"

"No," I said. I felt the eyes of the students and tutors on me even though they were supposed to be working in their pairs. I looked over at David Sherman and he smiled at me before he looked away as one of the girls at his table asked him a question.

Mr. Newman wasn't going to let it go. "What made you think that you wanted to start doing this, after the semester already started and without any of the training we usually offer?" he asked. "I'm not asking this to discourage you, but I am curious."

"I haven't done any community service and I need to start somewhere," I said. It was the truth.

"Well, we can put you to work," he said, moving away from his desk. "I want to make sure you know what you're getting into, though. You can't just quit if you decide you don't like it. If you're on board now, I need you to stay through the rest of the school year. Continuity is very important in peer tutoring. Right now I have two students assigned to one tutor, so I'm going to give you one of those students. We'll see how it goes. I may reassign if necessary, but this seems as good a fit as any."

He stopped by the desk where two girls were being tutored by David Sherman. "Amy," Mr. Newman said to one of them, "this is

Andrea Beckett. I'm going to reassign her to be your tutor. David, you've been doing a great job with two, but I think this will make it a little easier on everyone. Amy, why don't you join Andrea at the table in the back of the room?"

I could tell Amy wasn't too happy about her new assignment, but she didn't say anything. She picked up her books and walked to the back of the room.

Mr. Newman pulled me aside. "Amy has several learning disabilities. She has a really hard time with reading comprehension—retaining the things she's read. For today, why don't you get to know her a little and do the best you can in helping her with her homework. I'd like you to stay after school today and I'll give you some more specific information and resources."

I needed to get in my workout for track after school, but I nodded my head anyway. Now that I had an actual person to help and the word *disabilities* was being thrown out there, I realized that this was more serious than I had thought. Also, it wasn't all about me. It wasn't really about me at all, except that I was the vehicle being used to help this other person. I'd need all the help I could get because I've never had a learning disability and didn't know how to help someone who did. School has always come easily to me.

As I made my way to the back of the room, I sized up Amy the best I could. I hadn't seen her around or I hadn't noticed her if I had. She was very unremarkable and unobtrusive: a chubby, plain girl with no glaring disabilities, but nothing very intriguing, either. Nothing that would make you stop and look at her to single her out for teasing or something, but also nothing that would catch your eye in a positive way, either. Her long brown hair was pulled back in a ponytail, her jeans were faded and a little too short to be in style, and her T-shirt left too much of her pale, pudgy arms exposed.

She didn't look up as I approached her table; she just sat there, laboriously copying down biology definitions from the book in a pink spiral-bound notebook with a smudgy pencil.

I decided to take charge. "Hi, Amy," I said. "First things first. Let me sharpen your pencil so you can write neatly." I held out my hand for her pencil. She looked up, met my eyes, held out her pencil to me, and then turned away without saying anything.

I marched briskly to the pencil sharpener on the wall, sharpened her pencil, and then marched back to sit down beside her. I could feel David Sherman's eyes watching me. I handed Amy her pencil. She took it without looking at me.

"It looks like you're doing biology definitions," I said. "How many do you have left to go?"

Her pale blue eyes flickered at me. "Twenty."

"You'll never get done by the time class ends," I said. "Would it be easier if I read them to you a word at a time and you wrote them down? Then you won't have to keep looking back and forth between the textbook and your notebook."

She nodded, and so that was what we did for the rest of the period: I swallowed back yawns as I read the definitions slowly, word by word, spelling the difficult ones, while she ground her pencil into the paper and wrote them down. We finished right before the bell rang.

"Great!" I said. "Now your assignment is done. I'll see you tomorrow, right?" Amy nodded, again not looking at me, put her books in her backpack, and left.

"See you after school," said Mr. Newman as I passed his desk. "I've set up some one-on-one tutoring instruction for you with one of our best tutors. It will only be for an hour or two today since it's short notice, but it will help get you started."

After school, I hurried out to the track to tell Coach that I would be missing the workout. Since it's not even the regular season yet, he was fine with me missing, especially when I told him I would make up the run later that day.

"Does this have something to do with what David's doing?" he asked. "I know David is missing practice today too."

"It might," I said, surprised. I knew David was a peer tutor, but I didn't know he'd be considered one of the best.

It *was* David waiting for me back in Mr. Newman's room. "Are you my tutor for tutoring?" I said in a lame attempt at humor as I sat in the chair across from him.

"Did Andrea Beckett just make a joke?" David asked, smiling at me. "Yup. Mr. Newman asked me to hang around and give you some of the training that I've had. You know—he wants me to kind of give you a summary of some things that work. Plus I used to be Amy's tutor, so I know a little bit about her too."

Mr. Newman was sitting at his desk grading papers. He chimed in, "And I need to give you this." He stood up and came over, handing me a flier. "You'll need to attend this workshop that the school district holds about tutoring. It's an all-day workshop and it will be three Saturdays from now. You'll have to attend this if you want to stay in the class. Usually I make students complete the workshop before they can sign up." He walked back to his desk and lifted a stack of papers into his arms. "Now, if you'll excuse me, I'll need to go to my office to finish grading these tests. I need to concentrate, and you don't want to hear the profanity I'm going to be using based on how my classes are doing so far."

I waited until the door had closed behind him before I said, "This seems pretty intense. Is it really necessary to go to a workshop for this kind of thing? I mean, I've only been doing it for a day and it seems really easy."

To my shock, David's response was, "Then you're not doing it right. If it's easy, then you're probably feeding answers to them or doing most of it yourself. The whole point is that it's *not* easy for these guys, so we have to find out ways to help them, and that's not easy, either. It definitely takes more than one day."

"Okay," I said shortly, "since you're the master tutor, tell me what I should be doing." I've never liked being told what to do, and especially not by the class clown! "If there's one thing I know, it's how to study," I added, "but if you don't think I'm doing it right, then by all means tell me what I'm doing wrong."

David leaned back in his chair, smiling his warm, easy smile. "Oh, no you don't, Andrea Beckett," he said. "You can't get ticked off at me before I even get started or this is going to be the longest afternoon of both our lives."

It's impossible to stay mad at someone who's grinning like a madman at you. "Fine," I said, unable to keep myself from smiling back a little. "Go ahead. I'm receptive and responsive."

"First of all, I listened to what you were doing with Amy today and even though that's a great way to get through the assignment, it doesn't help her retain any of the information. Also, you didn't really even talk to Amy and that's important. You have to build a relationship with her, even if it's just a basic one." David leaned in and spoke quietly. "Amy takes a long time to do things, but she's not stupid. The way you were reading things slowly to her was embarrassing her. Didn't you see how red her face was getting?"

I felt *my* face getting red. This was supposed to be easy and now I was way out of my comfort zone. "No," I admitted brusquely. "I thought the point was to help her get her homework done."

"Yeah, but it's also to help her learn how to learn. You'll learn more about comprehension strategies and stuff when you go to the workshop, but Mr. Newman wanted me to give you a few of them now so you weren't floundering around. So let's pretend that you are the person being tutored and I'll help you with the same assignment Amy was doing." He slid a biology book and the worksheet with the definitions toward me.

"You've got to be kidding me," I said, staring down at the definitions. I thought with longing of the track team out running along the streets through the cold rain. I like the chilly weather; it makes me run faster and faster. It sharpens me. I could feel my legs itching to get started instead of just sitting there, thinking about how to help someone I didn't even know.

"Okay, Amy," said David in his deepest, most serious teacher voice. "Let's get started on these definitions." He marched to the chalkboard, lifted his skinny arm high over his head, and dramatically began to write on the board. "I'm writing down the first definition, and you should too," he said over his shoulder. I played along, copying the definition out of the book and onto my paper. "Now, you read it back to me." I did. "Now," he said, "draw a picture on your paper of the definition." He handed me some crayons.

"You've got to be kidding me," I said again. "I'm supposed to draw a picture of an amoeba? There's a perfectly good one right here in the book with all the parts labeled and everything."

"Doesn't matter," he said. "Drawing something yourself will help you retain the information. And you don't have to make it super scientific or anything. Just what you think is important and what you think will help you remember it later."

I drew a blob and labeled a few parts. David came over to inspect my work. "Great," he said. He walked me through a few more comprehension strategies like summarizing and retelling, and I could see how they might be helpful. After an hour and a half, Mr. Newman came back to lock up the room and kicked us out.

We decided to run our late workout together, so we changed and met on the track. We started jogging to warm up. I like running with guys because they're so much faster and it pushes me.

"This tutoring is more involved than I thought," I said as we ran. "I thought that all I'd have to do was sign up and I'd be in. Now I'm getting special tutoring myself and signing up for Saturday workshops."

David is gangly, but long legs make for a long stride. I could tell he was shortening it so that I could keep up. He looked over at me, the huge pom-pom on his ridiculous beanie bouncing chaotically as he ran. "But anything done right takes time and effort, right?" He grinned. "Why would tutoring be any different?"

"I thought it would be easy because I'm good at school, I guess," I said.

"Oh no, my friend," David said. "That's where you're wrong. Being bad at school actually helps more with tutoring because you understand how it feels to get things wrong and make mistakes. You can understand where the problems are coming from. That's why I'm so good at it. That and the fact that my rugged good looks make the ladies line up to be tutored by me."

I laughed, and he feigned hurt. "You don't think it's the truth?"

We were picking up speed, but he wasn't breathing hard at all. I was starting to have to work to keep my words from coming out choppily, but I didn't want him to know. It's so unfair that guys are naturally faster than girls.

We ran our intervals hard. We did ten 400-meter intervals, which was a pretty hard workout. We ran a lap of the track as hard and as fast as we could, then jogged a lap in between, then ran another 400-meter lap. It's a grueling combination of speed and endurance and, when done right, is a workout that can make you ache physically and mentally by the end.

David finished ahead of me on all the intervals, then waited to jog with me in the intermediate lap. We didn't talk much because we were both running hard in the intervals and trying to recover in the jogging laps, but it was nice to just have someone there and not be running alone.

After the last interval, I was beat; David was too. I'd just run one of the hardest workouts of the year on a stomach full of milk and cookies. Not exactly the food of champions. We finished our cool-down mile and sat on the bleachers for a minute to stretch. We still hadn't said much, but the silence was pleasant. It wasn't a cold or embarrassed silence, just companionable.

I pulled out the elastic holding my ponytail and shook out my hair, then raked it all back from my face. I caught David looking at me with admiration in his eyes. It made me feel good, which surprised me. I didn't know I cared much about what he thought. I'd thought he was immune to how I looked, but I guess he noticed after all.

"What?" I asked, more sharply than I meant.

"Nothing," he said. Then he got a mischievous glint in his eye, pulled off his beanie, and shook out his sweaty, disheveled hair. He started preening, making fun of me in a good-natured way. "How do I look?" he asked, trying to pull his hair into a ponytail.

I glared back at him, trying not to laugh. "I'm too tired to joke around with you," I said, stretching my arms out in front of me. "That was a hard workout."

"Yeah, it was," he agreed, but his irrepressible energy was already back. "Thanks for running with me," he said. "That would have been even worse if I'd been alone."

"Yeah, thanks to you too," I said. "And thanks for the tutoring pointers. I'll have to give them a try tomorrow."

"Good luck," he said. "I'll be watching. You'll do fine." He popped his hat back onto his head, clapped me firmly on the back, and said, "See you tomorrow." He broke into a run towards the boys' locker room.

I was still pretty exhausted—I'd run each 400-meter lap somewhere between 1:05 and 1:10, which was good for this early in the season. I walked back to the school slowly to pick up my calculus book from my locker.

I was surprised to see Amy standing near my locker, pulling things out of her locker. She looked up as I walked by.

"Hi, Amy," I said. "What are you doing here this late?" I asked, stopping near her and trying to seem friendly. It came out sounding kind of fake.

She didn't look at me, just mumbled something about retaking a test and closed the locker door, turning to leave.

This was going to be harder than I thought, I realized for the fiftieth time that day. "See you tomorrow," I called. She nodded and walked away, plodding down the hall.

Suddenly a line from a poem that was published in the school paper last fall flashed through my head. I'd kept the poem stapled to a page in my notebook all year because I'd liked it so much. Something about it had shocked me with recognition. I felt that same way as I watched Amy slouch down the hall.

I went to my locker, got my notebook, opened it up, and turned to the page where I'd stapled in the poem. I found the lines that reminded me of Amy (and of myself):

> *It's easier to let yourself drown.*
> *Why struggle and slip and swim and choke?*

I read the rest of the poem out loud to myself quietly, finishing with the last stanza, which was my favorite part:

> *But something in me still wants to rise up out of the dark water.*
> *Wants to feel the sun on my wet, cold skin.*
> *Something inside of me wants to put my feet on hot, grainy sand*
> *And run along the beach.*
> *Even though there is glass that might cut me buried beneath.*

I could picture exactly what the author was talking about. That poem was published a month or two after the Homecoming debacle. I could understand how much easier it would feel to quit coming to school and running hard and trying to be perfect all the time. It would be so much easier to slip beneath the surface and give up.

I guess I've already done that in a way by cutting off my family and being reserved and standoffish to almost everyone. But there really is something in me that wants to run along the sand and feel again. Grandma brings that out in me. So does David Sherman. Maybe I could bring that out in Amy if I worked hard enough at it.

I closed my notebook and turned around to see someone standing behind me. It was a girl named Avery; I think she has a crush on David. She was looking at me with a funny expression on her face. I was embarrassed to be caught reading out loud.

"Hi," I said, shutting my locker and sticking the notebook into my bag. There sure were a lot of people hanging around the school late today! Then I saw that she had some copies of the school paper in her arms.

She saw me looking at them. "Do you want one?" she asked in her brusque, take-no-prisoners voice. "We just finished printing them and I'm on my way to the newsroom to get them ready to hand out for tomorrow."

"Sure," I said. I took a paper from her and added it to my bag, then slung it over my shoulder. "Thanks," I said.

"Same to you," she said, which caught me off guard because it didn't make any sense. She walked away down the hall, her boots making a marching cadence as she went. I started walking in the opposite direction, and I found my stride matching hers in spite of myself.

CHAPTER 1 4

FEBRUARY

David Sherman

Absolutely ridiculous, you are. That's what Yoda would say if he had seen me flailing through this dating debacle. And no, I don't make a habit of thinking about what Yoda would say, although my younger brother, Eric, does. Eric is thirteen and he seems to be bordering on the obsessive with his *Star Wars* knowledge and interest. The fact that he often breathes in the same asthmatic wheeze as Darth Vader might be the first clue that he was pretty into it. The fact that he named his cat "Chewy" would be the second clue. I would worry about when Eric heads to high school in a year or so, but he also happens to be very tall for his age and plays football, so I think he'll be all right.

What's even weirder than Eric's *Star Wars* obsession is that he was a big help in my asking Andrea to go out on a date with me. Not just any date. I asked her to go to the ballet with me.

I got the idea when I heard her and Amy having a really animated conversation in tutoring about how no one does anything romantic anymore or classy on dates. They just go out for burgers or see a movie, weekend after weekend. I remembered how Andrea once told me about going to see the *Nutcracker* ballet at Christmas with her grandmother every year and how much she loved it.

But when I checked to see how much tickets were for the Pacific Northwest Ballet, I realized that there was no way that was going to work out, barring a large windfall coming my way. I don't have a hundred dollars to spend on a date—even for Andrea Beckett—not with my mission coming up so soon. I've been working extra hours after practice at the sports store at the mall to save money for my mission and college. I knew there was no way I could justify spending so much.

That job at the store has turned into a lucky break for me. Not only is it helping me save some cash for my mission, but it also helped me get up the courage to consider asking Andrea out on a date in the first place.

A couple of days ago I was at work and some little kid came in wanting to buy a baseball glove. He was going to start practicing with his dad so that he could play Little League in the summer. Well, that's the kind of customer I like best and so I was helping him find the right glove and talking to him about how much fun it was going to be.

There was a little old lady following me around and watching me and she looked really familiar. When I'd rung the glove up for the kid and sent him on his way, the old lady marched over to the counter where I was clerking. It was then that I remembered where I'd seen her before. She was Andrea Beckett's grandmother. They'd come in together once around Christmastime, and besides, there was no mistaking that perfect posture. It must run in the family.

Apparently, bluntness also ran in the family. "I need to buy a Nike Windbreaker for my grandson and you are going to help me," she said without preamble.

I went over to the running section with her and helped her pick out a Windbreaker for Ethan. Apparently his birthday was coming up. She made her decision and I carried her purchase to the front of the store. As I was putting it in a bag for her, she said the magic words that made me think I really could ask Andrea out.

"You are a nice young man," she declared. "I think you should take my granddaughter on a date."

"Do you think she'd say yes?" I asked, surprised and interested.

"Oh, yes," she said and picked up her bag. "Thank you for your help, young man. I think Ethan will quite like this." And she was gone. My own fairy god-grandmother.

Anyway, Eric wandered in just as I hung up the phone with the Pacific Northwest Ballet. I was muttering about how much tickets to the ballet cost, and he said, "Isn't it free?"

I said, "No, it's not free, it's fifty dollars a ticket! And that's for the balcony seats where you can't even see anything!"

"Why would anyone pay fifty dollars to see Addie dance?" he asked.

I realized that he had handed me the perfect solution. Addie is our eleven-year-old sister, the baby of the family and the only girl, so my mom has enrolled her in everything possible that is girly. Ballet is one of those things.

"Does Addie have a ballet recital coming up?" I asked.

Normally, we all—except for my mom—avoid Addie's recitals like the plague. And that includes Addie. The great tragedy of Mom's life is that her only daughter came last, not first, and has been turned by her older brothers into a tomboy who hates ballet and pink and dolls. The only reason Addie is still taking ballet is because Mom promised her a snowboard next winter if she keeps dancing until then. Addie's sick of using my old one. It *is* pretty beat up.

"Yup," Eric said. "Next weekend. She's been complaining about it forever. How did you miss that?"

Because I've had my head in the clouds thinking about Andrea Beckett, that's why.

Now that she does peer tutoring during her free hour like me, I see a lot more of her. I'm getting better at talking to her, but it is still going to be emotionally scarring to ask her on a date. But I have to do it. If I don't, I'll always wish I had and time is running out. The school year is flying by faster than you can say "decapitated Skipper."

"Eric," I said, "I think I might bring a date to Addie's recital. Do you think Addie'd care?"

"I don't think she'll mind at all. Mom will pass out with joy. But it'll be a pretty short date. Addie's recital starts at seven so it'll be over by eight for sure."

"I'll think of something else to do after," I said.

"You could have hot chocolate in the tree house by candlelight," suggested Eric.

I paused, thinking it through. "Where did you come up with *that?* The tree house is freezing this time of year!"

"Not if you put a space heater up there. Don't you remember how Dad would let us do that sometimes when everyone lived at home and we wanted to pretend we had our own room for a couple of hours? I'm sure we still have the heater and the cord."

I gave him a bear hug. Eric is going to do just fine in high school. Maybe I should hire him to do the asking out for me as well as planning the date.

• • •

I ran the idea by Avery Matthews the next day in journalism. Avery knows that I've been working up the courage to ask Andrea out for a long time. Say what you like about Avery's take-no-prisoners approach, it's sometimes helpful to know exactly what she really thinks about any given topic.

"What do you think?" I asked. "Does that sound like a decent date? Do you think she'd say yes?"

Avery gave me a considering gaze. "You've put a lot of thought into this, haven't you?"

"Yup," I said. "More than I'd like to admit."

"When are you going to ask her?" she asked. "It's Tuesday. Plus, it's Andrea Beckett. You'd better ask her today if you want to have a prayer of her being free on Friday. I'm sure guys are asking her out in advance all the time. When will you see her next?"

"We've already had peer tutoring today, but she's in English across the hall right now. I usually see her in the hall after class," I said.

"Ask her out then," Avery said.

"In public? In front of everyone?"

"This isn't that big of a deal," Avery said. "If someone hears you, so what? It's not that weird to be asking in the hall. I hear people asking other people stuff like that all the time."

"Everyone will hear if she rejects me!" I said as the bell rang and Avery and I gathered up our books.

"She won't reject you," Avery said. "Believe it or not, Sherman, I think she's kind of intrigued by you. You're a different breed than the guys she usually dates."

"I still can't do it," I said. We both caught sight of Andrea as she walked out the door. I waved at her and she waved back, and I stopped in the hall. Avery ricocheted off my backpack and sighed in annoyance.

"Ask her out, you freak," she hissed, and shoved me into the stream of people. I squished through them, a fish swimming against the tide, and made it to Andrea's locker.

"Andrea," I blurted, "are you busy this Friday?" Oops. Not very subtle. Maybe a little preamble would have been better. A little conversation and then a segue into the asking out. Too late now.

"No," she said. "I'm not."

"Do you want to go to the ballet with me and then have hot chocolate?" I asked her in a rush.

She didn't say anything. All she did was look at me in perfect silence, a look of absolute surprise on her face. I waited for a second, or maybe it was a year, in that excruciating silence, and then I panicked. "That's all right," I said. "Pretend I never asked." I patted her on the arm in a kindly manner—like a little old man in our ward or something!—and headed for the doors. I walked fast and with purpose, as though I had lots of places to be and lots of things to do and this rejection was no problem at all, just a little annoyance in the grand scheme of things.

I was partway down the hall when Avery caught up to me, running. She moves pretty fast, even though she's always wearing those clunky combat boots of hers. One of her friends called to her, but she said, "I'll talk to you tomorrow, I've gotta go." Then she grabbed me by the arm and made me slow down. She couldn't stop me, though, and I kept heading for the doors.

"What happened?" she asked. "It looked like it was going fine and then all of a sudden you started sprinting down the hall."

"She didn't answer me," I said. "I asked her and she just stood there. I couldn't take it, so I left." I started laughing in spite of myself even though it still didn't feel funny. "If I can't even ask a girl on a date without bailing, what on earth am I going to do on my mission when I have to wade through worse than this? I can't run out every time there's an awkward silence or I don't get the answer I want."

We were in the parking lot by then. "I know what you'll do," said Avery.

"How do *you* know?" I asked. "I don't even know what I'll do." I felt disgusted with myself.

"You'll keep trying until it works out," she said. She turned me around, just in time to see Andrea coming out of the doors of the school. She was walking straight toward us.

"Let me know how it goes later," Avery said. "Now . . . march." And, for the second time in under an hour, she gave me a shove. This time it was a little shove, and then she was gone.

Once an object is in motion, it stays in motion until something—like Andrea Beckett's eyes—stops it. I stopped.

"Hey, David," Andrea said.

"Hey," I said. "I'm sorry for taking off so fast."

"No, I'm sorry. I gave you the wrong impression. The absolute wrong impression. I was surprised and I didn't react fast enough. I didn't think you would want to ever ask me on a date in the first place. In the second place, I couldn't believe you were inviting me to do something so . . . thoughtful." She smiled at me a little bit uncertainly. "I'd be happy to go with you, if you still want to."

"Of course," I said. Then I paused for a second. "Why would you think *I* wouldn't ever want to ask *you* on a date?"

She looked embarrassed. "Oh . . . because of the whole Homecoming night incident. Or because I'm not really active in the Church. Or because you like girls who are funnier and more . . . alternative, like Avery Matthews. There's plenty of reasons."

I shook my head. "You shouldn't worry so much."

"Neither should you," she said. There was a pause while we looked right at each other. I didn't flinch; she didn't either.

"What ballet are they performing?" she asked.

"I'm not sure," I said. "We'll have to ask Addie, my sister. She'll know because she's in it."

"Your sister is a *ballerina?*" she asked. "Isn't she really young?"

"She's not a professional ballerina," I said. I realized I'd better clear up right away that we would be watching Addie and her dance class, not Baryshnikov. "She's just a kid in a ballet recital, but I think it will still be pretty good. Every ballerina has to start somewhere, right?"

Andrea gave me one of those measuring looks that she does every once in a while. They used to terrify me because I felt like she was holding up the person or thing to some impossible standard, judging it, and finding it inadequate or disappointing. Lately those looks haven't scared me as much because I'm starting to realize that she's just thinking about and analyzing things, not necessarily judging them. Still I worried that the analysis of this potential date might not come out in my favor.

"It sounds perfect," she said. "What should I wear?"

"Anything's fine," I said. "Jeans and a sweater, whatever. It's just a kid's ballet recital."

"I think we should dress up," she said firmly. "It will show Addie that we took it seriously."

"Okay," I said. "Can I pick you up at about six-thirty?"

"That sounds fine. I'll be at my dad's this weekend, though. I'll write down directions to his apartment for you tomorrow during tutoring."

"Sounds good," I said. "I'll see you at track later."

She nodded and was gone. I turned toward my car door to hide the grin on my face as I opened it to get my track bag. No one was going to be able to catch up to me in workout today, not even Ethan Beckett, because I was going to fly through those intervals like a man possessed. I threw my bag over my shoulder and headed toward the locker room.

FEBRUARY

Michaela Choi

It sounds like a question someone might ask theoretically to make conversation at a party or something: Which hurts more, a broken heart or a broken leg? After this month, I know the answer. A broken heart, hands down. Although a broken leg isn't a piece of cake, either.

At the beginning of the month, I felt as though I had a lot to look forward to—the indoor track meets, hanging out with Ethan and (probably) going to the Valentine's Dance together, things like that. At the beginning of the month, it looked like it was going to be the best February on record, and I was on top of the world.

February is usually the worst month of the year because it's still gray and cold and everyone is really sick of winter by then. And then there is Valentine's Day: the most tortuous holiday imaginable for a single teenager. This time, I thought, it was going to be completely different. I was actually looking forward to February.

The month had barely started when things began to go wrong. I don't know what the groundhog saw when he came out on

Groundhog Day, but I think we both wished we'd stayed in our bur-rows before too much time had passed.

Ethan went to his dad's new apartment in Bellevue for the first weekend of the month but he came home early for some reason. I was surprised because his dad had just moved back into town and I'd thought Ethan would want to stay the whole weekend, but he didn't seem to want to talk about it.

That Saturday night we all went bowling and he gave me a ride home afterward. Usually, Saturday nights are the ones I look forward to all week. We hang out with everyone, but our eyes are always meeting, we find ways to sit right by each other, we always laugh and flirt. We've been good about trying not to steady date, but everyone knows there's something there and that's more than okay by me. But something was off all night long. I couldn't tell what it was because Ethan was perfectly nice to me, but it was there. So when he offered Julie a ride home too, I was a little apprehensive.

Things seemed okay on the way to Julie's house, but I could still feel that underlying tension of something wrong under the surface of our conversation. We were talking about an article that had been published in the school paper that week by Avery Matthews, a girl in Ethan's and my English class. She had interviewed someone from most of the major religions represented at Lakeview High. She inter-viewed Elizabeth Andrade to represent the Mormons. Elizabeth is in my early-morning seminary class and she did a good job explaining our religion. She also did a good job describing early-morning sem-inary and why we bother getting up so early.

Julie was really excited about the whole thing and was going to show it to her parents. I had been happy with the article too, but it was hard to generate much enthusiasm about it right then when I was so worried about what was going on with Ethan.

After Ethan dropped off Julie, we were both quiet as he drove to my house. We made a couple of filler comments that I forgot as soon as we'd made them. He pulled into the driveway and looked over at me. The light above our garage flipped on (thanks, Dad!) but that didn't seem to bother Ethan. He was taking his time about saying something. I'm usually good at filling the silence, but this time I couldn't do it. My mind was misfiring, I guess, because nothing I could think of seemed to make sense, so I stayed silent.

He spoke quietly—my first signal that something was wrong. "You know the Valentine's Day dance later this month?"

"Yeah," I said, thinking that this wasn't a very promising beginning if he was going to ask me to go with him. There wasn't any excitement in his voice.

"I was kind of thinking I'd take Elizabeth." He wasn't doing a great job of making eye contact with me, I noticed, because I was staring straight at him in surprise. I felt more physically shocked than anything, like someone had slammed into me from every possible side and somehow I was still upright.

"Oh," I said. He had to know how much this would hurt me, didn't he?

He did. His face looked worried. "Mikey, I think we might be getting too serious. I've been thinking a lot about this. I mean, we do a pretty good job of hanging out in groups and all that, but I think you and I both know that we're basically together. And everyone else knows it too. It might be a good idea for us to go out with other people more and each other a little less."

It was hard to breathe for a minute or maybe it was way too easy to breathe. Whatever it was, it didn't feel quite normal. "What do you mean? Are you saying we shouldn't date at all anymore?"

The pause before he spoke was my answer. "Maybe we shouldn't, at least not for a while. We're more than just friends and that could get us hurt at some point. It's getting a little too serious for me. It seems like the best thing to do is to take a step back."

"Are you trying to tell me that you don't like me anymore?" I asked. "Because if you don't, you should just come out and say it and not try to let me down easy." I was a little mad, I'll admit.

"No," he said, moving a little closer. He was very earnest. "It's because I like you a lot that I don't want to date you anymore. I just don't want to be on the line like that because the potential for getting hurt is too big." Ethan was speaking very quietly and slowly now. "I've been thinking about this for a while and it makes a lot of sense to me. Can't you see what I'm saying? We can still be good friends and hang out with the group without going on dates and all of that."

All of that. All of that was holding hands on the bus after track meets. All of that was sitting together in his living room while he practiced his guitar and I did my homework.

It was having a food fight at a picnic with some friends one Saturday.

It was hanging out with other people now and then and having it not matter if I had a good time or not because eventually I'd go out with Ethan again and it would be wonderful.

It was the feeling of watching the minutes in chemistry count down until class was over, waiting for the few minutes in the hall we'd have together.

It was hearing the phone ring and knowing that it was going to be for me.

It was getting up in the morning and caring about what I wore because I wanted Ethan to like it; conversely, it was getting up in the morning and not caring about what I wore because Ethan would like it anyway.

It was daydreaming about our first kiss on the bus on the way home from the State Championships.

Most of all it was knowing that I belonged to someone who valued me for who I was. It's not like I was Ethan's property. It was that in the nicest, most comfortable way possible I felt like someone had chosen me and that I had chosen him and that we cared about each other.

It meant that when something bad or something good

happened, there was always someone to talk to who cared. That I would have a date to the dances and games and someone to hold hands with. That we both respected each other and our beliefs and helped each other uphold those beliefs.

I don't think adults understand how lonely it is to be a teenager. We can't embrace and cling to our parents for comfort; we've outgrown that. We've outgrown it from them but still need it from someone. We are looking for someone to fill that void.

But how could I argue with Ethan? He looked so sad, and so sure.

"What are you thinking?" he finally asked.

"I still don't understand," I said. "If you like me, and I like you, and we're not doing anything wrong, I don't understand the problem."

"I was at my dad's this weekend," he said, "and he's all alone, and it got me thinking about how hard that would be. I'm not ready for this stuff. I want everything to go back to the way it was." He stopped and said it again, more quietly, "I want everything to go back to the way it was."

• • •

Ethan was right about the fact that we would still hang out, but he was wrong about everything else. We were friendly and we still saw each other on the weekends when everyone hung out, but we both knew that everything had changed and so did everyone else. I hated that part of it most of all—the part where we were acting like nothing was different when the very foundation of our relationship, our friendship, had shifted beneath our feet.

I started hanging out more with Julie on our own and less and less with the group, just to avoid the weirdness and awkwardness and sadness I felt around Ethan. I also tried to be friendly to Elizabeth, whom Ethan *did* end up asking to the dance, but it was hard. I could tell that she felt strange about it too. For the first time, I was glad that Ethan and I weren't in the same ward. Then I'd have to see him every morning at early-morning seminary and every week at church.

As it was, seeing him in the halls and at running practice was enough daily contact for me. Somehow, though, even though he was there, workout became an escape for me. Ironically, as Ethan became harder and harder for me to understand, Andrea became less of a mystery. I could understand why she kept people at arm's length, why she always ignored the guys vying for her attention. It had to be easier that way, right?

I came to understand how frustration could be a powerful, motivating force for running. I was running faster and faster, even though my shins had been hurting me—and I mean *hurting*—for a few weeks. Coach and I both thought it was a bad case of shin splints, which I'd had before. I was trying to run through the pain but not overdo it, which is what worked for me before. In a weird way, the physical pain was a relief because then it was all I thought about instead of the heartache I was feeling.

• • •

The day before the Valentine's Dance was an especially cold day. No one had asked me to the dance, which I was alternately happy and sad about. I was glad because then I wouldn't have to go and see Ethan and Elizabeth together. I was sad because it would have been nice to be asked and to get all dressed up and show Ethan that nothing was bothering me.

Julie and I had plans to watch movies instead and make our favorite homemade salsa and smoothies. It wasn't a plan that would set the world on fire, I admit, but it would be fun, and I wouldn't be sitting home alone, which in my present mood was not a great idea.

As I dressed for our workout that day, I realized that I had forgotten a hat, which meant my ears were going to freeze. While we stood around waiting for Coach to organize our workout schedule, I spent the time covering my poor ears with my hands and trying not to look in Ethan's direction. We'd already had one little awkward, "Hi, how are you?" interaction in the hall today and that was enough.

I heard him say, "Mikey, do you want my hat?" and without looking at him, I responded, "I'm fine," and turned away. I didn't care if I hurt his feelings. He'd already hurt mine.

Suddenly Dave's face popped up in front of mine. "Here," he said, shoving a wool hat of his into my hands. "Your head is going to freeze."

"Thanks, Dave," I said gratefully, taking it from him. It was what I needed—a hat without emotional baggage attached. The fact that it came from another guy, even though that guy was David, didn't hurt.

So there, Ethan, I thought, pulling the hat over my frozen ears. I didn't care what I looked like, which was good since Dave's clothes are a little eclectic. This hat, for example, was a red and green Christmas tree hat with a giant yellow pom-pom star on top.

"Aren't *you* going to be cold?" I asked David. Out of the corner of my eye, I saw that both Becketts were watching our interaction closely, which was kind of odd. Why did Andrea care who Dave or I talked to? I turned to look at her and she looked away.

Dave shrugged. "I've got an extra one in my car. Almost anything you could ever need is in my car."

I laughed. "That's the truth." I remembered the time we'd all been waiting in line forever for a movie and he'd produced a game of Clue for us to play. He also had a package of stale Twinkies that no one had been willing to eat—except for Dave himself, who ate them with gusto while his character, Colonel Mustard, solved the game in record time. "Thanks for the hat, Dave."

"No problem," he said, and turned to jog to his car. He caught Andrea looking at us again and he gave her a little salute as he ran away. I saw her smiling back at him.

Coach told us that we were going to go on a three-mile run looping through the neighborhoods around the high school. It was an easy run, but one that would hurt my shins nonetheless, especially since I've been trying to keep up with Andrea for at least the first part of each run. I groaned inwardly a little as we started off. Andrea runs a little more slowly at the beginning of each run, but it isn't long before she's full steam ahead, and even the pace she was setting now at the beginning was hurting my shins today. Still, I stayed with her.

"Mikey," she said, about half a mile into the run when she started to pick up the pace, "you should probably take it easy today. Your stride is off. I can tell that this is hurting you a lot more than you're letting on."

She was direct, but her voice was pretty kind. "I think I'll be all right," I said.

She shook her head a little bit. "Suit yourself."

Andrea is merciless, with herself most of all, and I knew that. She never cuts anyone any slack—herself included—during workout. She wasn't going to make me quit and she wasn't going to slow down for me.

It hurt even more than usual to try to run with her. A sharp, stabbing ache shot through the length of my whole shin with every step. I felt some tears come to my eyes that weren't just from the cold wind. I told myself, *Just stick with Andrea until the end of this street. Then you can back off a little.*

We were almost there when it happened. It felt like someone took my leg in their big mean hands and snapped it like a twig. I fell down, scraping my other knee hard in my efforts to save the hurt leg. A sound came out of my mouth. I don't know what it was, but it couldn't have been pretty, because Andrea turned around instantly, a look of horror on her face. The girls behind us almost fell on top of me, but then they caught themselves and everyone stood around watching me crying on the ground.

I've never been speechless with pain before, but I was then. I just clutched my leg and sort of gasped and cried at the same time. It

Michaela Choi

hurt, and my other knee, bloody and full of gravel, hurt almost as much.

Everyone was talking at once. "What happened?" "What should we do?" "Mikey, are you okay?"

"No, she's not okay," I heard Andrea say. "I'm going to go into that house and use their phone. You guys stay here with her. I'll be right back." She was gone before she finished the sentence.

My friend Jana put her arm around me. "Mikey, hang in there. We'll get someone soon."

Andrea was back in a moment. "Mikey," she said, leaning in where I could see her, "I called for an ambulance. I called the school too. Coach Roberts is on his way over here right now."

An ambulance? Did I really rate that kind of intervention? I took a look at my leg and almost passed out; it was bent in a way that legs shouldn't really bend. My other leg was bleeding everywhere and Andrea wrapped her sweatshirt around it gently but firmly. Jana kept patting my arm.

Coach arrived just in time to ride in the ambulance with me. I don't remember very much about the ride, or the X-rays after, or the part where the doctor put the cast on my leg. They also stitched up my other knee, but that was the easy part. I think they gave me some pretty good painkillers at one point.

My parents arrived and took Coach Roberts's place before too much had happened. My mom told me later that Coach had stayed in the waiting room for a long time to make sure I was okay. Andrea hung around for a long time too.

The doctor later explained that I had been running with an injury all right, but it wasn't shin splints. It was tiny little stress fractures and the constant pressure and pushing through the pain had finally resulted in an actual break in my leg. Coach felt horrible. "I told her to keep running," he kept saying. The doctor told him, "She must have a very high pain threshold."

I've never thought of myself as having a high pain threshold, but

143

this month was making a believer out of me. My mom made a lame joke about how that would serve me well when I had kids, but the bottom line was that I was out for the rest of the season and I'd have a cast on my leg for a good long time.

This was turning into the worst February on record and it was taking the rest of the spring down along with it. When I finally got home, I went straight to bed, still a little dulled from the painkillers, but aware enough to feel very, very sorry for myself.

• • •

I had lots of visitors the next day—Valentine's Day. The first was Dave Sherman, who came at lunchtime with a big bag of sub sandwiches for my family and a pan of brownies that he had made himself. I managed to make it into the kitchen for his visit and propped my leg up on one of the chairs.

Dave didn't stay long, since he had to run some errands before he could take his sister snowboarding that afternoon. He promised he'd be back again to visit and said I should call him if I needed anything. He was a hit, as always, especially with my younger brothers. We dug into the sandwiches, which were delicious, and the brownies, which were . . . interesting. It's the thought that counts.

We were clearing up the paper from the sandwiches and deciding how best to dispose of the rest of the brownies when the doorbell rang again. My mom answered it and I heard voices talking. I wondered who it was. I hoped it was Ethan.

"It's Andrea Beckett," my mom said. "I had her sit in the living room. Then you can prop your leg up on the couch. You're not going to get a chance to rest with all these visitors."

I hobbled into the living room where Andrea was waiting. Even though my mom hadn't mentioned him, I had hung onto a little hope that Ethan was with her. He wasn't. She was alone, sitting on our couch.

"Hey," she said. "I came over to apologize."

"For what?" I said, sitting down carefully.

"For what happened yesterday. I was pushing too hard. I should have slowed down a little. I could tell you were hurting, but I figured you'd slow down if it got too bad. I feel like a jerk."

"It's okay," I said. "It's my own fault, not yours. How were you supposed to know how bad I was feeling?"

"That's another thing," said Andrea, smiling wryly. "I thought I was the biggest masochist on the team, but you've got me beat. How on earth were you running through stress fractures? That had to hurt like crazy."

"I don't know," I said. "I guess I kept thinking that it would get better if I just ignored it and pushed through the pain."

"Yeah," she said. "I can understand that."

We sat there for a second. I was trying to think of something to say when Andrea added, "You're still going to come to the meets, right?"

"I don't know," I said, trying to laugh. "What would be the point?" I gestured to my leg. "I wouldn't even be a very good cheerleader for you guys."

"Well, I think you should come," Andrea said seriously. "You're one of the biggest leaders we have on the team. All of the underclassmen look up to you and like you. That's why they voted you team captain and not me. You're really good at encouraging them. You're a better leader than I am."

"Thanks," I said, and I meant it. Andrea doesn't say things she doesn't mean, so it felt really good to hear her say that about me.

"At least think about coming," she said. "It would be really weird if you weren't there at the meets. Plus, you could still keep an eye on the competition for next season." And with that classic Andrea logic, she excused herself to leave, saying she was going snowboarding.

"Hold on a second," I said. I asked my mom to bring me Dave's hat from the day before, which was in a pile with all the other stuff we'd brought home from the hospital.

"Here," I said mischievously, handing the hat to Andrea. "Dave might need this snowboarding today, so could you give it to him?"

"Sure," she said. The look on her face was priceless. I could tell she wondered how I knew, but she decided not to say anything.

I laughed a little to myself. Even though I was sort of bitter about love in general, this Andrea and Dave thing could be fun to watch.

It wasn't too much later that the doorbell rang again. This time it was Ethan.

The good feeling I had from Andrea's visit vanished pretty quickly during Ethan's. It started out okay. He came in with some flowers wrapped in tissue paper. They were pink tulips, my favorite. My mom excused herself and went into the kitchen to find a vase for them.

"I feel so bad about what happened," Ethan said when we were alone. He looked like he didn't know what to do with himself. I would have liked a hug, or something, but he sat down on the chair nearest me instead. "Are you all right?"

It was a dumb, generic question, one that anyone could have asked, and still it managed to bring me close to tears. "Yeah," I said. "I'm fine." I didn't trust myself to say more.

"Your mom said you've had a lot of visitors," he said. "I hope it's okay that I came."

"Of course it is," I said. "We're *friends,* aren't we?" I wasn't acting like myself, or maybe I was. Maybe the real me was grumpy and prickly after all.

"Yeah, we are," he said. The gentleness in his tone made me feel great and terrible at the same time. I didn't know what to do with him. He looked like he wanted to say something else, but at the moment I didn't want to hear it. He was going to go off to the Valentine's Day dance with a really cool girl. I was going to stay home with my broken leg. Even though only half of that was his fault, I was still really hurt and angry.

"Well, you'd better go get ready for the dance," I said.

Ethan looked surprised, and then he looked hurt too. It didn't feel as good as I expected. In fact, it felt terrible, but I still didn't stop him. To my astonishment, he bent and gave me a quick hug. He was at the door before he turned back and said, "I still care about you a *lot,* Mikey."

I wanted to call after him and tell him I was sorry. But I didn't. I sat there feeling all kinds of bad and even more kinds of sad.

What with all my visitors, especially the last one, I was feeling drained. My dad carried me upstairs to my room and ordered me to take a nap. I tried, but my mind wouldn't let me, even though my body was exhausted. I wished there was a switch that I could use to shut it off. I came down from my bedroom even more worn out than before.

My parents suggested calling Julie to cancel, but I didn't. I really wanted to see Julie and talk to her. She has this peaceful, calming aspect about her. I don't know what it is. It's not just that she's a quiet person, it's something more than that.

When she arrived, Julie took one look at me and smiled sympathetically. "Maybe you should call it a night," she said. "You look a little worn out."

"That's what I've been telling her!" my dad interjected, poking his head in the doorway. "Honey, you really should take it easy."

"I will," I said. "I won't stay up too late. But if I go to bed now, I won't be able to sleep. I might as well do something fun instead of lying there being mad."

My dad left the room to make me a dinner tray. I felt bad about all the extra waiting on me my parents were doing, but it was kind of nice. They'd even farmed my brothers out to their friends' houses for the afternoon. The quiet had been nice, though I knew they were about to descend upon us again at any moment.

"So what do you think all the people who are going to the dance are doing right now?" I asked Julie. "They're probably starting to get ready." I imagined what it would be like at the dance as the couples, all dressed up, started walking through the door and out onto the dance floor. The music, the dim light, the smell of dozens of different colognes and perfumes and peppermint gum . . . it would all smell and feel like possibility. I felt extra sorry for myself at that moment.

"I wonder what Ethan and Elizabeth are going to do on their date. Do you think he likes her? I still can't believe he's taking her instead of me. It's so awful. And you'll never believe what he said to me today. He said that he still likes me. I just can't figure him out. We weren't being exclusive; we weren't doing bad stuff. I mean, we've kissed, but that's all right, isn't it? Why did he feel like he had to break up with me? Sometimes I'm so mad at him I almost hate him for being so confusing."

Julie paused for a second or two before she spoke. What she said was not what I had expected to hear. "Mikey, you're going to have to let go of all of this. He *is* being really confusing, but that's because he's really confused. He doesn't want to get too serious because he doesn't want to get hurt, so he's going to the extreme of not dating you at all. There's probably a lot going on with him right now with his dad moving back to town and stuff. But you can't control any of those things. You're just going to have to let it go for now and try to be his friend. What's so bad about that? You two have been friends before."

I couldn't believe it. What kind of a response was that? From a best friend no less? "It's bad because—" I couldn't think of why it was bad for a moment, and then I started to cry. "It's bad because it hurts so much. It's too hard."

Julie put her arm around me. "Mikey, do you remember what you told me when I said that there was no way I could be forgiven for what I'd done and for all the hate I had for my brothers? When I said that there's no way I could get rid of all the pain? I know that it isn't the same thing, but don't you think that Jesus understands you, like you said He understands me, even though it's different? Won't

Heavenly Father still help you because you're hurting? Couldn't you ask Him to help you?" She spoke hesitantly at first, and then with more and more assurance. "I'm sure you could. Look at everything that's happened to you in the past few weeks. First Ethan, now your leg. I'm sure Heavenly Father wants to help you through this. I'm sure you could ask Him for help."

Was *I* sure that I could? Was the answer to the void I was feeling really that simple? All these months I'd been telling Julie all about the gospel and about Jesus and our Father in Heaven. I'd been bringing her to activities and Church and meeting with her and the missionaries. Was I the world's biggest hypocrite?

I believed everything I told Julie, I really did. But why hadn't I thought to give it a try in my own life? Julie had had to tell me. Who really had a better understanding of the Savior's love, Julie or me? Member or non-member? Was my testimony so fragile that a couple of tough events could snap it the way the impact of my foot against asphalt had snapped my leg?

Part of me didn't want to pray about something so dumb. I resisted it. It was just a high school relationship and a broken leg, after all, and there were plenty of things going on in other places that were more serious, even though my heart was dark and my leg was aching.

Julie frowned thoughtfully. "Doesn't Heavenly Father already know that you are hurting? You just have to ask Him for help. And then you can show Him that you appreciate His help by helping other people. Like you've helped me."

I stared at her. Then I started laughing. "Julie," I said, "I don't think I've helped you to find out anything. I think you've known it all along."

Julie smiled at me. "We've both known it all along, somewhere in our hearts. But that's what friends do, right? We help each other remember." She took something out from under the pile of movies she'd brought. "Do you want to practice 'Come Thou Fount of Every Blessing'?" she asked, handing me the sheet music. "It always makes me feel better to sing this song. I can't wait to sing it in church, which is really weird. Usually I'm too scared to look forward to things like that."

I nodded. "I might cry through the whole thing, though," I warned her. "I mean, really cry. You'll just have to keep singing."

She looked back at me. "It won't be anything I haven't done before," she said seriously. "The crying, I mean."

So we sang, and then we watched silly movies all night. After Julie left, I prayed for help. I didn't pray that Ethan and I would start dating again, even though I thought about praying for that. I didn't pray for my leg to be miraculously healed so I could have the track season of my life, even though I thought about praying for that too. Instead, I prayed that I would be able to trust in the Lord to help me through the month of February and on into the spring.

That was all.

That was a lot.

FEBRUARY AND MARCH

Ethan Beckett

My dad had moved back. I still can't believe it.

Not moved back into our house—now that would be wild. He moved back to Seattle, to Bellevue to be exact, to an apartment and to his old job, at the end of January. He'd been talking about moving for a while, not that Portland was so far away he didn't get to see us often, but because he said he missed the day-to-day stuff, like coming to every race instead of just the big ones. Stuff like that. Even my mom seemed to think it was a good idea. They don't fight anymore, but I didn't think she'd be thrilled about him moving back to town. She was glad he'd be around for us kids more. And Grandma—well, she was over the moon. That's to be expected, though, I guess. He's her only kid, after all.

He expected us all to be excited.

Dad and I haven't had any serious trouble, not like he and Andrea have had. When he took the job in Portland right after the divorce, Andrea felt betrayed, but I honestly felt relieved. It made things so much easier. We saw him for longer chunks of time, and we didn't always have to be running to his house for the weekends and then back to Mom's during the week. I hated waking up and wondering where I was. Chloe was too little then to stay away from home overnight so she doesn't remember any of it. She's still too young to understand what the move means now.

And things are different now.

I really wasn't that thrilled when I heard the news. I couldn't tell why. Like I said, Dad and I haven't had any big fights or anything. I guess that it seems more complicated all of a sudden. Now he'll be at every race, not just the big ones. Now I'll run into him at Grandma's all the time. Now I'll have to stay at his apartment every other weekend (the custody has changed a little since we're older).

It had been kind of nice to have two different worlds all sectioned off into their separate compartments: the Portland world and the Seattle world; the vacation world and the real world. According to Dad that was exactly the problem. He felt like he was a vacation dad. "You have to give him credit for that," said my mom. I didn't feel like we had to give him credit for anything. You have to understand—I don't hate my dad. All I wanted to do was keep things uncomplicated and predictable.

The first weekend in February was the first one we were supposed to spend with him after his move back. Andrea was predictable and said that she didn't want to spend the weekend, but she was unpredictable when she actually agreed to at least have dinner that night at his place. That was a big step. I thought Grandma might have something to do with it, but I wasn't going to ask. I wanted Andrea there, even though it might mean a fight, because I didn't want to be one-on-one with Dad. Chloe was going to be there for her first weekend away and she was excited, but she's five. You can't exactly count on her for scintillating or even relevant conversation half the time.

"How are you going to get home after dinner?" I asked Andrea as we drove to Dad's. "I'll need the car until we come back Sunday morning."

"It's been arranged," she said snottily, then softened just a little. "Dave's coming to get me. We're going to the ballet." She gave me a look that dared me to say anything about either Dave or the ballet, and then turned to look out the window. I fought back a grin as I focused on the road ahead, not wanting to miss the exit. *Good for you, Dave,* I thought.

Dad's apartment was in one of the quiet areas of Bellevue. We rode the elevator up to the third floor, and of course Chloe wanted to push the button. Dad's apartment was down the hall, and Chloe begged to be able to ring the doorbell, but it wasn't necessary. Dad was waiting for us.

"Hey, you guys!" he said, guiding us into the kitchen. Chloe sprang at him like a small, pajama-wearing puppy. He picked her up and grinned. "Come on in. I just finished getting dinner ready."

My dad was a pretty decent cook before the divorce and living on his own has made him even better. Plus he likes to grill things and eat guy food. Sure enough, there were some ribs on the barbecue that smelled amazing and a potato salad I could tell he made himself. There was also a basket of some exotic fruits—papayas mostly. My dad served his mission in Brazil and has never quite gotten over it. It smelled like a picnic.

"Andrea, you're not a vegetarian, are you?" he said, looking panicked as he handed her a plateful of ribs.

She actually smiled at him and shook her head. "Nope," she said. I guess I hadn't realized how little they'd interacted since he'd moved if he didn't even know what she ate, but to be fair, it was mostly Andrea who had kept him at a distance. Still, dinner seemed to be going pretty well.

"Mom told you I was just staying for dinner tonight, right?" Andrea said, helping herself to the fruit.

Dad looked nervous. "Yeah, she did. I'm glad you could make it for dinner, though."

Andrea smiled. "I have a date tonight that I don't want to miss," she said, offering him more personal information in that one sentence than she had in three years.

His eyes widened in surprise at how open she was being. I could see him physically restraining himself from asking more. Meanwhile, I was still in complete shock over finding out that David Sherman was a date that Andrea didn't want to miss.

I could practically see the questions running through Dad's mind: Do I know him? Is he Mormon? Is he a nice guy? Where are you going? What are you doing? What time will you be home? But he's smart. He knew that asking for more information could be fatal. I saw Andrea visibly relax when all he said was, "That's great," and smiled at her.

Chloe, meanwhile, had dressed herself in barbecue sauce. My dad looked over at her and shook his head. "I hope your mom packed extra pajamas," he said, laughing.

"Me too, 'cause I still wet the bed," Chloe said matter-of-factly and then beamed at him when he laughed. I never know whether to be sad or happy for Chloe: sad that she never really knew what it was like for our parents to be together, or happy for her because she seems content with her life the way it is, not knowing what she's missed.

"So," I said, "how's the job? Same as you remembered?"

"Pretty close," he said. "It's the same job working in Portland or working here. I guess that's the benefit of staying with the same company. It sure is great to be back, though. I can't wait to see you guys run during the track season more often, go to more of Chloe's school stuff, you know. And it'll be good to see your grandma more too."

"Did you know Grandma sold her car?" Andrea asked.

"What?" Dad exclaimed. "She didn't tell me!"

"She did it yesterday. I guess she almost had an accident driving to the temple and she drove right over to our house and marched in the door and threw her keys on the table and said she was never driving again because she was too dangerous and it was too scary. I didn't think she was serious, but it looks like she was."

Dad shook his head. "That's just like her. Once she decides to do something, there's no holding her back. That's why your mother and I always thought it was a good thing that we'd named you after her because you're so much alike."

"I'm named after Grandma?" Andrea asked. "But our names are different."

"Well, they're not the same name, but they are similar and that's part of the reason we chose your name—to honor her. And you shared a lot of personality traits, right from the beginning." He laughed. "You're both a little stubborn. I remember trying to convince you that cowboy boots and a princess dress weren't the right thing to wear on your first day of school, but there was no arguing with you, and you ended up being fine. All the other kids thought it was great. And your grandma—when she decided she was going to leave her home and move out here to be with us, that was the end of it. You are two stubborn ladies."

Andrea looked at him with a raised eyebrow. "I guess I should take that as a compliment."

"You certainly should," Dad said. "Sometimes I wish I were more like her."

We cleared up dinner and had dessert, which was a birthday cake complete with candles. "Whose birthday is it?" I asked Dad in the kitchen.

"Nobody's," he said. "But your mom said that Chloe's really into birthday cakes and pretending there's a birthday, so I thought it would be fun to have a cake. Plus, we can practice for your birthday coming up."

Chloe loved it and decided that we should sing "Happy Birthday" to the cake itself instead of to me, so we did.

"Do you want to take a piece home to your mom? Or to Grandma?" Dad asked.

"Sure," I said. He set some aside in a plastic container.

"So, Dad," said Andrea, licking the frosting off her fork, "are you dating anyone these days?"

Dad looked surprised. "No . . ."

"I was just wondering, since I know you were dating in Portland."

"I only got here a couple of weeks ago. I haven't had time to meet anyone yet. I kind of hope I do, though. It would be nice to go out sometime."

I thought that sounded kind of dorky and ridiculous for a grown man to say, but Andrea didn't make any of the smart comments I thought she would. All she said was, "This cake is *really* good," and helped herself to another piece.

"It's awesome, Dad," I added, and had a third slice. Maybe I could gorge myself on cake for the entire weekend.

The doorbell rang and everyone looked startled. "That must be David," Andrea said, as Dad went to answer it. She stood up and smoothed back the one piece of hair that always escaped from her ponytail. She didn't look nervous, but I noticed she was wearing dressy black pants and a red silk shirt with the fancy red earrings Grandma had given her. I couldn't tell if she had dressed up for the ballet or for David.

"David!" Dad said. "How are you?" I could tell he was surprised. He had known Dave since he had been a crazy Cub Scout, a terror of a deacon. I'm sure Dad's seen him since then, though, at the meets or something, so he had to know Dave had grown up.

"Great," Dave said, shaking hands with Dad. "How's it going, Brother Beckett?"

Andrea went into the foyer and she and Dave said good-bye. I could tell Dave was nervous. He'd better be. The ballet and Andrea in one evening would be enough to make any guy on edge. What was he trying to do to himself?

Dad came back into the kitchen and sat down. "Andrea's going on a date with David Sherman? That kid is a total goofball. He's not a bad kid, though . . . his family is great. He's still active, isn't he?"

"Yeah," I said. "I think he knows what he's getting into with Andrea, as much as anyone can. He's on the team, you know, and he's in our ward so he knows how she is and that she hasn't been to church in a few years."

"Well, I hope they have a good time." I could tell Dad was relieved that the date Andrea had been looking forward to was with a member of the Church. Andrea hasn't dated members in a while. I don't think either Mom or Dad liked Connor much, even though he wasn't a terrible guy, but I think they figured the odds of a non-member reactivating Andrea were pretty slim.

Chloe decided that it was time to play a game. Specifically, it was time to play "Hungry Hungry Hippos," which she had packed in her overnight bag, and so we humored her. After a few rounds of chomping hippos, and a bunch of stories from my dad, it was time for Chloe to go to bed. We tucked her in her purple sleeping bag on top of the covers (she always sleeps like that) and then it was one-on-one time with me and Dad.

Dad suggested watching a movie or some basketball. I chose basketball. The Sonics were playing the Spurs and it was a decent game. "We'll have to get tickets sometime," he said partway through the game. "It's been a long time since I've been to a Sonics game. Since before Gary Payton left, in fact."

"Yeah, that would be awesome," I said. Inside, I was wondering how long this weekend would last. Playing with Chloe, making small talk, all the while wondering what was going on back in my real world. The guys were going to run a twelve-mile loop around the lake tomorrow and I wasn't going to be there. I wouldn't get to hang out with Mikey and the rest of the group on Saturday night. My dad moving back to town might be great for him, but some of us were just getting used to things the way they were.

"Daddy? Ethan?" said a small and teary voice. Chloe. "I want to go home."

"Oh, Chloe, are you sure?" my dad said, jumping up to hold her. "I can come in and read you some more stories, or sing you a few songs."

"No," she wailed. "I want to go home. I want to see Mommy."

"I'll take her," I said quickly. "Mom thought this might happen, just because she's so young and she hasn't tried it before."

"I can drive her, Eth," said my dad. "Then we can catch the end of the game or do something else."

"That's all right," I said, not looking at him and putting on my sneakers. "I've got kind of a lot to do at home anyway. We can all try again next time—in a couple of weeks or something."

He started to say something, but then accepted defeat. "Okay, if that's what you want. I'd love to have you stay, though." Chloe's crying was getting louder, so he helped me get her things together and gave us both hugs at the door. I kept moving fast, not wanting to look into his face, not wanting him to try to convince us to stay again. It's a good thing he isn't as stubborn as Grandma and Andrea. I was pretty worried that he'd put up more of a fight, but he seemed too quiet or resigned or something for that.

I looked back to say one last "See you later" after we'd gone out the door, but when I saw him with his head leaned back against the couch and his eyes closed, I didn't. I closed the door quietly and followed Chloe down the hall as she dragged her purple sleeping bag and hurried to push the elevator button. I drove her home through the night and she was asleep before we even got there. Mom came to greet us. "Oh, I thought this might happen," she said, lifting Chloe out of the car. "Was she okay for most of the time?"

"Yeah," I said. "She had a great time. She just couldn't sleep there."

"Thanks for bringing her home," Mom said. "You'd better head back before it's too late."

"I'm staying too." I said. She looked back at me, surprised. "Some of the guys are going on a long run, anyway, and I've got a lot of homework. It's just not a great weekend."

"Ethan," she said, "is your dad okay with that?"

"Yeah," I said, trying to shut out the picture of him sitting there alone on the couch with all the dinner leftovers in the fridge, waiting hopefully for us to eat them. I reached in the back of the car for my bag and followed my mom and Chloe into the house. The smell of rain was thick in the air and I felt melancholy. Even thinking about seeing Mikey tomorrow didn't cheer me up. I couldn't get that picture of my dad out of my head.

What is the point, I wondered, *if this is what love can do to you?* My dad was alone in an apartment that night, with no wife and no kids there. I don't know exactly what went wrong with my parents. I know that they fought and couldn't seem to fix it and weren't in love anymore. Neither of them were terrible people or had committed huge sins. I know half the marriages in the U.S. end in divorce and I know that the marriages in the Church aren't immune either, by any means.

So why get married, or put yourself on the line at all? In fact, why date at all if the potential for disaster is so huge? Mikey and I had gone out on our own, sure, but we'd also done a pretty good job of going out in groups and not being exclusive, having fun and being close friends as well as dating, but even so, maybe that was too much. The way I saw it, either we'd quit dating and that would hurt a little, or we'd date forever and get married (a long shot, I know) and then we'd end up like my parents. And that would hurt a lot.

I decided it would be better to make a preemptive strike and not date Mikey at all and save us both some pain later. I'd just keep it casual and go out with lots of different girls instead of going out with Mikey a lot and other girls some of the time. Even though the thought made me feel bad, it still was better than waiting around to get hurt.

Still, the breakup didn't go so well. She took it really personally. I think she felt like the morality of our relationship was being called into question or something. I tried to reassure her that things were okay because we'd gone out in groups a lot and we'd been careful about being alone in compromising situations, all of that. We had a good time together and a lot of that was because we both knew that we weren't doing anything wrong—just enjoying the chemistry and attraction that was there, which made dating her so much fun.

I think it really hurt Mikey and I couldn't seem to explain to her that it was more about me than about her. She went into her house mad that night and I couldn't seem to fix it.

Even when she broke her leg and I went to visit, I couldn't say the right thing. She looked really miserable and I knew that I was part of it. It made me feel awful. Even when I gave her a hug, that wasn't the right thing to do either. And going out with Elizabeth was strange too. She was great and we had a good time, but I thought about Mikey a lot and I think Elizabeth noticed. Somehow, in my effort to keep from getting hurt, I was managing to hurt a lot of other people. I wasn't getting off scot-free either. How had this all turned out so wrong? I watched Mikey hobbling down the hall on her crutches, and even though I'd had nothing to do with her broken leg, I still felt like we'd both been crippled somehow by the way I'd mismanaged things.

Then, she started to do better and to smile more and laugh at things again, and I couldn't figure out why I wasn't feeling the same way. I was almost mad at her for doing so well even though I was the one who'd wanted this.

My birthday was a month or so after the breakup and I really wasn't looking forward to it. Mom had invited Dad and Grandma over for cake and presents that night. I think she did it to be nice, so I wouldn't feel like I had to split up my birthday or something, but it didn't really change anything or make me more excited.

Turning seventeen isn't a big deal, at least not after sixteen.

Sixteen meant driving and dating, although I was now convinced that both were overrated. Dating was full of potential pain and driving meant being a glorified chauffeur for Chloe and practically engaging in mortal combat with Andrea every time I wanted to use the car. Seventeen didn't mean as much as far as I was concerned, and having a family party of any kind with all that fuss only made it stand out even more how useless it all was.

I got home from school early because there was a meet the next day and we didn't have a workout practice for track. Andrea dropped me off and then went back to school. She was staying late to tutor a freshman in chemistry, something she's been doing after workout a few nights a week. I learned not to ask her too much about that— Andrea's still a little prickly, even when she's doing something nice. *Especially* when she's doing something nice.

My mom's car was in the driveway, which was a surprise. She works at the school district office and usually doesn't get home until a little after three-thirty, which is when Chloe's kindergarten gets out and she picks her up.

"Hey," I said. "You're home early. Where's Chloe?"

"She's going to a friend's to play after school. It works out well because we're eating at five, and I still have to get things made." She hadn't started yet, but her apron was on and the cookbook was out. "There's a lot to do. I'm a little nervous about having everyone over here, but it made too much sense not to do it."

I thought of it all—Grandma fluttery and excited; Dad and Mom on their best behavior; Andrea being unexpectedly kind or abrupt; Chloe with her never-ending enthusiasm and energy wanting to sing "Happy Birthday" five hundred times; me having to express gratitude for every gift . . .

I plopped down in a chair. "Oh, Mom," I sighed. "What's the point?"

She turned and looked at me, stunned. "You don't want a birthday dinner?"

"It's not so much that as it is everything. What's the use of birthdays, or of getting up in the morning, or of any of that stuff?"

"What's getting you down?" she asked, trying to make a joke out of it. "Are you feeling like an old man now that you're seventeen?" Then she could see that I was serious. "Wait here a minute, Eth," she said and hurried out of the room.

When she came back, she was carrying her scriptures. I groaned, exactly as Andrea would have if she'd been there.

"Ethan, I know you don't want a lecture on your birthday, but I understand how you feel." She was serious with a "This-is-one-of-those-important-talks" tone to her voice.

"When your dad and I got divorced and Andrea stopped coming to church, I really felt down about things. I felt like a big failure since the two most important things in my life—my children and my family—weren't okay. Your dad had his share of blame for the divorce too, and I knew that, but it was really hard for me to feel so badly about myself and about the way things were going. I felt pretty hopeless sometimes. I didn't think I'd ever want to date again, or—"

"Let's not talk about your dating life," I said. She's been out on a date once or twice with guys in our stake and it's just too weird for words.

"Fair enough," she said. "I won't talk about my dating life, and I also won't mention that I know there's something going on with you and Michaela and that that's part of this."

I opened my mouth to speak but then closed it. Parents. Every once in a while they zero in on something that you'd rather they didn't.

"Anyway," she continued, "I decided to try to find some places in the scriptures where there were people who'd been through similar things and came out of it all okay. I had just been called to teach early-morning seminary and I felt completely inadequate. I knew that I needed to really search the scriptures and find some answers so that I could teach the students with confidence and not let my personal struggles keep me from doing the things I needed to do in my calling and in my family. So I started in First Nephi when Lehi is having a lot of trouble with his family and even begins to doubt the revelations he's received. I could really relate to that."

I laughed a little in spite of myself. "Andrea does make a pretty good Laman or Lemuel."

My mom glared at me. "Ethan," she warned.

"Sorry," I said, and I was. I didn't want her to think that I thought she was a failure as a mom or that Andrea was going to end up like those guys. I didn't think that at all. Andrea is surprising us all these days, in fact, so who knew what would happen with her.

"Anyway," Mom said, riffling through the pages of her scriptures, "the story about Lehi did bring me a lot of comfort and I kept reading. I read the part in Mosiah about the wicked sons of Mosiah and Alma and that made me feel better too. Not that I think you or Andrea or your dad are wicked or anything. Mainly, as mean as this might sound, it was good to see that people who were trying hard, like Mosiah and Alma the Elder, had trouble and trials too."

"That makes sense," I admitted grumpily. "It's always good to know you're not alone in your misery."

"More than that," Mom said, finally finding what she was looking for. "Listen to this scripture: Mosiah 27:29. It's Alma the Younger after he's had a change of heart and what he has to say is beautiful: 'My soul hath been redeemed from the gall of bitterness and bonds of iniquity. I was in the darkest abyss; but now I behold the marvelous light of God. My soul was racked with eternal torment; but I am snatched, and my soul is pained no more.'"

I shrugged. It was fine, but I wasn't sure what it had to do with me. My mom smiled at me with tears in her eyes. "I loved this because it made me feel so good to read it. I was in bitterness and despair and I knew I needed to open myself to the Spirit again. I really liked the image of myself, stuck in a big, deep, dark pit, being 'snatched' out by our Heavenly Father. I imagined a big hand reaching down and lifting me out by the collar and putting me back outside of the pit, out where I could walk around and be free and happy again. I just want you to know, honey, that there are hard days but there are great ones too. You'll make it through those tough times if you hang onto what's really important. And Ethan, one more thing." She looked right into my eyes. "Loving and caring about people, romantically or not, puts your emotions on the line and sometimes that will hurt. But it is worth the price. No one knows that more than the Savior, who loved and cared about us all and suffered because of it."

She handed her copy of the scriptures to me. "I know you probably didn't want a lecture on your birthday, honey, so maybe I should give you your present a little early to make up for it." Her eyes sparkled. "Come in here," she said, leading the way into the living room.

There was a huge, flat package on the top of the piano; that's where we usually put all of the gifts before we open them after dinner. "It's not car keys," I said, pretending to be disappointed, and she smiled. She knew that Andrea and I battled like crazy over the ancient beast of a Ford Taurus that we shared. I slid the wrapping off and found a painting of myself, running. It looked exactly the way running felt. And I looked triumphant, different than I pictured myself. It was definitely me, though. It was pretty great.

"Where did you get this?" I asked, surprised.

"I painted it," she said, a little shyly. "You know that class I've been taking on Tuesday nights?"

"Yeah," I said, "but I assumed that was another class toward your master's degree. I didn't know it was painting."

"I decided to do something that I'd always wanted to do. You and Andrea, and Chloe too, have so many talents. I thought maybe I should see if I had any, and I'd always loved art in school. I know it's not wonderful, but I've been working on it and having a lot of fun doing it."

"It's really great, Mom," I said. "How long did it take you to do?"

She laughed. "A really long time. Much longer than it took you to run that race. I'm happy that you like it. It's a little scary to show your work to someone. I'm kind of glad you're not opening it in front of everyone. But mostly, I'm just pleased that you like it."

"I really do," I said. "But I'm showing it to everyone tonight, so you're not getting out of it." I set it down carefully and studied it for a minute. "Do I really look like that when I'm running?"

She knew what I was asking. "Yes, you do. And I know you're going to triumph, Eth."

She gave me a hug. "Would you rather go to the pier for seafood tonight?" she asked. "I could call Dad and Grandma and tell them to meet us there and we could come back here for cake and gifts after. Seventeen deserves a celebration with lobster. We should splurge."

"Let's do it," I agreed. I took the painting and the scriptures up to my room for safekeeping. I laid down on the bed and put my hands behind my head, looking up at the glow-in-the-dark stars I'd put up years ago. I'd tried to scrape them off since, but it looked like they were going to outlast me. It was too light for them to really work, but I could still see their outlines on the ceiling and knew that they were there.

It was like Mikey these days. We pretended to be really casual when we saw each other, but I always knew exactly where she was on the bus on track trips and in the hallways. My plan wasn't working out after all. I was still hurting in spite of everything I'd done to protect myself. I reread the scripture Mom had given me and tried to hold on to that good feeling as my mind went over and over things—Mikey, my parents, the church, everything.

I must have fallen asleep because I jumped awake when my door flew open and the light flipped on. There was Andrea in the doorway. It had gotten darker. Groggy, I sat up. "Why didn't you knock?" I grumbled, reaching for my sneakers. "Is it time to go to dinner?"

Andrea nodded. "Almost. Mom's getting Chloe ready. It could be a while because Chloe can't find the birthday hats she picked out for all of us to wear. I hope she finds them because I think a Disney Princess birthday hat would really set off your eyes."

I laughed grumpily in spite of myself. I shoved my shoes on without bothering to tie them and stood up, but Andrea was blocking my way, holding out a present. "I wanted you to open this before we met up with everyone else. In case you thought it was dumb." She pushed it into my hands and folded her arms, watching me closely.

It had been a few years since Andrea had given me a birthday gift. Usually she stuck ten dollars in an envelope and wrote my name on it. This was an actual gift, wrapped in actual paper and wearing an actual bow. I tore it open curiously.

It was a scrapbook. I think that's what they call it, when there's lots of pictures and writing and cute paper and stuff. That might be a misnomer though, because this wasn't cute at all. It was every article from the school paper and from the local paper that mentioned my name. There were also several photos of me running. It was all done very professionally in black and white with crisp edges and clear headings. I turned the pages and went through every meet, remembering. Most of the pictures were ones I'd seen before, ones that Mom or Dad had taken.

Then, on the last page, there was a heading in Andrea's bold and perfect writing. "State Meet," it read and there was a full-color picture of me running, the same one Mom must have used as the basis for her picture. I hadn't thought about where Mom would have gotten the pose and the setting for the painting. I guess Andrea must have taken the photo, which was kind of a shock. I didn't even know she owned a camera.

The picture was of me in a kind of a hard place on the course, a spot in the trees on a hill that only someone else who'd run the course would really know about, a spot where the crowds are a lot more sparse than on the rest of the course. There wasn't anything else on the page, just the picture and the lettering.

It was weird, and cool, to see two different people's interpretations of the same person, the same picture. I sat there looking at the two things, the picture and the painting, for a minute.

"You took this?" I asked Andrea.

"Yeah," she said. "I was going to take a picture of that spot on the course because I felt like it was the hardest part and the part where I won the race. It's where I really started to build a lead. I wanted to remember that. And then I saw the guys coming, and there you were, so I took the picture with you in it."

I looked closer. "Maybe that's where I lost the race," I said, joking. "I didn't end up first like you. Are you trying to tell me I should work on that for next year?"

Andrea was impatient with me, but it wasn't the impatience-with-an-edge that it usually is when she is explaining something she feels is obvious. Maybe peer tutoring has taught her that it isn't particularly effective to be ticked off when you're explaining something.

"No, no, no," she said. "That's not the point of it at all. The point is your face and how alive it looks. This is the hardest part of the course. I think it's the part of the course that hurts the worst. I always gut it out and hate every minute of it and think about beating everyone else. You're not doing that. You're just running and enjoying it, even though you're working hard." She stopped. "It's corny, but you're enjoying the race, even though you don't know exactly what the results will be yet."

"Thanks," I said to her, wishing I could think of something better to say.

"No problem," she said. At the door, she paused. "Not to get too deep with you or anything, but don't try to control everything. I've made that mistake too often. It doesn't keep you from getting hurt."

I was in a little bit of shock after she left, both from the gift and from Andrea getting all philosophical and insightful with me. My mom called up the stairs for me to come out to the car. Andrea was already sitting in the back with Chloe, so I climbed in the front. I didn't have a chance to say anything more to Andrea because Chloe was in the car and she had plans, big plans, for the celebration that she *had* to tell me about. Then, when she was done, Mom started wondering aloud if the restaurant would mind that we were bringing our own cake and if they would light the candles for us there.

It wasn't until later, when the birthday cake was on its way out from the restaurant kitchen, that I could say something to Andrea. Everyone else was looking at the cake and so I leaned over and said, "That present was awesome." It still wasn't what I really wanted to say, but it was better. She smiled a real smile and then started singing "Happy Birthday" along with the waiters and my family.

My family. There they sat, in front of everyone else in the seafood place, a group of people wearing pastel Princess paper cones on their heads, singing vigorously as the elastic sawed into their chins. Grandma's hat was a little askew, giving her kind of a tipsy look, and Dad's was on too far forward.

"He's a unicorn," said Andrea, leaning over to help me blow out the candles, and Chloe, who was doing the same, asked excitedly, "A unicorn? Where?"

My laughter blew out the last candle.

MARCH

Owen Thomas

I posted the results of the auditions for next year's choirs on the door. Done. Let the complaining begin. One of the students who had made Chorale, the elite choir that we use in competition, stayed after class for a minute to talk to me. I was surprised because she's a shy kid. She doesn't really make a lot of eye contact with me and she's very quiet in class. Even then, standing in front of me, she seemed very nervous.

"I wanted to tell you, Mr. Thomas, that I really appreciate your not holding everything against me."

"What do you mean, Julie?" I asked. I smiled at her as encouragingly as I could, because I could tell this was hard for her for some reason. Meanwhile, I frantically replayed the year in my mind, trying to remember her possible offense. Nothing came to mind.

"You've still treated me fairly and been really nice to me, and I really appreciate it, especially because of my brother," she said. Her eyes were teary. "It's made a big difference to me and I wanted to tell you that."

I couldn't figure what on earth she was talking about. Who was her brother? Was he an especially good singer? "It's no problem," I said, trying to put her at her ease. "I'm excited to have you in Chorale next year. You're one of our best singers." She smiled at me with something extra in the smile—could it be relief?—and left the room.

I mentioned it to my dad in passing that night, as we sat around the dinner table. I had thought it might be a difficult situation to teach at the same school as my father, but our departments are separate enough that it has worked out well. Plus I was the only candidate who applied for the job when Mrs. Durham retired last August, so no one could accuse the hiring committee of playing favorites. They had to take their only option. Dad and I joke about how I'm carrying on the proud tradition, but I think we both do feel a lot of pride behind all the teasing.

"Who is Julie Reid's brother?" I asked my dad.

He was very still. "What brought that up?" he asked.

"Today she thanked me for being so nice to her in spite of her brother. She thanked me for not holding anything against her. I didn't know what on earth she was talking about, so I just said it was no problem."

"Owen," my dad said quietly. "Julie Reid is Kevin Cox's sister."

Kevin Cox.

"*What?*" I breathed. "You can't be serious."

"It's a blended family and Julie agreed to be adopted by her stepfather and take his last name. Kevin, who is a lot older, didn't feel the same way, so he kept his name. I didn't realize that his younger sister would be old enough by now to be in high school. I never actually taught Kevin but I've heard other teachers talk about the family in the teachers' lounge. He had another brother who was a lot like him."

"I put her in Chorale, Dad," I said. "I had no idea she was related to him."

"Is she a good enough singer to be in there?"

"She's a beautiful singer. But I can't have her in there now. I can't teach looking at her every day, knowing that . . ."

"Knowing what?" my father asked.

"Knowing that her brother killed Mom," I said angrily. If he needed it spelled out, so be it.

He flinched a little at the use of the word "killed," but he is familiar enough with my anger and with his own sorrow to recover quickly. He lives with both every day. "Owen, Julie didn't have anything to do with that."

"I don't think that matters," I snapped. "Should I have to look at her every day and think about what happened over and over again?"

"She already thinks you've forgiven her. She thinks you've been able to look past that and see what *she* is, not what her brother is. She has probably been saddled with his reputation all her life and then to have a fresh chance from you of all people—can you imagine how that must feel to her? It's no wonder she stayed after today to thank you even though it must have been hard for her."

"I can't keep her in Chorale next year. It's going to be hard enough to get through the rest of this one, now that I know. I've got to find some way to fix this." My voice was louder than I'd anticipated. "I can't believe that I didn't know."

"I shouldn't have told you. I thought you were enough of a man to forgive someone for a crime they didn't commit."

And with that Parthian shot, he left me alone at the table.

I only saw Kevin Cox once. The case was so obvious, with so many witnesses, that our family hadn't needed to testify. The prosecutor asked us once if we would; it would gain a lot of sympathy, he said. My father silenced him with a look.

On the day of the sentencing, though, I did go to court. I was the only member of my family who went. Evan wanted to go, but my dad talked him out of it, telling him that it was not going to bring the kind of closure Evan was looking for. Ryan didn't want to go at all and, of course, neither did my father.

But I was feeling angry and vengeful, and I wanted to see that Kevin Cox paid the maximum price for what he did, even though any price paid could not possibly be enough. Even though my father didn't agree with my going, he didn't try to prevent me.

Kevin Cox slouched in his chair. He didn't look as villainous as I had expected, especially from his mug shot, but he also didn't look like a saint. Looking back, I can see a slight resemblance to Julie, but none so obvious that I would notice it based on appearance alone. Kevin didn't seem to see me at all. I was just a few years older than he was; our paths had probably crossed in the grocery store or when we were in high school.

When the sentence was given, his face showed a twinge of some emotion—I'm not exactly sure what. He turned to his lawyer, who whispered something to him. I didn't wait to see him led out. I had put a face to my mother's death and it was one I could safely hate. He hadn't cried, he hadn't offered a heartfelt apology for what he'd done. He had made it easy for me to keep on hating him. I had made it easy for myself.

The day after Julie's revelation, I sat in Principal Downing's office. "I need to ask if I can give Ms. Claythorne the Chorale class next year," I said.

"What?" she said, surprised. "Why would you do that? It doesn't make any sense. She's part-time, you're full-time, you have more musical background, and the Chorale group is the best of the best. It's not adding up."

"I know," I said. "It's for personal reasons. I realize I'm asking a lot as a first-year teacher, but I really would rather not be in charge of Chorale next year."

"You're going to have to give me a little more to go by for me to even consider making such an unprecedented change."

"There's a student in one of my classes and her brother is the one who's in jail for killing my mother." *Is that personal enough for you, Principal Downing?* I thought harshly.

Her face changed. "I can't imagine," she said slowly. "But you made it through this year with her—why is it a problem now?"

"I didn't actually know who she was until yesterday," I said. "She stayed after class to tell me that she appreciated my not punishing her for what her brother did, I guess, and I ended up figuring it out from there."

"Owen," Principal Downing said, "I can't imagine how difficult this is for you and it's none of my business, but this seems to me like an opportunity worth taking. This student has done nothing wrong and thinks that you are willing to look past everything and see who she is for herself. Don't you think you can try to understand her, even though you may never understand—or forgive—him?"

She sounded like my dad. I told her I would think about it and left. I was afraid I would say something I'd regret. What does she know about this kind of thing?

In class, I tried to be as normal as possible with Julie, and it didn't seem like anyone noticed anything. But it was hard; it wasn't something I'd like to do on a daily basis for the next year.

Even though I was still angry with him, and he with me, I relayed my conversation with Principal Downing to my father that night. We were sitting in the study at our opposing desks, working on our lesson plans for the next day.

"She has a very good point," he said quietly, looking across at me. "And she knows a little about working through forgiveness herself. Did you know, Owen, that her cancer was initially misdiagnosed? She could have been given a much better prognosis and not endured the double mastectomy and all the chemotherapy if her doctor hadn't missed an obvious problem."

"I didn't know that," I said. "I knew she had cancer because of that special faculty meeting at the beginning of the year, but that's all I've heard about it." Then I got mad enough that he would throw her example in my face that I decided to ask him something I'd wanted to for a while. I didn't care if it hurt him or invaded his privacy.

"That's another thing," I said. "How do you know so much about Principal Downing? Are the two of you dating? I know you've been out together before. Is that how you found out that she's a paragon of forgiveness?"

"We've been to dinner twice; I wouldn't call that dating. And, no, I don't think she's perfect, but she is a very good human being." He looked down as his desk for a moment, and when he looked up, his voice was tight. "I am still mourning your mother, but Lindsay understands what it feels like to have a hard time moving on from something difficult, and I appreciate the understanding we have." He cleared his throat and paused for a moment.

I didn't break the silence, ashamed of my outburst.

"She's not telling you to do something she hasn't herself done, Owen. I know she's been very angry with her first doctor and she's had a hard time working through that. She's been focusing on some of the good things that have come out of it, like a greater appreciation for each day."

"It's not the same situation. I'm not saying hers is easier; I'm saying it's not the same."

"That's true," my dad said. " But it's still something to consider as you're figuring out what to do. I'll be honest with you, Owen. My motive in wanting you to let this go is purely selfish. It has a little to do with wanting Julie to be happy, but mostly it has to do with you."

"What do you mean, Dad? I can get another job. It wouldn't be the end of the world if I went to work somewhere else."

"No, but this is the perfect job for you—you've said that a hundred times. You've always wanted to work at Lakeview. I'm worried that you'll let this anger eat away at you. You'll let Kevin affect you in a way that I think you will regret later. That's all."

"Later? Right. Why is everything supposed to happen *later?*

When does *later* happen, Dad?" I said, clenching my fists in anger. "When can we stop thinking about it a hundred times every day?"

My dad's voice was shaky. "I don't think that will ever happen," he said. He looked me in the eyes and I saw such deep sorrow there that it made me catch my breath. "Whatever you decide to do, Owen, please choose your next steps carefully," my father said quietly. "You'll have to live with them forever. We all will."

I didn't sleep very well that night. I wonder if Kevin Cox even has any idea what he's done. He must. He knows he was drunk. He knows he shouldn't have been driving. He knows someone died. He is serving his time, but I wonder if he has the capability to put himself in our place. Does he have the power to imagine himself rolling over at night and reaching for someone and finding that they are gone? I know my father has done that. Does he have the power to imagine all of our different achievements being forever shadowed by the fact that our mom is not there? I don't think he does and that makes me even angrier.

I know I don't have the ability or the desire to put myself in Kevin Cox's shoes. I'm sure there are people who think I should forgive him, but right now it is safest for me not to think about him very much at all. But I'm starting to imagine myself in Julie Reid's place. A decent kid, average in every way except for a pretty singing voice, walking into my classroom that first day and wondering what would happen. Living in the shadow of what other people have done her entire life. Trying to decide whether or not to try out for Chorale. Deciding to do the audition and making the cut. Realizing that I wasn't going to punish her for being Kevin's sister. Getting up the courage to thank me for something that she really believed I had done.

The next day, Julie and Michaela came in and asked if I would help them for a couple of hours after school with a piece they were singing at Michaela's church that weekend. Even though I'd been trying to do the right thing, I hesitated for just a minute before saying, "Yes." They wanted to make sure they were singing the parts correctly—Mikey would be singing alto, which she doesn't usually sing.

Julie helped Mikey prop her crutches against her chair and I caught myself watching, wondering if Kevin were capable of anything thoughtful like that. I shook my head. Back to the music at hand.

I sat at the piano and started playing. It was a song with which I was not familiar, but it was a simple melody and I could sight-read it easily. Michaela started singing and then Julie joined in, her clear, soft voice carrying to the corners of the room.

I have heard and sung music's great religious pieces many times. But for some reason, the lines that Julie sang caught my heart:

Prone to wander, Lord, I feel it,
Prone to leave the God I love;
Here's my heart, O, take and seal it,
Seal it for Thy courts above.

Several times music has hit me like a physical force, so hard that I can't really breathe or see or think, only *feel*. I am a musician; I am moved by music quite often. But it doesn't happen with that magnitude every day. I stopped playing the piano.

Julie turned to look at me. "Did I do something wrong?" she asked.

I swallowed hard. "No," I said, "you didn't. I'm sorry. Let's start again."

I stopped by Principal Downing's office before I went home and told her to forget about our conversation from the other day and that I would be happy to continue with the Chorale class. She just nodded and said, "All right, Owen. Thank you."

I am prone to wander, like that song says, from Something I can't quite name. Maybe it is God; I don't know. There has been a lot of anger inside me for two years. It is a little frightening to let some of it go without being entirely sure what will take its place. But there is a great deal of beautiful music in the world; if I can listen to it, if I can find it.

CHAPTER 18

APRIL

Tyler Cruz

Sometimes it stinks when you get what you ask for. When I talked my parents into letting me stay for the basketball season, I'd been on cloud nine. They arranged it so that my mom would stay with me while my dad moved up to Seattle. Now we're all here, basking in family togetherness, and I have to live up to my end of the bargain by being cheerful and giving Seattle a fair chance.

Anyway, now I kind of wish that they had said no to my brilliant proposal. Now that I'm here, I kind of wish that we'd gone ahead and moved right away. Basketball is what I'm best at doing. It's how I stand out in the crowd. No one here knows that (even though they might be able to guess, since I'm 6' 4"). Our team in Phoenix had a great season and I guess I'm still glad I waited, but I don't really know how to define myself here without basketball. Maya told me that it would be great to start over fresh, but it's actually kind of hard. I keep having these little introductory conversations with people, but I haven't made any actual friends yet. I told her this the last time we talked on the phone and she reminded me, "You've only been there a week. Keep trying."

I woke up to my mother's voice, as always. The curse of being an only child is that they focus all their energy on you. There isn't anyone to engage in diversionary tactics with you or take the heat.

"Tyler!" she called. "I need your car today. Dad's wouldn't start, so he took mine. I'll drop you off at school."

Wonderful. Today we were going on a biology field trip to the Seattle Aquarium. That meant that my mom was going to drop me off and pick me up right where everyone would be meeting the buses for the trip. I knew it would do wonders for my social standing.

For someone who likes to get other people up in the morning, my mom is always running late. She always has a number of things she absolutely *has* to do after she's said that she's ready. I used the time to nap in the car, which, of course, ticked her off no end when she finally did climb in the front seat.

"The *least* you could do is help me get out the door! It was *your* breakfast plate I was clearing in there!"

I didn't bother to point out that I had been going to leave it there and use it for a snack when I came home from school. Her idea of efficiency and mine are not the same.

Sure enough, Mom dropped me off in the back where the buses for the field trip were parked. I could see a crowd of kids and biology teachers. The kids were filing onto buses and the teachers were checking them off a list. No one seemed to notice when I got out of the car and Mom was in such a hurry that she didn't wave good-bye and honk her horn like she usually does. So far, so good.

I saw my teacher and headed for her bus. Ms. Carl said, "You're late, Tyler. There's no room on my bus anymore. I think Mr. Walsh has a few seats left on his." She pointed me toward another bus and I headed over to it and climbed on.

Rows and rows of faces stared back at me. "Hurry up and sit down!" the bus driver barked. "We're going to be the last to go." Who knew bus drivers were competitive? I started walking down the aisle.

Where was I going to sit? This could get embarrassing. It would be way too weird to ask some *guy* I didn't know if I could sit by him, and a girl might think I was trying to hit on her. I'd been a little self-conscious about my "player" reputation since Maya called me on it back in the fall, and I thought maybe that might be a good reputation to ditch. Besides, the only girl I really wanted to impress lately was . . . you guessed it. Maya. Sitting by a girl would probably be the lesser of two evils.

There was a girl I didn't know sitting alone. "Anyone sitting here?" I asked.

"I don't think so," she said, sliding over.

"What does that mean?" I said, not sure if I should sit down.

"My friend Michaela might be coming." She looked up at me. Like I said, I'm six four and she was sitting down so she really had to look up. "Sit down, though. It's fine. If she's not here yet, she probably isn't coming. She's been sick and wasn't sure if she would be here today or not."

I shoved my backpack in the overhead rafters and sat next to her. "I'm Tyler Cruz."

"I'm Julie Reid," she said. "You must be in a different class than me. I don't think we've met."

"Yeah," I said. "Ms. Carl didn't have room on her bus, so she sent me over here. And I'm new. I moved here a week ago."

"Really?" she said. "Where are you from?"

I'd had this conversation so many times in the past week I'd gotten sick of hearing it. "Phoenix," I said. "My parents got jobs here, so we moved."

"I've never moved. I've lived in the same house my whole life." She smiled shyly. "Pretty boring. So what do you think of Lakeview? Are people being friendly?"

The bus pulled out of the parking lot. "Yeah," I said, wondering when the polite conversation would die and we would be able to read our own books or do our own homework or *something*.

People who haven't been new at a school don't get it at all. They have no idea how many connections they have all built up over the years. Even though some of the past history isn't good, it's still history. Just try starting all over without knowing anything about that history and trying to fit in. It's a joke. I hadn't told Maya all this in our e-mail or occasional phone conversations, though. I wanted her to think I was making progress, even though today, with the rain coming down thick and gray and no one I knew in sight, I was tempted to chuck it all and give up. Until basketball season came around, anyway.

"I would love to be able to start all over like that," Julie said. "Then no one would know about me or anything."

I laughed. "What on earth could *you* have done?" I asked. She didn't look wild at all.

"I have these two brothers," she said. "Everyone thinks I'm going to be like them when they first meet me and then they're surprised when I'm not. You have to understand. They're not just jerks. They're criminals."

"Really?"

"Oh, yeah," she said. "Everyone knows about them. You'd have heard about it sooner or later."

"Bad news travels fast here too?"

"Yeah," she said. "I guess that's the way at every high school. But I don't want to talk about that. I don't know why I brought it up. Sorry."

She was cute, in a quiet sort of way.

"So tell me about Phoenix," she said, turning to look at me directly.

"It's hot. And it's really big. My high school was bigger than this one."

"No, not that kind of stuff. What did you do there? How long had you lived there? Did you leave a lot of friends behind when you left?"

She was the first person to ask me the second layer of questions—the ones that come after "What's your name?" and "Where did you move from?" Sure, she'd asked me those too, but she had bothered to ask more. It was kind of nice.

I told her about the heat that bakes through you in Phoenix, and how we would run across the hot tar on the pavement in our bare feet as it melted in the sun. I told her about the way the desert looks, how you can see much more sky than you can here, where all the trees get in the way. If a thunderstorm is coming, you can see it for miles, and the clouds turn black and purple, which they don't seem to do here, even though it rains. I told her about the difference in the rain—here, it keeps things green and lush; there, it rescues plants and people, then lets them wait and sweat it out before it comes again.

I talked about the people I knew and had left behind, my best friends and even a little about Maya—how I didn't see her often and now I didn't know if I'd ever see her again. Arizona and Washington are pretty far apart. It felt good to say my friends' names again and remember that they had existed for me and me for them. I told her about camping with my dad and how I'd like to go camping here, but we've been too busy to get a new tent or find any cool places. I told her about my old house and how it had a huge cactus in the front yard that we used to string Christmas lights on during the holidays. I told her how I can't figure out which world feels more unreal right now—the one I left behind or the one I'm stuck in now.

The bus trip was an hour long. We talked for almost the whole ride. She kept asking questions, and I kept answering. It was easier to talk to her than I would have thought. Maybe too easy. I didn't shut up. "Sorry I talked so much," I said, as the bus pulled into the parking lot of the aquarium. "You probably had no idea what you were getting into when you let me sit here."

She laughed. "It's been fun to hear something new."

As we climbed off the bus and began to herd through the doors, some guy fell into step behind us. "Hey, Julie," he said. "Who's your new boyfriend? You sure get around, don't you?" He started laughing.

Julie's face turned bright red. I turned to see who was talking to her. One of the football players, I think. Some guy named Everett, who I could tell the first time I met him had serious attitude. "Didn't take you long to figure out who was easy, did it, buddy?" he said to me, laughing.

I looked him in the eye. He was bigger than me, but shorter. I could take him. Besides, who was he to talk to Julie like that? "Doesn't take me long to realize who's a lowlife, that's for sure," I said, glaring pointedly at him. "Get lost."

He didn't like that. He got right in my face. "I should take care of you right now," he hissed.

I didn't say anything. I also didn't back down. We kept on standing there, glaring at each other. People were starting to gather in interest when Ms. Carl saw us. "What's going on here, boys?" she demanded.

"Nothing," I said, but I didn't turn away. I waited for Everett to turn away first, and he did. I looked around. Julie was nowhere to be seen.

"Come with me, Tyler," Ms. Carl said. "The tour is starting and you need to take notes." She basically babysat me for the rest of the tour, probably thinking I was going to start a fight. I didn't care. I did what she told me, marching through the exhibits.

Finally, at the end of the tour, I was able to ditch her. I wandered by myself for a few minutes, pretending to read the plaques and informational displays.

"Hey," said a guy next to me. "You new here?"

I turned around. "Yeah," I said. He was tall, even taller than I am. I wondered if Everett had sent one of his friends over.

"You play basketball? Some girl heard me talking a minute ago and said there's a new kid who plays basketball. I figured you must be him."

"Yeah, I used to play for my high school team in Phoenix."

"Are you busy this weekend? Like tomorrow? There's a three-on-three tournament downtown and one of our guys can't make it. I've got to find someone who can fill in."

"Yeah," I said. "I could do it. My name's Tyler."

"Hey," he said. "Sorry about that. I'm Nic Hollist." He stuck out his hand. Just then, an announcement came over the intercom. "Lakeview High students, please report to your buses. You need to return to your buses immediately."

"Whose bus are you on?" Nic asked.

"Walsh's."

"I'm on Craig's. We're meeting tomorrow before the tournament to practice. Do you have a pen?" I pulled out my notebook and he wrote down an address and a phone number. "We'll see you there and make sure we can all play together. Some other guys have been mouthing off that they're going to beat us, and I want to waste them." He grinned and jogged off to his bus, waving.

I looked at the piece of paper. I didn't know where this street was or even what neighborhood it was in, but I was sure I could find it. Hopefully, Mom's car would be fixed by then and I wouldn't have to have her drop me off to play with my new little friends. I couldn't help but grin. It would be great to play ball again.

I walked down the aisle of the bus again, still alone, but feeling better. Julie was sitting alone again, talking to a girl across the aisle. When she saw me, she sat back and smiled. "Hey, do you want to sit here again?"

"Sure," I said, jamming my backpack into the rafters once more and plunking down next to her again. "Hey, did you tell some guy named Nic that I played basketball?"

She flushed. "Yeah," she said. "He was talking to one of my friends about how they needed another guy for the three-on-three tournament and how anyone who was any good was already on another team. I told him that you were new and had played ball before. I told him you were wearing a Phoenix Suns T-shirt and that you might want to play on his team. Was that okay?"

"Yeah, that was fine," I said. "Thanks. I thought maybe you were mad at me from before, when I said something to Everett. I was trying to be, you know, a good guy and look out for you, but maybe you didn't want me to get involved in your business. I wouldn't blame you for being mad."

"I wasn't," she said. "I was embarrassed. I thought you would think I was . . . well, what Everett said I was. I can't believe you stood up to him like that. That was really nice of you. I get so embarrassed when Everett acts like that. I wanted to get out of there as fast as I could. I shouldn't have left you standing there."

"What's the story, anyway?" I questioned. "If you don't mind my asking."

"I used to date Everett last year," she said. "Maybe dating isn't the word." She looked away. "We hung out a lot on the weekends and stuff. Last year I decided that I was going to be like my brothers and live up to their reputation, since being good didn't seem to change anything. Nobody believed I was good anyway. My parents were always checking up on me, even though I hadn't done anything wrong, and I couldn't stay out late or anything. I decided that since I was going to get punished anyway, I might as well earn it. So I hung out with Everett a lot."

"What made you change your mind about him?" I asked.

"I realized that Everett was even worse than my brothers in some ways, so I decided to quit seeing him." She paused. "I wanted to go away to school this year, but my parents wouldn't let me."

"But would you really leave now if you could?" I asked.

"Not now," she said. "I have a best friend and school's going a lot better. She talked me into trying out for the school's elite choir group and I actually made it. She also helped me find out that you don't have to punish yourself forever for the things that you do.

There's a religion that I'm looking into that has helped a lot, the Mormon religion."

"You're Mormon?" I asked. What was it with me and these chance meetings with Mormon girls?

"Not yet," she said, looking surprised. "Are you?"

"No," I said, "but Maya—that girl I was telling you about—is. And I went to her church once, to hear her cousin speak. It was pretty cool."

"Yeah," Julie said. I got the feeling there was more she wanted to say, but she didn't.

We rode for a little while in silence before Julie said, "I am going to leave someday, though. I just know there are places I need to go. Maybe I'll go to Phoenix. I'd never thought of it. There's a lot of places I've never even thought about and things I never thought I'd do that are starting to seem possible."

It was almost dark outside. We sat on the bus, looking out at the lights of the cars. When we went over the bridge, it was as though we were rushing through nothing, connected to nothing, with only water on both sides. Then we hit the other side and the land appeared. We were connected to everyone else again. I felt like this past week for me had been me alone, surrounded by nothing on either side, until I touched down over here. It's different from where I started, that's for sure. I don't mind being alone, but I really hate being lonely.

Julie fell asleep on my shoulder as we were driving. I was listening to my headphones and I didn't wake her up. It was cool to know that someone felt that comfortable around me.

The bus lurched to a halt at a stop sign near the high school. Julie opened her eyes and looked at me, embarrassed. "Sorry about that," she said.

"No problem," I said. We were getting close, so I slid my arms into my jacket and noticed a hole in the sleeve. "Stupid coat," I said. "I'd better get a new one. Where can you get a good rain jacket around here? There ought to be plenty of places since all it ever does is rain."

"That's not true," she said. I was surprised at the spunk in her voice. "People always think that. It does rain a lot. But all the time—that's an exaggeration. Today was beautiful. And it's not raining now, is it?" She gestured to the window.

"I stand corrected," I said. "But I still need a new coat."

She smiled. "I guess you do. There are lots of sporting good stores around here. In fact, my mom works at REI, so I know they've got good stuff. You could get a great new tent there for camping too. One that can fit you and your dad."

I laughed as the bus pulled into the parking lot. "It's going to have to be a pretty big tent." The door screeched open and students started to pour into the aisle and out the door. I reached up and got Julie's backpack for her. It looked a little worn. "I should take you with me when I go," I said without thinking. "You could use a new backpack."

She laughed. "Yeah," she said. "This one's about eleven years old. It's probably about time to retire it."

"Monday?" I asked.

"What?" she asked, looking confused.

"Do you want to go on Monday after school? My dad has the day off because he has to work this Saturday on a big project. The three of us could go. We're not so hot at directions yet, so you could show us where the store is."

She seemed surprised. "Really?"

"Yes, really. Unless you have something better to do."

She thought for a moment, then nodded. "With any luck, my mom will be working there that day and we can get her employee discount."

"Now you're talking."

We stepped off the bus and I heard honking right away. It was my mom, sitting in her car, waving at me happily to get my attention.

"Who's that?" Julie asked, laughing.

"Can't you guess?" I rolled my eyes and Julie grinned.

"Thanks again," she said. I waved to her and took off for the car before Nic or someone saw me getting into the car with my mother. The paper with Nic's address and Julie's phone number written on it was deep in my backpack for tomorrow. And Julie was right. It wasn't raining. There were even a few stars in sight.

CHAPTER 19

MAY

Avery Matthews

When I went to interview Principal Downing for the newspaper article, I was a lot more nervous than I thought I would be. After all, it's not like I haven't been in her office a few times before, but this time it was for a legitimate purpose. Rumors had been floating around school about Principal Downing all year long—that she was on drugs, that she was sick, that she was having a mental breakdown—because she often looked like she didn't feel so hot and because she vanished for a couple of weeks in the middle of the year. I didn't really know what to think about any of it. Back in November, I was sure she was on something, but I might have been projecting. I admit it.

Mr. Thomas cornered me at the beginning of journalism one day and told me, "I have an article in mind for you. It's going to be pretty big news and you'll need to interview Principal Downing since she's the subject. I'm going to send you down there right now to do the interview. She's waiting for you."

"Why me?" I asked. I was genuinely curious. I'm still the newest staff member and something like this sounded like an article he'd

189

usually assign to one of the editors. I was also a little suspicious. Was this just a ruse to get me to the principal's office? I racked my brain for something I'd done wrong lately, but the only things I could think of were minor. Nothing that would be grounds for going to the principal's office for a suspension.

"Principal Downing is going to tell the student body the truth about what's going on this year, which is that she has been battling cancer. I want the article to be the best it can possibly be. I also want her to be treated with respect in the interview, which I assume you can do without any problem." Mr. Thomas is a nice man, but he doesn't pull any punches. I know he knows about my history with the principal's office. "And," he added, "she requested you."

That was a surprise. I wondered why on earth she would have picked me. Mr. Thomas watched me for my response. "Are there any specific questions you want me to ask her, or am I on my own?"

"I trust you to ask the right things," he said. "Are you ready to go now? This is the only free time she has today."

I made a point of bopping Dave on the head on the way out of class with the little tape recorder Mr. Thomas had given me. "Where are you going?" he asked. "I thought we were going to work on an advice column together." That was his latest brainchild. I can't even begin to imagine who would want to get advice from the two of us, but Dave is convinced it will be a raging success. Dave is delusional. It's one of the things I like best about him.

"Special assignment," I said snootily and ducked out the door. I don't want Dave to figure out that I have this ludicrous crush on him. I want us to stay good friends. He is not my type at all: he's goofy, churchy, and into athletics and journalism. I'm more interested in the guys who can play guitar or bass or who are a little more alternative, a little less mainstream, a lot less class-clownish.

If only he didn't like Andrea Beckett. How do you compete with Andrea Beckett? You don't. Not if you're me, anyway. I still fight all the time, but not battles I don't think I have a chance of winning.

I'm trying to do a little more picking-and-choosing when it comes to fights I want to spend the time and energy on these days.

"Come on in, Avery," said Principal Downing, ushering me into her office and indicating where she wanted me to sit. She looked a little rough, but not as bad as she had earlier this year. I glanced around her office. It was the same as I remembered—big desk, lots of plants and books. It had been a while since I'd been hauled in here, which was probably a good thing. I know my parents certainly thought so.

She saw me looking around. "You haven't been here in a while," she said, smiling. It was a warm smile.

"I've been too busy destroying school mascots," I quipped, and instantly regretted it. Maybe she still didn't see the humor in that situation.

"That was quite a day," she said, laughing. "Poor Mr. Thomas. He was playing with fire, putting you and David Sherman together. He's a brave man." She settled down in her chair behind her desk. Her smile faded just a little. "Did he happen to tell you why you're interviewing me today?"

"He told me that you have cancer and that you want to tell the student body about it." I started the tape recorder, fiddling with it a little more than necessary to avoid looking at her. *Cancer.* I'd thrown it right out there on the table. It looked like we were going full steam ahead with the interview, and this was one interview I wanted on tape for sure. I wanted to be able to go back and check the facts. There was no way I was going to mess up something like this.

"That's right. There are too many rumors floating around school, so it's time to come clean. The faculty has known all year, but I need to do what I should have done at the beginning and tell the truth to the students as well."

I glanced up at her. She was looking right at me, which startled me for some reason. I wished I'd brought a list of questions so that I could pretend to be reading from a list. It made me uncomfortable to be quizzing her about her terminal illness. It seemed like some kind of cruel joke, but I guess she was willing since she had agreed to—and asked for—the interview. So I looked her in the eye and asked the first question that came to mind.

"Why didn't you tell us at the beginning of the year? I mean, I can understand why you would want to keep it private, but it seems like it would have been easier in some ways to tell everyone and then they could help you out."

"I didn't tell everyone immediately for a lot of reasons. There's a lot of pressure on someone in my position, as a woman in the administration field, which is predominantly male. I didn't want other schools, or parents, or the students to feel as though I couldn't operate at full capacity, or to feel that I wasn't capable of dealing with everything if word got out.

"And I was proud. I didn't want to seem weak. I wanted to be tough. I didn't want people to think I was a wimp or to give me special treatment. I also didn't want you students to think that I wasn't going to be able to do my job and make you all toe the line." A wry smile. "Finally, I think I was in denial. If I could pretend for part of the day that the cancer wasn't really happening, that was an escape for me."

"What kind of cancer is it?" I asked, hoping it wasn't too intrusive a question.

"Breast cancer." She said the two words quietly. I wondered how they had sounded when she first heard them applied to her condition. Had they echoed in the room, sounding louder and louder with each passing minute and taking on extra significance as she thought about them? Or had she not really heard them at first? It would be almost too much to take in, I thought. Had she been alone when she heard them? Or had there been someone to hold her hand? Had she gone home and cried? It was hard to picture her crying, but I'd be the first to know that a tough exterior might be a front for something else going on inside.

I didn't say any of that, but I asked another question that was still pretty personal. I worded it as carefully as I could. "And what is the . . . prognosis?"

"Right now, it's good. In fact, it's in remission, as of a few weeks ago. That could change at any time, though."

"Is that scary?" I asked in spite of myself. Then I frowned. That wasn't the kind of question I would really want someone to ask me. Of course it would be scary.

She was watching me. "I'm sorry," I said. "I don't really know which questions to ask."

"You're doing fine," she said. "That is a tough question, but I knew you wouldn't be afraid to ask questions like that. I wanted this to be an honest interview with honest questions; that's why I asked Mr. Thomas to send you. I've been reading your articles this year, Avery, and there's a lot of candor in them, but there's also a lot of empathy too. The article you wrote about the different religions at Lakeview was especially good."

"Thanks," I said, not sure what to do with the praise but liking it nonetheless.

"To answer your question," she continued, "it is scary. It was the worst at the beginning, though. It was hard to make plans because I didn't want to look too far into the future. It's still a little frightening, but I'm learning to put fear on the back burner so that I can get on with living my life, however much of it might be left. Right now, I feel like there is quite a bit."

"You look a lot better," I said. "Are you planning on being back next year?"

"I'm planning on it."

"How are you feeling?"

"Not perfect, but much better. It's not such a struggle to get through the day anymore. It's not so hard to put one foot in front of the other when I walk down the hall or go shopping or out on a date. Before, I had to concentrate on getting through every small task.

Now, whole minutes go by where I don't think about how I feel. It's a great feeling."

Even though I don't have cancer, I could understand how she felt. My problems were more . . . psychological, I guess, but I definitely knew how it felt to have to drag yourself through every task every day.

I remember when I found Andrea Beckett reading my poem to herself and being shocked. Out of all the people in the school, she was the last person I would have thought would relate to how I felt, but I was wrong. Mr. Thomas had been the first to teach me that there were a lot of people carrying significant amounts of pain around with them but still managing to help others. Ms. Downing was the most recent person to teach me the same thing. It was both sad and encouraging to realize how many people were hurting but still making the effort.

"Who helps you with your cleaning, your shopping, your doctor's visits? All that stuff?" I wondered aloud.

"The faculty have been very helpful, Mr. Thomas in particular. I also had some nurses when I was really sick and a cleaning lady. I don't have any children, and my parents have passed away, so I was on my own at the beginning. What I've learned is that there is an invisible net of people waiting to catch you, to help you when you fall.

"When I first became principal a few years ago, I didn't feel that way at all. Instead, I felt like there was a very visible net of people out to get me. It seemed like every move I made, every policy I changed, upset people. Multitudes of people were ready to go up in arms about anything and everything. I'd never felt so hated in my whole life as I did that first year.

"But now, I've never felt so loved. I've learned that there are people willing to help, to give, even when they don't know what's wrong. People like the students who gave me a piece of gum when they heard me throwing up in the bathroom one day. I'd been too weak to make it back to the office bathroom when the nausea hit; I was so humiliated. They didn't know what was going on, but they did the best they could to help a little bit when they found me in trouble.

"There are people like the night-shift nurses who brought me crushed ice that they picked up from the Pizza Parlor on their way to work because ice was all I could eat and they knew I liked that better than the cubes they had at the hospital. People like Mr. Thomas, who takes me out to dinner once in a while when he can tell I've had a hard day. Sometimes he bakes me a batch of cookies because they're one of the only things that taste really good to me right now. I want the student body to know that they are surrounded by people like that, and that *they* are people like that. All people have a great potential to be good to one another." It was quiet for a few minutes. She had tears in her eyes, but her voice had been firm throughout the whole thing.

I stared out the window, blinking a lot harder than usual. "I think the students are going to be really supportive," I said. That made her smile.

Just then her secretary came in and said, "There's a parent here to see you, Ms. Downing."

I snapped off the tape recorder and stood up. "Thank you, Ms. Downing," I said. "I'll drop by a copy of the article for you to approve before I turn it in to Mr. Thomas in case there's anything you want to change." I started to leave, not wanting to overstay my welcome, but she called me back.

"Avery?" I turned around. "Was there anything else you wanted to ask me?"

I shook my head. "You said it all perfectly. I want to get it down before I lose the feeling I had when you were saying it."

She looked surprised, then pleased. "All right. And you don't have to worry about having me approve the article. I know you'll do a good job. Just make sure Mr. Thomas remembers to send me a copy of the paper in that red wagon of his."

I grinned back at her and ran up the stairs to the journalism room to start typing.

MAY

Ethan Beckett

When I was younger, I used to imagine myself receiving the greatest honors imaginable. Back then it was always some sports championship. I spent a lot of time in my backyard single-handedly winning the World Series or the Super Bowl and a lot of time at the basketball standard in the driveway doing the same with the NBA Finals. Then when I got into soccer, it was the World Cup where my last-minute heroics saved the day. And lately, ever since State, I have to admit that I've been dreaming about holding that first-place trophy next year. But I don't know if I'll ever have a greater honor than Julie Reid asking me to baptize her.

When her parents finally gave her permission to be baptized, she called us all up and we went out for ice cream to celebrate. We drove to the temple grounds to sit and talk and it was then that she asked me to baptize her and Dave Sherman to confirm her. We were both in shock, in a good way. Of course, we both said yes.

Later, Dave and I were talking. "This just makes my mission even more real," he said. "It's not so far away. Hopefully I'll be baptizing and confirming people all the time then. This is really something else. I've got to be ready for this."

I felt the same way. Knowing that I was going to baptize Julie made me think about everything I did in a different way. I didn't want to do anything that would make the experience less than perfect for her.

Mikey, Julie, and I all drove to the chapel together on the day of Julie's baptism. Julie's parents would be coming later with Mikey's parents. Initially, they had given Julie permission to be baptized but hadn't planned on attending. Julie told them that she wanted them to be a part of it and finally they agreed.

"Are you nervous?" Mikey asked Julie as we pulled into the parking lot.

"Not really," Julie said. "Actually, I feel calm."

I looked over at her. She did look calm: calm and peaceful and serene.

That was good, because I was terrified. I couldn't get all of the details of the baptism straight in my mind. I didn't want to mess up the words, so I kept saying them over and over in my head. I kept reminding myself to completely immerse Julie in the water so that we didn't have to do the baptism again. I've had to repeat the sacrament prayer in church before and it was embarrassing. This would be a hundred times worse if I messed it up because it would affect Julie too.

"Is Mr. Thomas here yet?" Julie asked in a whisper as we entered the room.

"There he is, kind of sitting on the side," Mikey said quietly. "It looks like his dad came with him. I'm so glad he agreed to accompany me during my song."

"I know. I really wanted to invite him to my baptism, but I wasn't quite sure how to do it. I'm glad you thought of this. You're a genius!"

Mikey laughed softly. "Well, he seemed like the obvious choice, since he came up with that new arrangement of 'Come Thou Fount' for us to sing at the choir concert." She grew serious. "It's great that he's here."

I saw the new guy at school, Julie's friend Tyler, standing awkwardly at the back. He looked really uncomfortable in his khakis and button-up shirt and tie. I was going to go over to say something to him, but Andrea, who was sitting near the back, gestured for him to sit next to her. I saw relief wash over his face. I was impressed that he'd come. When Julie told me she'd invited him, I had been skeptical. "Do you think he's really going to come?" I'd asked her. "I mean, no offense, but if I were him, I don't know that I would want to go to someone's baptism at a strange church."

"I think he'll come," Julie had said. And she had been right. Tyler slid into the seat next to Andrea and started messing with his tie immediately, trying to loosen it. "This thing is choking me," I could hear him say quietly, and Andrea laughed.

Dave came over to us. "Hey," he said to Julie, giving her a hug. "This is going to be a great day for you."

Julie smiled back. "I know," she said, returning his hug. She left for a moment to say hello to Tyler. Dave stood there next to me, scanning the faces in the room.

"Who are you looking for?" I asked. "It's almost time to start."

"Avery Matthews—you know her? I asked Julie if I could invite her, but I don't see her." He turned back around. "Hey, do you want to go somewhere and say a prayer together? This is the first time I've confirmed anyone and I want it to be perfect for Julie."

"Sure," I said, and we went out into the hall and into an empty room. At first, I didn't really listen to Dave's prayer very carefully because I was still so nervous, but then I noticed that he was just praying for Julie, not for him or for me. He prayed that Julie would feel the Spirit and that she would know that she was loved, and that her baptism and confirmation would be the experiences He had in mind for her. That really snapped things back into focus for me. I decided to quit thinking about how nervous I was and start thinking about how happy Julie was instead.

We went back into the room. Julie saw her parents and gave them a hug, and then we all went to sit on the front row. Of all of us—me, Dave, her parents—Julie seemed the least nervous.

I'll remember the night that she told us she could get baptized for a couple of reasons. First, because of how happy she was as we all sat quietly on the grounds of the Seattle Temple, watching night fall around us and talking in soft tones. "I thought I was going to have to wait for two years to get baptized. I thought my parents would still be upset," she kept saying. "But not only have they given me their permission, they're even going to come!"

"What changed their minds?" I asked.

"I asked them the same question and they couldn't really answer me," Julie said. "They said it was mostly just watching me change into a happier and better person over the course of the school year. My mom said that most of her concerns slowly faded away." Julie smiled a little. "She still is a little worried about the whole temple wedding thing, but I've told her that we'll cross that bridge when we come to it. I'm still hoping that maybe she'll want to investigate the church and someday we'll be here together." She gestured to the temple behind her, rising tall and clean out of the night, illuminated by the floodlights.

The other reason I'll always remember that night was because it was the night that I decided to ask Michaela if we could start dating again. Dave and Andrea and everyone else decided to go see a movie, but Julie wanted to get home to see her parents and Mikey and I were both running the first race of the track meet the next day, so we needed to get more sleep. I offered them both a ride home, hoping that they'd both accept, and they did.

I dropped Julie off first. She'd been sitting in the front seat, so when we dropped her off, Mikey climbed out to take her place and give her a hug. "Congratulations again, Julie," I called out as she turned toward her front door. "This is the best thing to happen all year."

"I think so too," said Julie. "And it's been a pretty great year." Mikey gave her one last hug and Julie went inside.

Mikey sat in the front seat next to me, and I backed out of Julie's driveway. I didn't do a great job of it and ended up making one of those seven-hundred-point turns to get headed the right way. The silence was awkward. We'd been hanging out in the same group again lately, and it had been getting easier, but this was the first time we'd been alone and I didn't know where to start. I thought I'd figured out what I wanted to say but I couldn't quite get the words out.

I glanced over at Mikey as I drove and I could tell she was trying to think of something to say too. The headlights of a car coming toward us illuminated her thick dark hair and made her look kind of mysterious. I was reminded of that night on the bus in the dark after the State meet. Well, that was as good a place to start as any.

"Remember last fall, on the bus?" I asked.

She turned to look at me. "Yeah," she said cautiously and a little quizzical, like she was wondering where I was going with this.

"That was another great night," I said. My words hung in the air. She didn't say anything. She just waited. Apparently she was going to let me suffer through this and not give me any help. I was glad that I was driving so that I had the excuse of staring straight ahead and keeping my eyes on the road.

"Mikey, would you mind if we went out again sometimes? You can say no. I know that might be weird after we broke up and everything." I paused in case she wanted to say anything. She didn't, so I went on. "I've missed you."

"What's changed your mind?" she asked softly. I slid a glance over to see what she was doing, and she was looking right at me. Whoops. Eyes back on the road before she could see how nervous I was.

"I think I'm getting a little more comfortable being uncomfortable." She laughed, and I hurried to explain myself. "I mean, I'm realizing that I'm not going to know how everything turns out down the road, so I'm getting better at trusting myself to make the right decisions for now. I guess I'm learning to have a little more faith and not be so worried about controlling everything." I made a feeble attempt at a laugh. "Andrea and I have the same genes, you know."

"That would be fine," Mikey said. "I've missed you too."

Relief washed over me. "So . . . do you want to do something right now? I have plenty of quarters for Space Invaders."

Mikey started laughing at me. It was a great sound. "I thought we were going home early so that we'd be ready for our races tomorrow."

"That was a ploy on my part," I admitted.

"I can't believe I fell for it," she said, still laughing. "Okay, Ethan. That would be fun."

The sounds of the prelude music snapped me back to the present. "Whoa," I said. "The pianist is playing pretty loud." Even as I said it, the music softened. I leaned back to ask Mikey in a whisper, "Hey, isn't that Mr. Thomas playing the piano? I thought he was only accompanying your song."

"He was supposed to," she whispered back, "but the pianist didn't show up, so he's sight-reading the music. He's doing a great job."

"Brave man," Dave muttered. "You couldn't pay me enough to play in front of all these people. You couldn't pay all these people enough to listen to me play."

After the opening hymn, one of the sister missionaries went up to give the opening prayer. She smiled at Julie before she began. "Our Father in Heaven, we are thankful for the opportunity we have to gather together for Julie's baptism today. We are so grateful for Thy gospel and for Julie's acceptance of it in her life. We are thankful for the opportunities for repentance and love that have been provided to us by Thy Son. Please bless us this day that we can have Thy Spirit in our hearts and appreciate the blessings of baptism and of the gift of the Holy Ghost."

Sister Choi gave a simple talk on baptism based on the scriptures. She talked about the concept of baptism, about starting over and being able to repent. She talked about the water of baptism figuratively washing our sins away. She talked about the Savior and how he was the living water of the gospel. "The Savior spoke to a woman of Samaria at a well during his ministry. When he asked her for some water, he was able to teach a wonderful lesson in John 4:9–14:

"'Then saith the woman of Samaria unto him, How is it that thou, being a Jew, askest drink of me, which am a woman of Samaria? for the Jews have no dealings with the Samaritans.

"'Jesus answered and said unto her, If thou knewest the gift of God, and who it is that saith to thee, Give me to drink; thou wouldest have asked of him, and he would have given thee living water. . . .

"'. . . Whosoever drinketh of this water shall thirst again:

"'But whosoever drinketh of the water that I shall give him shall never thirst; but the water that I shall give him shall be in him a well of water springing up into everlasting life.'

"Jesus taught this woman, who had been a sinner, that He loved her and that His gospel was for everyone, of every race. He taught her that she was worthy of His gospel and His love, in spite of her past, and that she was of worth. This is a lesson that we should never forget: we are all worthy of His love and He has living water—a gospel—for us that can quench our thirst forever."

Julie's eyes brimmed with tears. I knew that this was what she loved best about the Savior and about the gospel. Michaela's mother continued, looking at Julie and smiling.

"Julie, today you will be immersed in the waters of baptism. Every time you see water, you will have a reminder that will trigger all of your senses. You can see the water as it moves boats, as it falls on the hood of your car, as it runs over rocks in a waterfall. You can smell the rain. You can hear waves crashing, rivers running, drops hitting the pavement. You can taste the clear, pure flavor of it. And you can feel it, Julie—you can feel the water on your hands and face, on your eyelashes and hair. When this happens, think of the waters of baptism and of the living water of Jesus Christ. You have the opportunity to be reminded of His love for you, and of His love for *all* of us, all of the time. He truly is the fount of every blessing."

Mr. Thomas had been listening so carefully to the talk that he almost missed his cue. Michaela was already at the podium before he stood up, music in hand, and hurried to the piano. She turned to make sure that he was ready, and they began.

I looked around at everyone while the music was playing and Mikey was singing. Everyone seemed different today. I don't know if it was because we were at a baptism and I usually didn't see all of these people at church, or if it was something about me. Julie's parents were watching with tears in their eyes. Back in his pew, Mr. Thomas, the older Mr. Thomas, had his eyes closed and was letting the music wash over him like waves. I closed my eyes to do the same.

I never imagined that it would be so quiet when we stepped into the water. Julie walked toward me in the font and neither of us could stop smiling. People she loved and who cared about her were all around. It was time, and she was ready.

CHAPTER 21

MAY

Julie Reid

I've never kept a journal before, but Michaela gave this to me as a gift for my baptism. She said that today would be a day that I'd want to remember forever. She was right. I want to write everything down so that I don't forget a thing, but I'm sure I won't be able to write things as beautifully as I would like. It feels good reliving today, though, even if I can't do it justice.

I have been waiting so long for my baptism that it feels like Christmas, or the first day of summer. When you wait so long for a day like today you wonder if you've built it up to be more than it could ever be. I wondered if Mom and Dad would ever let me get baptized. I knew they would be happy for me if I could only get them to understand. Even if they didn't understand the whole gospel, I knew that if they could understand why it was so important to me, they'd be happy for me. It took a long time, but they do see what it is about the Church that appeals to me. It's the love and forgiveness and the sacrifice of the Savior that made it all possible. Once they could see that, they understood. I think that what helped them to understand was seeing the difference it made in me.

I've never felt so good. The water was so warm. It was so quiet. I could hear every little movement of the water and feel every beat of my heart. My friends were all there, smiling at me. My family was there, supporting me, at least some of them anyway. I did think about Kevin and Mark as I stepped into the water. I wondered if they would ever get to feel as clean and happy as I knew I would feel. I didn't feel angry or bitter or mad. Just hopeful. It was a good feeling.

Being confirmed gave me so much comfort. When I first heard that the Holy Ghost was called the Comforter, I thought that was the best name anyone could choose. I love knowing that there will always be someone to comfort and help me as long as I do my part. Both Ethan's voice when he baptized me and David's voice when he confirmed me sounded so strong and sure. I knew they both knew that what they were doing was true. They'll both be great missionaries.

When I asked Ethan if he would be the one to baptize

me, he got tears in his eyes, which I didn't expect. He told me that baptizing me was the greatest honor he had ever had. I couldn't believe that someone would feel that way about baptizing me, but now that it's happened, I think I understand. Helping someone feel as happy as I do must be truly rewarding.

A few of us went to walk around the grounds of the Seattle Temple later, after a little gathering of friends at Mikey's. I've been to the temple grounds before, lots of times, to collect my thoughts and watch people go in and out of the temple. It's where we went when I found out that I would be able to be baptized after all. Even before I had a testimony, I knew that the temple was a good place to be. Soon I will be able to go there to do baptisms for other people, which is an incredible thought.

Even more incredible is the thought that someday I could be married there. Me! I remember a couple I saw there a few weeks ago who had just been married. They were more than happy as they came out of the doors of the temple and posed for their pictures—they positively glowed. The flowers and trees were thick and lush. It was sunny, and they were happy because they had been married in the best possible place and in the best possible way. It made me excited for the future.

There is so much to look forward to in this life and

beyond. I didn't know that a few months ago. I hoped that it was true—that the world could be a beautiful place in spite of trials and problems—but now I KNOW.

JUNE

Andrea Beckett

Thousands of people were watching to see if I would make a mistake. I was *not* going to think about the last time I was in front of this many people, which was Homecoming—oops. I held on tight to the piece of paper with my speech written on it. If I lost that, I might as well walk off the stage and out the door like I did last fall. Oops again. There was just one more musical number before it was my turn to speak. I'd known that I would be the valedictorian for two months now—and I'd wanted to be the valedictorian for twelve years—but I was still petrified.

Maybe I was actually fossilized. I hadn't changed position at all and I realized suddenly both my legs were falling asleep. That would really be the way to deliver a memorable valedictory address. Stand up and collapse, then army crawl to the podium and cling to the microphone, legs dangling.

My imagination has been occupied with only two areas of thought lately. I know it's not very healthy, but sometimes it happens. First, I have been thinking about my grandmother, who died this past month.

She had dinner with us one night at Dad's and had laughed at the antics of my sister Chloe. She talked to me about my "wonderful honor" (being valedictorian) and told me how proud she was of me. She asked Ethan about his latest race. She mentioned (for about the hundredth time, but who could blame her?) how glad she was that Dad had moved back to Seattle. Then she went home and didn't wake up the next morning. She died in her sleep sometime during the night. That great, grandmotherly heart of hers just stopped.

From talking to her this winter and spring, I had learned that her greatest fear was that she would lose her mind and slip away into shadow, losing us and herself in the process. But it wasn't how she died, thank goodness. She was clear and coherent right up until the end. I know she is with my grandfather now and I know that they are happy together. That is the knowledge that she often told me she had, but that I never thought I had for myself. To my surprise, I am finding that there is more and more that I do believe about the Church. I thought I didn't believe any of it. Grandma is the one who helped me start asking again. I miss her.

The second train of thought, of course, was regarding the graduation speech. How was I going to write it? What was I going to say? Who would even care? All the other students would be thinking about what they would do after graduation, what parties would be going on, how much they were going to drink, and so on and so on. I was scared that no one would pay attention to me and terrified that they would.

One thing was better than the Homecoming experience, though. I had friends again, people who cared about me and were rooting for me to succeed. There were people I cared about sitting in the audience. My family, of course, and Dave, and the members of the track team, who I'd finally gotten to know on the bus trips and in the meets this year, and the girls from church, and others.

My speech didn't even really exist (except in the form of a terrible rough draft) until the night before graduation. I was so stressed out that people were starting to get *very* worried about me. David, who had to speak at seminary graduation earlier in the week, brought me a book of inspirational thoughts and quotations from people like Nelson Mandela. He also took me kite-flying at the park to relieve the stress. Standing barefoot in the green grass by the water with my kite flying higher and higher did help. My dad kept suggesting poems that he thought were profound. My mom took me out to buy a new dress to wear, even though my graduation gown will cover most of it. Chloe made me a drawing and slid it under my door. It was of a princess giving a speech at a tea party, she informed me later. Ethan kept coming up with sports analogies he thought I'd be able to use.

I was sitting in front of my computer, trying for the millionth time to think of something effective to say as an introduction, when my mother came in, holding an envelope and smiling at me.

"Here," she said, handing it to me. I looked at it. It was written on thick, cream-colored paper. My grandmother once had the world's most beautiful penmanship. Now the writing on the envelope—*Andrea Beckett*—looked whiskery and shaky. It seemed that there were a hundred ways that I could miss her each day.

"What is this?" I asked.

My mom smiled at me with tears in her eyes. "Your dad found it in that carved wooden box on top of her dresser. She wrote one to each of us. Dad said there was a note with them, saying that the letters were to be given to us on our birthdays this year. Dad thought that since this was a special occasion, you should receive your letter early. I told him he was right."

After she closed the door, I sat on my bed and opened the letter.

To my beautiful oldest granddaughter,
I can't begin to tell you how proud I am of the young woman you've become. You were my first grandchild and I

couldn't believe how perfect you were when I first held you. I still find you perfect now.

In your life, Andrea, you will hear a lot of talk about your future and what you should do with it. I want to tell you, Andrea, that those who tell you that the future is up to you are dishonest. The future is not always up to you. But those cynics who would tell you that the future is not up to you are also lying. What, then, is the truth? It is very complicated, as I have found in my eighty-plus years of living and as you have, no doubt, found in yours. I will do my best to tell you some of what I have discovered in the hopes that it will be of some help to you, my wonderful, beautiful granddaughter.

The truth is that your heart will be broken. People you love will die. Dreams you had will not work out the way you intended. People are capable of cruelty that will wound you deeply. At the end of your life, as I am finding, your body will be old and out of your control. This is if you are lucky. There are those to whom this happens when they are young, which to my mind is one of the saddest things that can happen. You will be scared. In the world in which you live, people will murder and degrade and hurt other people in ways that are incomprehensible to you. You will wake up in the middle of the night and feel a weight on your chest and in your soul that you don't know if you can shake.

So what, you may ask, makes life worth living? There is so much, Andrea, that makes life worth living. I have known for years and still know that the gospel is true. Jesus Christ died for us and He and our Father in Heaven love us more than we can imagine. You will hear babies laugh. You will love people, and they will love you. One night, you will wake up and hear the quiet and you will feel peace. People are capable of kindness and goodness and they will show it to you and you will show it to them. You will learn things. Dreams that you have had will come true. Not all of them, but some of them. You will have moments of joy at just being alive that will fill your soul. You will have to decide if these things outweigh the others. It is my experience that they do. But you cannot be lazy. You cannot expect good to happen to you and think that you do not have to contribute.

Our prophet, President Gordon B. Hinckley, once quoted a man named Jenkins Lloyd Jones as saying the following, which I believe to be very true:

"Anyone who imagines that bliss is normal is going to waste a lot of time running around shouting that he has been robbed. The fact is most putts don't drop. Most beef is tough. Most children grow up to be just people. Most successful marriages require a high degree of mutual toleration. Most jobs are more often dull than otherwise. . . .

"Life is like an old-time rail journey—delays, sidetracks, smoke, dust, cinders, and jolts, interspersed only occasionally by beautiful vistas and thrilling bursts of speed.

"The trick is to thank the Lord for letting you have the ride."

I hope that some of the idealism and exhilaration you feel as a young woman stays with you forever. I hope that it is tempered and made more realistic by experiences you have. I hope that it is not destroyed but instead grows stronger and more resilient. I have confidence that you will walk your own path and create your own ripples in whatever pond you choose to swim. I have confidence that you will remember to thank the Lord for letting you have the ride and that you will appreciate those vistas around you because of the cinders you have endured so far.

But pay attention to those around you. Do not take your association with others lightly, without thinking about what effect you might cause. Don't let this cripple you; let it empower you and make you think. You can't do things only for other people; you also can't do things only for yourself. It will ruin you either way. Your life is going to be wonderful if you embrace wonder and worthwhile if you embrace things that are of worth. Remember that one of those things is service, something I have learned again recently myself.

Andrea, I love you dearly and want you to know that I have confidence in you. I am very proud of you today and always. You have been a wonderful part of my "ride" here on this earth—and forever.

> Your grandmother,
> Anna Beckett
> P.S. Please read Isaiah 40:31

I opened my scriptures and read the verse she recommended: "But they that wait upon the Lord shall renew their strength; they shall mount up with wings as eagles; they shall run, and not be weary; and they shall walk, and not faint."

At first, I didn't know why Grandma had given me that scripture. Was it because I'm a runner and she thought it might speak to me? As I sat and reread the letter and the scripture, I began to understand what I needed to do to move forward with my talk and with my testimony. All I needed to do was rely on the Lord and take it one step at a time, maybe walking instead of running to begin with. I also needed to perform more service for others. Tutoring other students was a start, but I had years of selfishness behind me to erase. And maybe, if I truly waited upon the Lord, he would help me make that glorious transition, the one I'd always dreamed about—the transition from running to flying, from good to great, from believing to *knowing.*

It scared me. I bent my head to pray. Then I began to write my talk, keeping the scriptures and Grandma's letter by my side.

After I was finished, I sat for a long while rereading the letter and looking at her signature, still beautiful even though it was not as steady as it once had been. I thought about those hands, shaking a little as she had gotten older, as they prepared me a snack of Hostess cupcakes and hot chocolate from her hot plate. Even though I could practically feel the sugar coursing through my veins, I still ate them and enjoyed the feeling of being taken care of and cherished.

One thing that surprises me about older people, living as they are at the end of their lives, is that most of them seem to be able to give a lot of time. You'd think they would be less generous with it, seeing as they might not have much left. But Grandma was willing to give me a great deal of time. We talked about many things— important things I didn't even tell my parents or my best friends and silly things like who my favorite authors were or where I would like to live someday. I wasn't trying to keep them a secret from other people; it's only that no one else had the time to ask about them.

I find it especially appropriate that my grandmother gave me the gift of time. When she retired from teaching, the faculty and staff presented her with a beautiful clock. I have always thought of her as being similar to that clock. She had a beautiful, clear, bell-like voice, like the clock; she was exact and methodical in marking down those things that mattered to her; she was unhurried but full of motion.

One of the things that broke my heart after her death was finding her bird-watching notebook with each bird she'd sighted listed with the date and location of the sighting and her opinion of their song. It also was one of the things that made me laugh until tears ran down my face. I was skimming through all the annotations like, "Although a common birdsong, the robin's is nonetheless one of the most beautiful, since I hear it and know that spring is here" and "The mockingbird's mournful sound is a beautiful dirge," when I came to the annotation about the blue jay: "It is a truth universally acknowledged that the song of a Stellar's jay sounds like crud." I never heard her use language like that in real life and it gave me a glimpse of someone I knew in a different, funnier light. I pointed it out to my father and he and I laughed until we cried. Now all I have to do is say, "It is a truth universally . . ." and he can't keep a straight face. It's been a long time since we've had a joke to share; I like to think of it as one of Grandma's last gifts to us.

It was time. I could hear the very last strains of the musical number fading into nothing and silence taking its place after the applause. Principal Downing looked expectantly at me.

Grateful that my legs weren't asleep anymore, I stood up and walked toward the podium. I was the last speaker and so the crowd was ready to be gone. The brief silence turned into a low murmur of talking. I didn't mind because the heartbeat I could feel coursing through me would surely be picked up by the microphone and maybe the talking would cover that.

When I finally got to the podium, I stopped. I waited until the students became a little uncomfortable and stopped talking to one another and looked up at me. I unfolded my paper and began to speak. My voice, to my surprise, sounded like . . . my voice. Just a little louder and more powerful than usual.

"We are graduating today," I said, "and I have thought many times about what you might like to hear and what I might like to say. I have decided that I would like to share with you part of a letter I received."

I read the part of Grandma's letter where she quoted Jenkins Lloyd Jones and then I discussed what we had all learned in the ride through high school. We'd learned things from our teachers— practical knowledge and more. We'd learned from Principal Downing and her fight with cancer and her discoveries from it. We'd learned from athletics and band and other activities. We had learned from our parents and from each other.

I read the last sentences of Grandma's letter, changing them slightly to say, "Our teachers, families, and friends have confidence that we will walk our own paths and create our own ripples in whatever pond we choose to swim. It is my hope tonight that we can earn that confidence and instill it in others. I hope that we can all serve each other and those we meet, and that we can enjoy the ride of life and help others enjoy it as much as possible." The walk back to my seat was much shorter than the walk to the podium.

I sat down as they applauded. I looked up at all the faces around me and stopped holding my breath and began to smile. It felt wonderful, even though I had tears in my eyes. It felt like flying.

CHAPTER 23

JUNE

Yearbook Entries

From Tyler Cruz's yearbook

Ty-

Next year will be awesome with you on the team. State Champs, baby!

Nic

P.S. Until then, I'll waste you in practice.

Tyler—

I'm so glad you moved here from Phoenix. This year has been more than I could have ever imagined and you have been a great friend from that first meeting on the bus. It will be fun to watch you next year in the games. Also, thank you so much for coming to my baptism. I know that it wasn't exactly the most comfortable thing for you to do, but I know you did it because you're a real friend and you knew that it was important to me. Thank you for being so awesome.

Julie R.

Yearbook Entries

• • •

From Avery Matthews's yearbook

Dear Avery—

It is always hard to write an entry to a student whose writing I, myself, admire. Your poetry has been thought-provoking; your work on the newspaper has been exceptional. I have associated with many good writers, a few great writers, and several who are that combination of great writer and interesting, refreshing person. You are one of those people and will go far. Even though I'm retiring this summer, I'll be reading the newspaper next year with great interest. I am glad you have agreed to be one of the editors. Please continue writing as much and as often as you can.

Sincerely,

Mr. Thomas

Avery—

It will be weird to go to college and leave Lakeview and the newspaper behind—but I know I will live on in the red wagon. Take good care of her for me. (Maybe you could suggest naming it the SS Sherman. Or the SS Skipper. Run that by the new journalism teacher, will you?) I will see you around this summer for sure. Keep in touch.

Dave

• • •

From Andrea Beckett's yearbook

Hey,

I won't get too nauseating here, but I want it documented in your yearbook that you are something else. It's a good thing I can make you laugh or I think I would get thrown over for some handsome movie star when he finally heard about how beautiful you are. Or by some good-looking reincarnation of Steve Prefontaine when he heard about how fast you run. Or by a future president of the

USA who heard about that mind of yours. But what they don't know is that, as great as all of those things are, there's even more to you. And that the most beautiful sound in the world is your laugh. Let's laugh a lot this summer.

Dave

Dear Andrea,

You were a great tutor this year. I was nervous when I found out you were my tutor because I knew you were smart but then you turned out to be nice too and that was great. I did a lot better once you were my tutor. Good luck in college and with everything. I'm glad we're going to keep in touch.

Sincerely,
Amy Walters

. . .

From Ethan Beckett's yearbook
Hey, little brother—

It's so weird that this is the last day that we'll be in high school together. At least we have this summer, right? It will be strange at college without you, but I'm trying not to think about that too much. Losing Grandma has made me think about our family, about all of us. I won't give you another version of my valedictory speech here, but I love you and will miss you and I know you're going to make Grandma very, very proud. I know she's watching us.

I also wanted to tell you not to worry so much about everything. (It's a lot easier to write this stuff than to say it—you know I have a problem with that. So I'd better write fast before I lose my nerve.) I know that you are trying hard to live right and be worthy, but as I've learned the hard way, we can't control everything that happens to us, no matter how hard we try. That's the great part about life—there are always going to be surprises—but that can be scary too, unless we rely on our testimonies and our faith. Maybe we will go on our missions at the same time! What a thought. I can't imagine a better missionary than you.

I want to tell you something I've been meaning to tell you for a while. This year, at the State meet, when you won second place, I really learned something from you. You got more joy out of winning second than I did from winning first and I wondered what was wrong with you. How could you be so happy when you didn't win? Later I realized that there was something wrong with me, not you. You were happy with your win because you knew you had run a good race and fought hard and because you loved what you did and because you cared about the team too. I won, but it was for all the wrong reasons—selfish reasons—and so I still wasn't happy. I have a lot to learn from you in so many ways. I want to be more like you, living for others and fighting for the right thing for the right reasons. Thank you for being an example.

I love you.
Andrea

Dear Ethan,

What a year. I wonder what we'd say about each other if we had to write our autobiographies again next year. I'm very glad that we are still friends, that we are dating again, and most of all, that we have both grown so much this year. I think that I felt like I had grown up or something, like my testimony and my life were in perfect order. What I learned this year (what you helped teach me) is that it's important to keep growing. Thank you for a wonderful year, Ethan.

Love, Mikey

• • •

From Dave Sherman's yearbook
Dave—

I wish I could tell you how I feel in person, but I'm taking the easy way out and writing it instead. You're in love with Andrea. I can see why and I know it's not just because of how beautiful she is, so I can live with it.

I wanted to come to church with you a lot of times, but I think I wanted to come for the wrong reasons. I wanted to come to be with you and not necessarily to find out the truth for its own sake. I think I will go next year when you're away at college so that I know I'm going for the right reasons. I hope you understand. Tell those missionaries that you're always talking about that I'm not ready yet, but maybe I will be. Just give me a little more time.

I hope this wasn't too much honesty for you to handle and that we can still be friends. I wanted you to understand why I kept putting you off. You've been a great friend to me and I want to give this church of yours a fair chance. After all, you gave me a fair chance and it has meant a lot.

Avery

Dear David,

It's been a pleasure to have you in journalism these past few years. I mean it. You have made me laugh many times when I truly needed a bit of levity. I appreciate your humor and I appreciate the warmth and kindness you show to other students even more. Good luck in the future. I would be interested to hear about your church assignment when you receive it.

Sincerely,
Mr. Thomas

Dear Dave,

You're writing in my yearbook, so I know the deal is that I'm supposed to be writing in yours right now. But it's hard to think of how to say what I want to say. You've always been better at this kind of thing—you can talk to anyone and make them laugh or smile. In fact, right now you're sitting there writing and grinning away and now I'm smiling too, just from watching you. I guess that says it all. You bring a lot of happiness into my life and I love being with you.

Andrea

• • •

From Mr. Thomas's yearbook

Hi, Dad!

I know you didn't want to have students sign your yearbook because it makes you too sad, but I found it and I disobeyed you (probably not for the last time). I took it to my room and had my students sign it—the ones who had you too—and David Sherman took it around to some of the newspaper kids. I hope you don't mind. I love you.

Owen

Dear Mr. Thomas,

There are a lot of students who say that you are the best teacher they have ever had, and at the beginning of the year, I didn't agree with them. I thought that a good teacher had to have bells and whistles and different activities every day. I was wrong. You taught us by caring about us and by giving us all a chance without giving us a handout. You are the best teacher I have ever had.

With respect,

Avery Matthews

Dear Mr. Thomas,

I still think that pink Barbie car would have been a smooth ride for the newspapers, but you know best. Thanks for putting up with me all these years. You have been a great teacher and a lot of us have looked up to you and learned from you. I know I sure have.

Dave Sherman

Dear Mr. Thomas,

I'm very glad that I got to be in your class before you retired because you are such a legend and rightfully so. Thank you for all the help you gave me from the first autobiography assignment to the last paper. I think I'm a much better writer now, thanks to you. I hope you enjoy your retirement. Your son is a great teacher too. You must have taught him everything you know. ☺

Sincerely,

Michaela Choi

. . .

From Principal Downing's yearbook

Dear Principal Downing,

I asked your secretary if I could sign your yearbook and she found it for me. From all the signatures in here, it looks like I'm not the only person to do this. I wanted to say that I think a lot about how courageous you are. I know there is a lot of pressure that comes from being in the spotlight and I admire the poise and confidence and courage you exhibit. Here is a copy of the quotation you asked for from my graduation speech and a copy of the talk that I found it in. I hope you enjoy both. Thank you again for being our principal and our example.

Sincerely,

Andrea Beckett

Dear Principal Downing,

I've ruined your mascot and caused a lot of other havoc at your school and you've still been a good sport through it all. Someday when I'm rich I'll donate a titanium Skipper head to the school in your honor and then no one can ever destroy him again. Still, he won't be as tough as you (I mean that in a good way). There're a lot of us rooting for you. Go Downing!

David Sherman

Dear Principal Downing,

Well, this is surreal. If someone had told me at the beginning of the year that I would end up signing your yearbook, there's no way I would have believed it. Some of our interactions at the beginning of the year involve things I would like to forget, but there are even more that I want to remember. I especially know that I will never forget interviewing you in May. I was (and am) honored that you would choose me to help tell your story. I'll be thinking of you this summer and hoping everything is going well. See you in the fall.

Avery Matthews

. . .

From Michaela Choi's yearbook
Dear Mikey,

I should probably write this fast because Ethan is standing here waiting for his turn to write in here—and I know you'll want him to have a chance to sign. ☺ I've never written in a best friend's yearbook before so I'm not quite sure what to say, except thank you. There's so many fun memories from this year—hanging out with the group and getting ice cream, practicing music together, making our world-famous salsa and smoothies for movie night, calling each other for homework assignments and then forgetting to actually talk about them. And the most wonderful memory of all—my baptism. I'm glad I could be there for you at least a little because you've been there for me so much.

Love,
Julie

Mikey—

We have both changed and gotten stronger this year. I'm so glad you're still in my life. I don't know what's ahead, but I know that I will never regret this year with you.

Love, Ethan

Michaela,

Thank you for introducing me to that beautiful song and for being an exceptional student. I look forward to teaching you and

Julie, and learning from you both, in Chorale next year. I appreciate all you students have done in making my first year of teaching a memorable one.

Sincerely,
Owen Thomas

• • •

From Julie Reid's yearbook

Julie,

You were my first friend here and I really owe you one for that. Thanks for inviting me to your baptism too, it was really cool. Thanks for always cheering me on. See you around this summer.

Tyler

Julie!

What would I have done without you this year? Whoever thought a best friendship could happen because the principal threw up in the bathroom? It must be destiny for us to be friends.

You taught me more about the gospel than I taught you—that's for sure. When you reminded me that I could pray for help with my pain, you taught me something I'd forgotten. Or maybe I'd never had a chance to learn. I kept telling you that we all have our trials for a reason, but you showed me how to actually apply the words that I thought I understood. I know you're always saying how much I helped you this year, but I honestly don't think that anything I did can even compare to you, Jules.

You have been courageous about acting on the truth that you know, step by step. Watching you discover the gospel has helped me to discover it too. It's like this ornament Ethan gave me for Christmas. I could tell it was beautiful in the box, but when I held it up to the light, it was exquisite. I think the gospel was like that for me. I knew it was good and true, but then you came along and helped me take it out of its box and showed me how much more to it there really was.

Someday when I am rich and famous and they make a movie out of my life, you will have a very big part. Actually, what will really happen is that they'll make a movie about *you,* and I hope that I'll get to be in it. And they'll put both of our pictures from the yearbook in the opening credits and we'll be sitting in the theater together eating popcorn and surrounded on either side by our fabulous husbands and we'll look at each other and laugh.

Or maybe we'll be collaborating on a great work of literature in your kitchen and we'll be covered in flour from making cookies for our kids, who are outside in the backyard playing, and then we'll all go camping and look at the stars and sing, even if our voices get creaky and rusty. And when we're old and on missions in faraway places, we'll write to each other and tell each other how things are.

That's how it's going to be, Jules. I have this feeling about it.

Love,
Mikey

LAKEVIEW
HIGH SCHOOL

School was over and everyone at Lakeview High had taken something with them.

Michaela Choi had taken the prism ornament that had hung in her locker since January. The flat, metal background of her locker would be exchanged for the sunlit window in her parents' kitchen, where everyone could see it. After she lifted it out of her locker, she turned to Ethan Beckett, who was standing next to her. He took her hand and they walked out together. Ethan was carrying his backpack, which for the first time all year was empty and light, free of the weight of a dozen books and all his worries.

David Sherman had taken home the papier-mâché eye that had once belonged to the Skipper. He was planning to send it to Avery for Christmas, along with a Book of Mormon, just in case she hadn't been to church yet.

Andrea Beckett had thrown away a lot of items from her locker—straight-A report cards, clippings about her races from the school newspaper, old running shoes. To her surprise, she had found her Homecoming tiara in there with a note from David: "I kept this for you. I know someday you might have a little girl as wonderful as you who wants to use it for dressing up." Andrea's eyes filled with tears. The crown had gone home with her.

Principal Downing took home a yearbook full of messages from students. Pressed between two of the pages was a foil gum wrapper.

Tyler Cruz had a letter of interest from BYU that had been forwarded to him from his school in Phoenix. He wanted to ask Julie and her friends what they knew about BYU's basketball program. He knew they would know—it was a Mormon school. It was in the same state as Utah State University, where Maya would be starting college next year.

Since he was retiring, Mr. Thomas took home piles of books, papers, and files. But he left one of the most important parts of himself there—his son.

Owen Thomas brought home the music he'd borrowed from Julie. He was going to work on a full choir arrangement of "Come Thou Fount of Every Blessing" over the summer for his class next year.

Avery Matthews took the Pass-Along card David had given her with the phone number for a free Book of Mormon written on it. She put it on her mirror. It reminded her to pray, which she tried to do occasionally, even though it didn't feel entirely comfortable yet.

Julie Reid took home the Book of Mormon that she'd kept in her locker since January and thought about who she could give it to. Kevin kept coming to mind. She knew it would take a lot of prayer and faith, but she thought that with help she could take the next step in the long process of letting go of her anger and pain.

The door had closed behind them once, twice, a thousand times. They had brought heartaches and fears and ideas and doubts and testimonies and everything that a teenage mind and a backpack can contain. Everyone had something to offer and something to learn. Some testimonies had deepened; some had just begun to grow; some were dormant, but seeds had been planted. Each face in the yearbook had a story to tell.

Stories were everywhere.

The bell rang in the empty hall.

ABOUT THE AUTHOR

Allyson Braithwaite Condie received a degree in English teaching from Brigham Young University. She went on to teach high school English in Utah and New York for several years. She loved her job because it combined two of her favorite things—working with students and reading great books.

Currently, however, she is employed by her two little boys, who keep her busy playing trucks and going to the park. They also like to help her type and are very good at drawing on manuscripts with red crayon. In addition to spending time with them and with her husband, she loves reading, running, eating, and traveling. *Yearbook* is her first book.